THE UNITED FEDERATION MARINE CORPS

BOOK 2: SERGEANT

Colonel Jonathan P. Brazee, USMC (Ret)

Semper Fi Press

Acknowledgements:

I want to thank all those who took the time to pre-read this book, catching my mistakes in both content and typing. A special shout out goes to my comrades at VFW Post 9951 in Bangkok for their help and to Dr. Alan Whiting, CDR, USN (Ret), my old Naval Academy roommate and physicist and astronomer extraordinaire, for his assistance in astrophysics. And once again, thanks to my editor, Anne Gentilucci for making me a better writer. All remaining typos and inaccuracies are solely my fault.

Original Cover Art by Almaz Sharipov

PART 1

Jonathan P. Brazee

SOREAU

Chapter 1

"Look sharp, Tizzard! Keep your team up," Sergeant Ryck Lysander sent to Corporal Rey, his First Team leader.

Ryck knew that was easier said than done. The squad was moving down a wide boulevard to the Tylarian government house, but with thirteen Marines in the squad, all in Personal Integrated Combat Units, or PICS, they easily filled the road. Add in the civilians lining the edge of the road, and it was a pretty tight fit.

Those civilians were none too happy, and they didn't hesitate to let the Marines know that. The locals didn't appreciate "foreign mercs" in their country, which seemed ironic to Ryck as the Marines themselves were not mercenaries, but they were there to get mercenaries out of a jamb.

The Foreign Legion might be semi-official, but in this case, they had been hired on as mercenaries no matter how it was cut. A negotiating team from the Legion had arrived to work out a contract with the Tylarian government, evidently without the support of the people.

A flash on his visor grabbed Ryck's attention. After four years in a PICS, the electronic displays on the visor were second nature to him, but this signal was different. He swung his head and looked past the images to the real world beyond. Something trailing smoke had arched up and was coming back down. Ryck spun around, weapon ready, as the Molotov cocktail registered in his mind. It hit Lance Corporal Teung in the back with a burst of flames as a blanket fire spread over him.

"Keep it steady, keep moving!" Ryck sent over the squad circuit, anxious to avoid a violent reaction.

Marines were not good at inaction. They were trained to react and react with extreme prejudice. However, a Molotov cocktail wasn't going to do anything to a Marine in a PICS, and their ROEs[1] were very clear. No action against the locals unless it was life or death. A few flames did not fit the bill. Teung didn't even falter. He just kept marching as the flames burnt themselves out.

Ryck wondered what the people would do if they knew that, Teung, their first target, was actually a native of Tylaria. Would they have held back, or would that have inflamed them even more?

The Navy intel officer had laid out the political situation on the planet during their briefing aboard the *FS Chappa*. Tylaria was one of three countries on the planet Soreau. The nation shared a 1,650km-long border with New Guangzhou, a border where skirmishes had broken out over the last several months as New Guangzhou was making noises about a "reunification" of the two countries that comprised the planet's main landmass. With only a small militia, the Tylarian government called upon the Legion for help. The arrival of the negotiating team was widely broadcast in both countries, probably to both bolster the Tylarian public resolve and lessen the resolve of the New Guangzhou people.

That might have made sense, but the government was obviously out of touch with public opinion. If the masses around Ryck's squad were any indication, the people of Tylaria wanted reunification, and they didn't want anyone from off-planet there to force their hand one way or the other.

Ryck watched his visor display. Each Marine was identified as a blue avatar. He wanted to see a nice, even pattern. What he saw was a bunched-up group, almost a gaggle. With a blink, he zoomed out, and Second Squad's avatars appeared, displayed on the next street over where they moved parallel to his Third Squad. They were even more bunched, given they had a much narrower avenue of approach. The lieutenant was with them, too, and the Marines in the squad looked like they were forming around him almost as bodyguards even if it wouldn't be obvious to someone outside of the platoon to identify him as anything other than a Marine in a PICS.

---

[1] ROE: Rules of Engagement

"Grubbing Legion," Ryck muttered under his breath.

Ryck actually had nothing against the Legion. Sure there was the Marine-Legion rivalry, but on the whole, they were good guys. They might have had better equipment, and they certainly were paid better than the Marines, but a grunt was a grunt. He just didn't understand why a Marine company was being sent in to rescue a Legion negotiating team.

From a practical standpoint, it made sense. Golf Company had been going through routine jungle training on Ho`oku`i on the other side of the globe. When things started getting dicey for the Legion team, the Legion brass on Camerone made a request to the Federation Council for assistance, and here they were. Ryck didn't object to breaking from training, and he didn't object to an operational mission. What he did object to was the principle of the thing, which was, using government assets for the Legion's benefit. More than that, the ROEs were not only limiting, but also downright dangerous. The aggressiveness that gave the Marines their effectiveness was taken away.

If a government organization had to react, it should have been the Federation Civil Development Corps. The FCDC handled civilians, not the Marines. Marines were trained to close with and destroy the enemy, not to play riot police.

As if to buttress his thoughts, a woman rushed out in front of the squad point man, Lance Corporal "Lips" Holleran. Lips was a busted-down corporal, but one of the steadiest Marines in the squad. Ryck wasn't sure what the 50 kg woman thought she was going to do against the 945 kg PICS, but it looked like she was going to try and latch herself onto Lips' left leg.

The Marines had been briefed to keep movement slow and steady and not to stop. Lips didn't stop. The woman was flung to the ground as he walked his suit forward.

"Uh, I think I squished one," Lips sent to Corporal Beady, his team leader.

Ryck, as squad leader, had ears on all the circuits.

"One-six, this is one-three. We've got a civilian woman down. She looks pretty bad, over," Ryck passed to the lieutenant.

If one of his Marines had gone down, the lieutenant, in his PICS-C, would have known immediately, but the civvies were not in the system other than as featureless grey avatars, and the PICS' sensors couldn't even determine an accurate count when they were bunched up so closely. Ryck knew the platoon commander had to pass up the incident immediately so the JAG[2] could get involved as soon as the situation was secured. If she were still alive, she would be in for a pretty hefty payment. All for being a grubbing idiot! What did she expect?

A hail of rocks came over the edge of a roof to shower the Marines. One rock bounced off Ryck's helmet. He blinked to an infrared scan and saw several signatures. If any of them had something more powerful than a rock, they were in a pretty good position in which to employ it. Ryck ached to call in a Wasp strike. He had been trained to take out potential threats instead of waiting for them to strike.

He couldn't call in a Wasp, though, even if they were under a real attack. The initial plan cobbled together was for the two Marine Wasps that were part of the combined unit going through the jungle package at the Mona Loa National Park training area to come in hot and heavy, leading the way for the PICS Marines. A Navy Experion fighter would have been better, but to civilians, the Wasp would still be pretty intimidating. The powers that be, though, nixed that. "Too aggressive."

Instead, the company's two heavy platoons were walking to the government building uncovered, or at least as uncovered as a Marine in the Corps' most modern fighting suit could be.

"Uh, Sergeant Lysander, do you see what I see?" Lips passed over the squad circuit.

Technically, Lance Corporal Holleran should have used standard radio procedure, but with the circuit's frequency jumping and scrambling, and with the displays indicating who was sending, communications tended to slide to a more normal speech pattern at the squad level.

---

[2] JAG: Judge Advocate General, the "lawyers" of the military.

In front of Lips, beyond the people lining the road and the scattering of people milling about in front of them, approximately 50 or 60 civilians were shuffling to block the Marines way to the square in front of the government building. Lips, closely followed by his team, was closing fast. Their orders were to keep moving, but not to hurt anyone. As far as Ryck could tell, the two orders were diametrically opposed to each other. He had to make a decision.

"Third Team, halt! Form in a line, but do not push into them yet. First and Second, get on line with Third. It's going to be tight, so squeeze it in."

Ryck took a second to blink up the larger picture. To the south of the building, but still 500 meters away, the three squads from Second Platoon were making their way forward. To his left, Second Squad was stopped, and beyond them, First Squad was still moving forward.

"Push it forward, Stillwell," he sent to the PFC in Second Fire Team. "Don't hit anyone, but use your bulk to get in line with Peretti.

"OK, now, elbow-to-elbow, slowly, and I mean *slowly*, shuffle forward. Do not raise your feet. We don't need to be making pancakes out of any of them," he said to the rest of the squad as they came online.

The squad had managed to fill the entire street. About 20 meters ahead of them was the square in front of the government building. Between the square and the squad, though, were 60 or so shouting civilians. Ryck had a sudden urge to sound a charge and scatter them, but orders were orders.

"Form on Holleran. I don't want any space between us. Corporal Beady, give us a cadence, slow and steady."

Ryck was standing one pace behind Lips, and with Beady giving a cadence, he could focus on what was happening.

"One, two, one, two, one, two . . ." the team leader intoned as the Marines did a shuffle step forward.

The PICS were not made for elbow-to-elbow formations, nor were they designed for shuffling. The Marines were clanging against each other as the line lumbered forward.

"Corporal Rey, what do I do with this negat?" PFC Hartono asked his team leader over his comms.

Ryck switched to put Hartono's visor view on his own visor. A young man with a red bandana across his face had taken a few steps into Hartono's path, then launched himself up with a spinning kick to the Marine's chest. What he expected that to accomplish other than maybe breaking his foot, Ryck didn't know. What happened was that the man bounced off Hartono's carapace, not even budging the Marine.

"Ignore him. He's going to fall flat on his arse," Rey replied.

The man tried to take a few steps back for another go at Hartono, but the mass of people kept him from getting too far. He ran up to level another kick, but just as Rey had predicted, he slipped and fell to the ground. Hartono switched from a shuffle to lift his feet and carefully step over the stunned man.

Ryck switched off Hartono's viewpoint. They were only 10 meters now from the square. The press of people was such that the first rank of civilians was right up against the Marines. They were being pushed back by the advancing Marines, but more Tylarians back of them were pushing forward. Some were trying to turn around and get out of the way, but that was not going to be happening.

An obese man in what looked like old-fashioned lederhosen tried to lower his shoulders to stop Lips as if he were a rugger joining a scrum, but as he put his legs back to push, they buckled. He went face first down on the pavement. Lips shuffled over him, the man's big body bouncing between Lips and Lance Corporal Martin off Lips' right side. He was dragged forward a meter or so, his body too big to easily slide between them, but like toothpaste in a tube, the man finally squeezed past to lie motionless on the road.

To Ryck's right, a body came flying forward. It was Hartono's bandanaed nemesis. Now behind the line of Marines, he had a cleared area in which to run, and he had built up a head of steam before launching himself once again, kicking out against the PFC's weapons pack.

Despite himself, Ryck was pretty impressed. The guy really had no chance to rock a Marine in a PICS. The gyros kept the PICS upright, and it would take more than a 70kg martial arts wannabe to overcome that. But the guy had sure jumped up pretty high to slam his kick on the Marine's weapons pack.

Ryck was tempted to slap some sense into the guy, but as the civilian wasn't armed, Ryck decided that ignoring him was the best option given their ROE.

Ryck quickly toggled to a wider view. Second Squad had been delayed in their movement: they were still a good 50 meters from the square. First Squad, on the other hand, had already entered the square and looked to be forming to advance on the government building itself.

"Squad, listen up," Ryck began. "We're going to push out into the square two meters and halt. Keiji, you're going to refuse our right flank. Peretti, you've got our left. Between you and Stillwell, don't let anyone get in our way on the left. We need to look like the crowd has stopped us, let them relax even just a bit. When I give the order, we're going to give it a military left face and move our asses, and I mean *move them*, in a column to join up with First Squad. We need to surprises these people, then leave them in the dust. Peretti, that means you're going to be leading us. Get us past these rock-apes, but steer clear of the civvies who are holding up Second Squad. We need to get past them before they realize we're coming. All of us, keep it tight! Assholes to belly buttons! Got it?"

A green check appeared under 11 of the avatars on his visor display. Ryck waited another few seconds.

"Khouri, do you understand?" he asked his 12th Marine. "We're waiting!"

A green check belatedly appeared under the lance corporal's avatar.

"Sams, this is Ryck" he passed to the First Squad leader, knowing that the lieutenant, Staff Sergeant Hecs, and Sergeant Pope Paul, "Popo," would be listening in. "In about two mikes, we're going to hightail it to your position to link up. I'm hoping there will be some scatter when the civs see a PICS squad rushing them, so that should give us an opportunity to present a more formidable front and maybe get up into the objective. You copy that?"

"Roger than, Ryck. Sounds copacetic. We'll mill about smartly here until you arrive, then let's push it forward," Sams replied.

"Good thinking on your feet, Sergeant Lysander," Lieutenant Nidishchii' passed on the circuit. "Staff Sergeant Phantawisangtong, you've got command of the two squads. We're kind of bottled up here, so I don't think we can get there to join you until after the fact. Remember the ROE, though. No civilian casualties."

"Aye-aye, sir," the platoon sergeant acknowledged. "Get your butt in gear, Ryck. More rock-apes are on their way."

The lieutenant was new to the platoon, and his enlisted time was in the Second Marine Division, so he was somewhat of an unknown entity. Both Sams and Staff Sergeant Hector Phantawisangtong were well known to Ryck, though. Sams was Sergeant Bobbi Samuelson, and Ryck had served with him when they were both privates over in Fox Company. Staff Sergeant "Hecs" had been Ryck's heavy hat at recruit training back on Tarawa. Despite the years that had passed, Ryck still thought of him as "King Tong."

The squad pushed into the square. Lips went slightly deeper than two meters, but along the edge of the square, tables and chairs were cluttered in front of what had to be restaurants. Even though a Marine in a PICS wouldn't notice crushing a table, there were people grouped there as well, and his squad needed to have a clearer shot to First Squad.

The squad halted. In front of them, the crowd, which had been slowly retreating in the face of the Marine advance, eased to a stop as well. A few of the braver sorts took a step or two closer to the Marine line, but staying out of arm's reach. Behind the squad, more civilians gathered and began to press forward. Ryck knew he had to move before they pushed up against the Marines.

"On three," he passed over the squad circuit, "left face and move out."

All twelve Marines acknowledge the order by activating their checkmarks.

"One . . . two . . . three! Move it!"

A PICS was not an extremely nimble piece of equipment. It had significant mass, and even with each Marine's physical movements augmented, the suit was not as agile as a Marine not meched up. However, once they got going, they were surprisingly fast. Within a few steps, the Marines were running at almost 60 KPH, far faster than any human could match. They left the protesters facing them and were able to dodge in back of the protesters surrounding Second Squad before those civilians could react.

Just as Ryck had hoped, when the protesters around First Squad saw the advancing Marines coming at full tilt, they scattered like a covey of quail. First Squad immediately started moving forward.

Stopping a PICS from full speed was an exercise in physics. Nine-hundred and forty-five kilograms at 60 KPH created beaucoup momentum. There was a trick to bringing the beast to heel. Ryck leaned back and thrust one foot forward, the LTC coating on his PICS heel digging a furrow through the stone cobbles of the square, individual stones dislodging to fly through the air. He pulled up to a stop exactly where he had intended.

Hartono was not as skilled. As the newest member of the squad and new to his PICS, he didn't get enough braking resistance, and he crashed into Keiji. Ryck knew the PICS' gyros would keep their suits upright despite some pretty serious impacts, and the suit's themselves were pretty sturdy, but a collision like that could damage sensors or even the weapons packs. Ryck had no time to check out either Marine's PICS, though. First Squad was on the move, and they had to get up to the objective before the protesters could shift with enough mass to impede their progress.

The square was covered in cobblestones, which didn't impede the progress of the Marines as they trotted up to their objective, but it slowed down the ability of the protesters to react to the Marines' movement. Ryck could see several small civilian groups trying to interspace themselves between the Marines and the building, but they were not going to be able to close in time. Nearly a hundred people were at the bottom of the steps, but the vast majority of the protesters had previously flooded out to plug up the streets and were now out of the Marines' path.

It took about 30 seconds to cross the big square. A single line of protesters tried to stop them, but the Marines slowed down and easily pushed their way through the crowd. The civilians didn't even try hard. They seemed to have given up, at least for the moment. Ryck knew they hadn't thrown in the towel, though. Getting into the government building was only part of the mission. The Marines had to get out again, with the Legionnaires, and the protesters were undoubtedly going to try and stop them. To the protesters, the Marines reaching the government house was probably considered only a temporary setback.

Staff Sergeant Hecs led the two squads up the many steps to the main entrance. About 20 nervous-looking local militia manned two crew-served weapons which were sandbagged on either side of the big bronze doors. One soldier raised his rifle to aim at the Marines before another soldier knocked the muzzle back down.

Staff Sergeant Hecs moved forward and addressed the soldier who had stepped out from behind the sandbags.

"Staff Sergeant Phantawisangtong, Federation Marine Corps. I think you are expecting us?"

"Yes, sir! Lieutenant Xie, uh, militia, uh, Tylarian Militia, I mean. Yes, we're glad you're here. Please, come inside," the flustered militiaman managed to get out.

He nodded at another of the soldiers who picked up a landline and quietly spoke into it. A few moments later, the big doors pulled open. The 27 Marines almost casually walked through them and into a very large, ornate rotunda.

Ryck listened with half an ear as Staff Sergeant Hecs reported in to the Lt Nidishchii'. Ryck was in awe of what he was seeing. Back on Prophesy, the government building was more of an office building, perhaps befitting a planet that was colonized by a corporation. This was more in the lines of an old-fashion capitol building, with statues in the cornices and an intricate tile mosaic covering the vast floor. Ryck took a step further into the room, then stopped, conscious of his big PICS crushing some of the tiles underfoot.

They waited only a few moments before a Legion captain, wearing his T34 Parade Dress uniform, came hurrying down one of the large staircases. Staff Sergeant Hecs had activated his rockers[3] on his PICS arms and went right to him.

Staff Sergeant Hecs opened up the input to his speakers to the two squad leaders.

"Staff Sergeant, I am Capitaine Pichon. Thank you for your arrival. I understood, though, that a full Marine Company was coming?"

"Sir, Staff Sergeant Phantawisangtong here. The company commander has been held up outside by the mass of civilians. Our ROE is very clear that we are to avoid civilian casualties, so for the moment, we are the only forces to reach this building."

"Ah, just so. Well, if you could, please follow me to meet Commandant Gruenstein, our senior negotiator."

The captain started for the sweeping stairway before stopping and looking back at the Marines.

"Ah, perhaps you can evacuate your Personal Combat Systems? They may not be so maneuverable upstairs," he said.

Ryck tried to decide if there was a condescending note to his voice. It was taken for granted that the Legion's Rigaudeau-3s were better combat suits than the Marines' PICS, but Ryck didn't think the legionnaire was in a position to dismissive of Marine Corps gear.

"Ryck, strip and join me," Staff Sergeant Hecs told him, already starting the procedures to release the back seal so he could get out of the PICS.

It took almost a minute before Ryck could perform the Cirque du Soleil maneuvers necessary to hitch his legs up, then back down outside his PICS. He disconnected the hood interface, and he was free of the big beast, feeling naked, and not only from shedding his PCS, but also because his longjohns were so tight and thin as to leave nothing about him to the imagination. He checked his small Ruger 2mm, holstered it, and followed his platoon sergeant up the stairs.

---

[3] Rockers: slang for the insignia of a staff sergeant. The "rockers" are the curves lines under the "stripes."

An armed militiaman guard standing outside the door leading into Conference Room A came to attention and presented arms. The captain made a cursory salute and entered the room.

Inside, Ryck saw four more legionnaires and two men in civilian clothes. The civvies looked relieved at the sight of Staff Sergeant Hecs and Ryck. The legionnaires showed no reaction one way or the other.

With their longjohns on, neither Ryck nor Hecs had on any indication of rank. Without hesitating, though, the tall, hawk-nosed commandant stepped forward, hand outstretched.

"Major Nicholas Gruenstein. It is good to meet you."

The major could have come from central casting for a new Legion flick. Ryck noted that he used the Standard "major" instead of the Legion rank of "commandant," unlike the captain who had insisted on using "capitaine" for his rank.

Score one for the major, Ryck thought.

"Happy to be here, sir," Staff Sergeant Hecs told him. "Staff Sergeant Phantawisangtong nd Sergeant Lysander. We've got two heavy squads inside this building. My commander, Lieutenant Nidishchii' is outside holding a few hundred civilians in place. Captain Davis, our company commander, is directly behind this building with another platoon of Marines. I've been tasked with preparing your team for evacuation so we are ready to move out as soon as Captain Davis arrives."

He looked around the room before continuing, "I was lead to believe that there were going to be more Tylarian personnel to evacuate?"

One of the two civvies looked embarrassed as the major said, "I'm afraid that Mr. Gelan and Mr. Liu are all that are left. Their, uh, *superiors*, decided that after the first group of protesters made it in the building, they didn't want to draw any more here to put us, their guests, in any danger."

"So you are saying they diddiho'd out of here, sir?" Staff Sergeant Hecs asked.

"Yes, I think that phrase is an apt description," the major said, only a slight hint of scorn in his voice.

Ryck wouldn't have done so well in hiding his opinions of the officials who had fled.

"If you think it feasible, we can move to the rotunda, sir, so we can prepare for the evac. We've got about a klick to go to our pick-up point," the platoon sergeant told him, careful not to make it sound like an order.

"Sounds good, Staff Sergeant Phantawisangtong," the Legion major said, actually doing a pretty good job with the platoon sergeant's name. "Lead on."

The five legionnaires, two civilians, and two Marines walked out the room, down the hall, and back down the stairs, but not before the major told the lone guard to rejoin his unit.

In the rotunda, Sams was taking some uniforms out of Lance Corporal Andersen's buttpack. The PICS buttpack, which was actually more of a small-of-the-back-pack, allowed a Marine to carry cargo with him. The problem with them, in typical Marine logic, was that there were impossible to reach while inside the PICS. The pack could be dropped and then accessed, but the fingers of the PICS were a little big to handle smaller items that might be carried. Once dropped, the pack could not be re-attached without outside help. Most Marines simply used them to carry some extra chow and an emergency coldpack, the small gel piece of gear that kept a PICS from overheating on the inside.

Sams brought the uniforms from Andersen's pack over to Staff Sergeant Hecs.

"Sir, please have your men change into these utilities. They will offer you some protection as we leave," the staff sergeant told the major.

Major Gruenstein reached out and took one of the skins tops, fingering it before asking, "You've already inserted the armor protection in these, correct?"

The armor, what was called the "bones," was 23 separate pieces of what looked to be cardboard or feltboard that instantly hardened upon impact of a projectile. They were lampreyed onto the trousers and blouse, the skins, and rendered the uniform system proof against most small arms.

"Yes, sir," Staff Sergeant Hecs answered. "They're ready to go."

"As I understand it, your armor is custom made for each individual, correct?" the major asked.

"Well, yes, sir, they are. But we took a bunch of different sets, and with most of the Tylarian negotiators gone, we have plenty to pick and choose."

"I appreciate the consideration, but I hardly think that wearing ill-fitting clothing leaves a good impression. I think we will remain in our parade dress. If that leads to an injury, that will be on my head," the Legion officer said with an air of finality.

Either Mr. Gelan or Mr. Liu (Ryck never got which one was which) stepped to face Staff Sergeant Hecs and hurriedly spoke up, "Um, officer, we would like to put on your uniforms."

The platoon sergeant nodded to Sams, and the two Tylarian functionaries began to paw through the skins and bones looking for a close fit.

"If you will wait a moment, sir, let me get back into my suit so I have full comms and can report back to my command for an update," Hecs said, stepping back and moving to where his empty PICS stood like an empty insect molt. "You, too, Sergeant Lysander."

Getting back into a PICS was easier than getting out of one, but it still took a bit of dexterity. Ryck had to connect his hood, then push his arms in first and squirm up until he could bring up his legs to clear the opening. There were two handles inside the PICS up near the shoulder that made donning the PICS much easier. Some enterprising armorer had installed a set some years back when the PICS was first introduced, and now they were standard to the combat suits. Ryck grabbed the handles, pulled up, bringing his knees up past his belly, then slid his legs back down inside the PICS. He hit the closure button, then watched as his lights indicated the check process. Twenty seconds later, he was combat-ready.

He checked on his platoon sergeant. Staff Sergeant Hecs didn't look much different from the other Marines as they stationed themselves near the entrance and around the rotunda, but from the slight forward tilt of the platoon sergeant's PICS, it was clear that he was in intense comms with the lieutenant or the skipper.

The two Tylarians had selected their skins and stripped down. One was in his skivvies, the other was going commando. Ryck couldn't help but hope that it wasn't his set of skins that the skivvie-less man had selected.

There was the ever-so-slight click as Staff Sergeant Hecs came on the open circuit and activated his speaker.

"Sir, our drones are showing thousands of people converging here. Captain Davis, our commanding officer, has been ordered by higher headquarters that we need to move now. With thousands of people out there instead of hundreds, they don't think we can extract you without harm to the civilians, and they do not want to bring in air assets to the city proper to try and extract from the roof," Staff Sergeant Hecs said.

"Captain Davis is going to push forward to just short of the rear of this building, trying to attract as many of the protesters as possible. Lieutenant Nidishcii', our platoon commander, will move into the square to the northwest in an attempt to draw those right outside the entrance to them. As soon as we see the ones outside begin to draw away, clearing the entrance, we're to move out and run directly to the northeast as fast as we can go. There will be ground transport about four klicks away that will take you to an LZ[4] outside of town where you will be lifted off and taken to where a French packet ship, the *Améthyst*, is waiting in orbit. Mr. Gelan and Mr. Liu, you will be met at the LZ by one of your own representatives."

Ryck saw one immediate problem. There was no way five legionnaires in parade dress and two Tylarian politicos were going to keep up with PICS Marines. Major Greunstein had evidently realized the same thing.

"Staff Sergeant Phantawisangtong, I am afraid that 'as fast as you can go' is much faster than we will be able to go. How do we get around that?" he asked.

---

[4] LZ: Landing Zone

"Yeah, that's the thing, sir. It's been discussed, and with the concurrence of the captain of the *Améthyst*, who has taken command the French side of the operation, you are going to have to ride us," Staff Sergeant Hecs, said, waiting for a response.

"Capitaine de corvette Blanchard is in command? I am senior to him, but that is not your problem," the major said, sounding miffed. "We will ride you? How?"

"The best we can come up with is piggyback, sir," Staff Sergeant Hecs said, sounding unsure.

"Piggyback? Like a child on papa's back?" came the incredulous response.

"Yes, sir, like that."

As is in punctuation, a large rock crashed through one of the rotunda's windows. One of Sams' Marines moved to cover the new opening. Chanting could be heard from outside.

"Piggyback," the major said with a shrug. *"C'est la guerre, mon* staff sergeant. If you can show us how to ride, you, then that is what we will do."

They needed seven "mounts." Staff Sergeant Hecs took three from First Squad and four from Ryck's Third Squad. This wasn't the first time PICS had been used to carry people. A PICS was a pretty good platform from which to go into the line of fire to take out besieged Marines, so this was something almost everyone had trained for at least once.

Staff Sergeant Hecs had them drop their weapons pack, leaving each of the Marine's back bare of anything extra. The clips on the shoulders to which the tops of the weapons packs were attached functioned as handles, even if they were not designed with that in mind. Below the PICS chest carapace and above the girdle, the waist narrowed, making a natural place around which a rider could latch his legs. It took only a few moments before the method became clear to the seven passengers.

"The ride will be quite rough. You will be jolted around, so you have to hold on tight. We haven't seen anything out there that can damage a PICS, but you are not PICS, gentlemen. A rock thrown off a roof can kill you, so we need to get you out of the area as soon as possible," Staff Sergeant Hecs told them.

"Jolted" was an understatement, Ryck knew. The one time he had ridden a PICS in training had shown him that. The seven men would be hard-pressed to stay on, and they would undoubtedly suffer bruises and cuts as they bounced around the hard-backed PICS.

"Are you ready, sir?" Staff Sergeant Hecs asked the major.

"This is not quite as I would have wished, but yes, we are ready."

Ryck would have felt more comfortable if all the passengers were in skins and bones, not just the two Tylarians. He hoped the major's vanity, if that was what it was, would not result in someone getting seriously hurt.

"Sergeant Samuelson, I want just one Marine watching outside. Everyone else step back out of sight. We don't want to play our hand too early," the platoon sergeant said.

"Lieutenant Xie," he called out to the militia commander. "The word from your higher headquarters is, I'm sorry to say, that you are on your own. My commander suggests that you leave with us. You won't be able to keep up all the way to the rally point, but you should be able to get out of the square, at least, before we pull away."

And if anyone had to fire on possible pursuers, Ryck realized cynically, it would be better if it were Tylarian militia rather than Federation Marines.

Staff Sergeant Hecs passed to Captain Davis that they were ready. The men in the rotunda stood around, doing nothing, basically waiting. Within a few minutes, though, the noise from outside shifted somehow.

"Some of them civvies is moving to the right," Lance Corporal Jurić from First Squad said as he watched out the window.

"Your right or their right, Jurić?" Sams asked his Marine.

Jurić, inside his PICS, moved the big suit back and forth, arms out, as he tried to figure out which direction was right and which was left.

"Our right," he said after a moment.

"Captain Davis is in position, and he says he can see the crowd gathering in front of him," Staff Sergeant Hecs reported.

Suddenly, Ryck's comms with the company opened up. Staff Sergeant Hecs must have switched both squad leaders onto the company command net.

Ryck knew both Staff Sergeant Hecs and Sams could see what Jurić was seeing, but as their lone set of eyes was in First Squad, not Third, Ryck didn't have that capability.

"Sams, can you slave me to Jurić's visuals?" he sent on a P2P[5] circuit.

"Sure thing," Sams said, and a moment later, Ryck was able to see Jurić's vids displayed on the upper right quadrant of his visor.

There were still about 50 people right outside the front entrance of the building. One man was talking to several other, pointing back at the entrance. He had the posture of someone in authority. Captain Davis' plan, if it was even his and not something higher headquarters was throwing at him, had not drawn everyone away from the building.

In the distance, more people were gathering, but those should be the protesters around the lieutenant and Popo's squad. Ryck wanted to tell Jurić to pan and zoom in to focus on them, but that wasn't his place to do that.

"Sams, Ryck," Staff Sergeant Hecs said over the command net, one linked to just the three of them.

"These civvies aren't moving. We can push through them, but our cargo is going to be at risk. Until we get everyone out and we can get up to speed, those yahoos out there can do some serious hurt to them. If they have any small arms, they really can't miss at that range, and rocks, or even just yanking their asses off of us could be pretty serious. We need a distraction, for at least 20 or 30 seconds. Any ideas?"

"What about sending a team, like out to join the lieutenant," Sams offered. "Think they would follow the team?"

"Nah, I don't think so. The team would be through them and gone," Staff Sergeant Hecs said.

Right then, Ryck knew what would work, but he hesitated to say it. As a new private on Atacama, in his first engagement, Ryck

[5] P2P: Person-to-person, a direct communication line between two people.

had seen the results of when miners had managed to knock down several PICS Marines and cracked them open with LTC drills. The sight of those Marines, opened up like a can of sardines, had stuck with Ryck through the ensuing years, a phobia that Ryck tried to suppress.

"We need someone to take a dive," Ryck said reluctantly.

"A dive?" Sams asked.

"Yeah. If a team runs through them out there, the staff sergeant is right. No one will follow. But what if two or three Marines make a dash, like they are making a break for it, but one Marine falls down? They'll swarm him, jump all over him."

"Shit!" Sams said, his opinion of the suggestion clear even over the circuit.

"No, I think Ryck's right. We need a distraction that'll keep their attention," Staff Sergeant Hecs said. "That would probably do it. We just need a few moments. I don't think they could actually do anything to us in that amount of time."

"What about if one of them has a toad?" Sams asked, referring to a hand-held incendiary that could slowly burn through about anything, including aPICS.

"That's a chance I think we have to take. We haven't seen anything to suggest that they might have something like that, and if they do, then our bait will just have to get up and out of there."

"So, who's going to do it?" Sams asked. "Who's going to take the fall?"

"I will," Ryck said immediately.

It was his idea—it was his responsibility to take the risk.

"No," Staff Sergeant Hecs said. "You're a squad leader. I need you for control. You need to bring up the rear, keeping everyone together, and trying to keep Marines between the bad guys and our cargo. Who else you got?"

Ryck thought for a moment. Ling, Stillwell, Khouri, and Hartono were "mounts" for the dash out of there. Peretti would be a good choice, but Ryck wanted him to help cover the rear. That left Holleran as the best choice. Knowing him, he would probably even think it was fun.

"Sams, give me one guy to go with Holleran, like two are making a break for it. Holleran will take the fall," he said.

"You gonna ask him if he volunteers?" Sams asked.

"Don't need to. He'll do it. And sometimes, you just need to pick the best person for the job anyway," Ryck said.

"That's it, then," Staff Sergeant Hecs said.   "I'll tell Lieutenant Xie to bring in his men outside the door to encourage the civvies to focus on Holleran. Let me pass this up the chain, and you go tell Holleran. Sams, who're you sending?"

"Lopez. That mother can really get his PICS flying."

"OK, good. Get ready. I want to leave in two mikes," he said before flipping back on the command circuit.

Ryck could hear him reporting to Captain Davis their plans as Ryck grabbed Holleran and briefed him. As expected, Holleran was up for the idea. He thought it would be "fun." Ryck couldn't help but think of Sergeant Nbele lying out on the ground on that Atacama mine pit, his PICS opened up and half of his guts spread out all over the dirt.

It was closer to three minutes before the seven passengers were mounted up and everyone was in position. Staff Sergeant Hecs gave the command, and Holleran and Lopez pushed out the main doors while the five militiamen slipped back inside. Ryck had Holleran's visuals on his visor. The lance Corporal bounded down the steps in front of him, startling the surprised protesters who then started to move back. Suddenly, the projection tumbled, making it hard to tell what was going on.

"Falling" while in a PICS was actually pretty hard to do. The gyros kept PICS upright through most forces thrown at it. The gyros had to be bypassed, and with them off, controlling the PICS took much more skill, skill Ryck hoped Holleran really did possess.

A loud "fuck!" sounded out as Holleran yelled, making sure his speakers were on. For a moment, the visuals steadied with a view of the sky. Then images started crowding forward as they shouted for the Marine's blood. A couple of men actually jumped on Holleran's chest, making the visuals too jumbled to make much sense from.

"Now!" Staff Sergeant Hecs passed, and Sams' first fire team and then the mounts-with their cargo onboard—pushed out the door to start running along the broad walkway that ran along the front of the building.

One of the legionnaires shouted "giddyup" as they started to move, to Ryck's annoyance.

Ryck had to wait several moments before he, as the second-to-last one to leave, got outside. About 20 meters beyond the bottom of the steps, a mass of people was attacking the prone Holleran. Several of the crowd, though, had stopped when they realized more Marines were pouring out of the building. A few were starting toward them.

To his left, Ryck saw that the way was clear all the way to the end of the building. Marines had already reached the edge and were disappearing down the stairs to ground level. He counted the seven mounts, their piggyback cargo still secure on their backs. As he took that in, a couple of the militiamen scooted past him and started running pell-mell after the lead elements.

"OK, Holleran," he passed. "Get out of there now!"

ROE be damned. If Holleran had any problem, Ryck was going to charge, his 8mm hypervelocity gun ablaze. Bodies were going to fall.

A few of the protesters who were still focused on Holleran seemed to lose their footing. The welcome sight of a PICS Marine rose from the mass of people. It lurched forward, looking like at least one protestor was under its bulk. A few steps forward, and Holleran broke free and started into a lumbering run along the bottom of the stairs parallel to the route Ryck was now taking. Two protesters tried to stop Holleran, but they went flying like pinballs after colliding with him.

At the end of the building, Ryck ran down the steps into the square. Along with the rest of his squad who were not acting as mounts and joined by Holleran, they formed a rough arc in back of the last of the cargo.

"Vehicle at our two o'clock!" Corporal Mendoza passed.

Ryck looked to see a hover picking up speed as it crossed the square, heading for where the Marines were entering the street that led deeper into the city. A quick mental calculation, and Ryck knew the hover could crash into the last of the Marines carrying the legionnaires and the two civvies before they could get out and into the street. A hover at speed could probably only damage a PICS if it crashed into it, but the same impact could be deadly to any unprotected passenger.

He was about to tell Prifit, one of the squad's heavy gunners, armed with the 20mm HGL[6], to take out the hover when a burst of fire sounded behind him. He didn't have to look back. His visor identified the outgoing fire as coming from two of the militiamen. The sparks flashed off the hover, then it fell to the ground sending even more sparks as it slid along the cobbles.

"Rey, Prifit, Keiji, slow down a little. We're going to cover those militia until they can at least get out of the square," Ryck passed to First Fire Team.

They might not be highly trained, but the militiamen, already being left in the dust, had stopped to remove a threat to the Marines. Ryck was not going to abandon them.

It seemed like forever, but it probably only took another minute until the militiamen, with the four Marines covering them, made it to the edge of the square. Lieutenant Xie gave Ryck a sloppy salute, then followed his men as they disappeared into the warrens that surrounded the area to the northeast of the square.

Ryck immediately sped up his team and caught back up with the rest. The same warrens that gave the militiamen cover provided the same cover for anyone trying to stop the Marines, so all senses were on full alert.

Ryck only half-listened to the recall of Captain Davis and Lieutenant Nidishchii's groups to turn and move to their respective rally points. They didn't have unprotected people riding Marines.

An explosion sounded in front of Ryck, and he caught a glimpse of a body being blown off one of the Marines. It wasn't much of an explosion, probably a home-made grenade of some sort, but Ryck's heart fell. Losing one of his charges was not supposed to happen. But much to Ryck's surprise, the passenger got back to his

---

[6] Heavy Grenade Launcher

feet. It was one of the Tylarians. The skin and bones he had put on had saved his butt. He shakily got back up on Hartono, and the group was back on the move.

Despite the confined route to the rally point, they were able to move pretty quickly, only having to stop twice for one of the legionnaires who was having a hard time staying on his Marine.

Eight minutes after leaving the square, they arrived at the rally point, which was a parking lot for a large Tesco store. Two Tylarian armored personnel carriers were there waiting. The five legionnaires and two Tylarians climbed off their Marines—gratefully, Ryck thought. The legionnaire who had fallen, a captain whose name Ryck hadn't caught, had messed up his uniform pretty badly. It was torn, and one sleeve was hanging off. Major Gruenstein was rumpled, and his nose was bleeding where he had probably slammed it into the back of his ride, but he had somehow managed to keep the blood off of his uniform. None of the legionnaires looked good, uniform-wise. Looking at the two Tylarians, even the one who'd been blown off Hartono, Ryck thought the legionnaires would be looking much more presentable if they had put on the skins.

"Well, Staff Sergeant Phantawisangtong, this was, shall we say, an adventure?" Major Gruenstein said, walking stiffly to the platoon sergeant.

"Glad to be of service, sir," the platoon sergeant said. "You should be at the LZ in another 10 or 15 minutes, so in less than an hour, you'll be on a French vessel."

"Yes, and in the arms of dear Capitaine de corvette Blanchard," he said dryly.

Ryck laughed, despite himself. The major had escaped what could have been a serious situation. He'd been beat up on a long run riding piggyback on a PICS. He looked like shit. But still, inter-service rivalries and personal dislikes trumped all of that. It was good to know that the Legion was just like any other service.

The major might have a feather up his ass, but Ryck found he kind of liked the guy. He wished him well, at least.

Major Gruenstein loaded up his four legionnaires, then turned and saluted the Marines before getting in himself. A moment later, the personnel carrier roared out of the parking lot and disappeared down the road in a cloud of black smoke.

"Good job, everyone," Staff Sergeant Hecs said. "We accomplished that part of the mission, but it's not over yet. We've got another five klicks to the rest of the platoon before we can get out of here. The ROE is still in effect. We will avoid any situation that can get ugly. Any questions?"

"Yeah, anyone got any charge on them?" Sams asked Ryck and Staff Sergeant Hecs on the command circuit. "What?" Staff Sergeant Hecs asked.

"Charge. On your PA. Money."

"What the grubbing hell for, Sams?" Ryck asked.

"Coke. That's a Tesco there. They've got to have Coke. I want a Coke."

Ryck started laughing, choking it off as Staff Sergeant Hecs flipped them back to the platoon circuit.

"If no questions, let's get the hell out of here," Staff Sergeant Hector Phantawisangtong, Federation Marines Corps, passed on to his men.

Alexander

Chapter 2

"You ready for this shit?" Sams whispered out of the side of his mouth to Ryck.

"Quiet in the ranks," Lieutenant Nidishchii' hissed, shutting Sams up.

The entire battalion was formed up in front of the nine of them: Captain Davis, the lieutenant, Lieutenant Lauer from Second Platoon, Staff Sergeant Hecs, Sams, Ryck, Lips Holleran, and Fab Groton, one of the squad leaders from Second.

The PA system was not working well. With galactic travel a long-accepted fact of life, Ryck thought a simple PA system should not be beyond their capabilities. At least the battalion adjutant was able to project his voice.

"Personnel to be recognized, front and center . . . march!" he called out, his command clearly reaching them in back of the formation.

"Detail, right face," Captain Davis ordered. "Forward, march."

The eight Marines marched to the far-right side of the formation, in back of H & S Company, then performed a column left and marched up alongside the formation. They conducted another column left after clearing the battalion, marching along its front to the center before halting.

"Detail, right, face. Present, arms!" the captain ordered.

Nine Marines saluted the three men in front of them. One of the men was the battalion commander. The second was none other than Major General Praeter, the division commanding general. The third was a Général Denis Bellerose, a Legion three-star. Général Bellerose was short, wiry man. His grayish dress uniform was understated despite the colorful medals on his chest, but the scrambled eggs adorning his kepi was pretty impressive. Ryck tried to keep his eyes locked forward, but he kept looking at the legionnaire through the corner of his eyes. He'd read the general's bio on the ceremony program, and it was pretty impressive. He'd served in seemingly most Legion conflicts over the last 30 years, commanding everything from a platoon to a division.

The fact that the Legion had sent a three-star to Alexander for the presentation was a message in and of itself. With the current tension between Greater France and the Federation, the Legion was showing that civilian leaders aside, there was a brotherhood of warriors. The cynic in Sams kept insisting to Ryck and Popo that the French were just trying to win over the Marines for political purposes.

The three officers returned the salute, and the captain brought them to order arms. There was a pause, then the adjutant's voice rang out.

"The *Commandant de la Légion Étrangère*, Général Alain Plessey, takes pleasure in authorizing the *Croix de guerre des théâtres d'opérations extérieurs* with bronze star to the following United Federation Marines for service in Tylaria on the planet Soreau on June 14, 366 Standard Reckoning:

"Captain Prentice K. Davis."

Ryck had been told that the award was the equivalent to a Federation Battle Commendation Second Class. If a Marines was awarded a BC, even a Third Class, a citation describing the action was read before presenting the medal. Not so with the TOE, which was the nickname of the French medal. Each recipient was mentioned by name in the battle dispatch, but not to the detail as in a Federation award citation.

A Legion lieutenant stepped up and presented the medal in a platinum box to the general as the flag officer stepped up to the captain. He pinned the white and red medal to the captain's dress blue blouse. As he stepped back, Captain Davis saluted, which the general returned. The French general took a step to his right to stand in front of Staff Sergeant Hecs while General Praeter slid in front of the captain.

"First Lieutenant Robert Lauer," the adjutant called out as the same procedure was followed to pin on the medal.

"Second Lieutenant Bertrand Nidishchii'," "Staff Sergeant Hector L. Phantawisangtong," "Sergeant Fabio Groton," and "Sergeant Bobbi Samuelson" followed. Ryck had to keep from sniggering at Sams' real name. Sams detested having a "girl's" name, and only answered to "Sams." It was as simple enough procedure to change a name. He could be "Duke," "Butch," "Rock," whatever, but he refused, saying Bobbi was the name his father gave him. He wouldn't let anyone use it to call him, though.

"Sergeant Ryck Lysander," the adjutant called out.

The Legion general took a step to stand in front of Ryck. He took the medal and started to pin it to Ryck's chest.

"That was aggressive thinking, sergeant. Major Gruenstein was quite impressed. Rumor has it that you were originally planning to join the Legion back on your home planet of Prophesy," he said quietly in his French-accented Standard.

How did he know that? Ryck wondered. Standing at attention, he stared straight ahead at the general's forehead, not responding.

"If you ever have second thoughts, I imagine we would have a place for you," the general said.

With the medal pinned on his blouse, Ryck saluted. A salute was an all-encompassing action, one that forced the officer to stop what he was saying to return it. It was the simplest thing for Ryck to do to change the subject.

"Lance Corporal Laste R. Holleran," rang out as the general took another step to his left.

Ryck let out a breath he hadn't realized he was holding. One general might have passed him, but now his division commander was in front of him. Ryck saluted, figuring that was usually a safe move.

General Praeter had started to reach to shake Ryck's hand, then when Ryck saluted, had to reverse course and bring his hand up in a salute. That done, he stuck out his hand once more.

Ryck didn't think he could shake hands while in the position of attention, but when a general officer offered his hand, it was best taken.

"Good job, Ryck. You made the division proud."

What is with these flags? One knows about when I enlisted, and here another is calling me by my first name?

The familiarity was making Ryck uncomfortable. General Praeter's attempt seemed forced, and that was even more disquieting. Ryck was glad when Lips' medal was pinned and the officers stepped back.

"Detail, present, arms!" Captain Davis ordered.

The three brass returned the salute, and the captain had them order arms, left face, and forward march. They got back to behind the formation, and within minutes, the battalion commander had turned the formation over to the sergeant major who dismissed the battalion.

The formalities were not over, though. The Legion was hosting a social at the O-Club, and each awardee was to attend. A number of Marines wandered over to take a look at the French medal and offer congratulations, and the platoon sergeant had to remind everyone to get to the club. He addressed the enlisted, but made sure the three officers heard him as well.

"So, Ryck, what do you think?" the staff sergeant asked once everyone was moving toward the club. "This legion medal mean as much as your Silver Star or BCs?"

"I don't know, Staff Sergeant. I mean, its kinda zap, I know, what with not many Marines having one."

Even after all these years, Ryck still had a problem addressing his former drill instructor. The staff sergeant was low-key, not at all like he'd been on the drill field. He called Ryck by his first name on a social basis. But to Ryck, Staff Sergeant Phantawisangtong was still "King Tong." His actual name was too unwieldy, and Ryck didn't feel comfortable calling him just "Hecs," so it was usually "staff sergeant" or rarely "Staff Sergeant Hecs."

"Still, we got the froggies out without too much damage to the locals, right?"

"But it isn't like we were really in too much danger. Not like on Luminosity," Ryck countered.

Ryck had earned a Silver Star on Luminosity as well as his second trip to regen. Staff Sergeant Hecs had earned a Navy Cross. A Navy Corpsman and another Marine had been awarded Federation Novas, one posthumously, the first time since the War of the Far Reaches that two Novas had been awarded for the same battle.

"True," Hecs replied. "But we saved lives, and sometimes, that is our mission."

"If you two can stop jabbering, we're here. The caic[7] is that the Frenchies have brought some real French wine and cognac, and I'm itching to try some of that," Sams said, pushing past the two to climb the steps to the club.

Ryck had never been in the O-Club. It was forbidden territory, not open to mere NCOs. As they entered the big double doors, he looked around eagerly—and was a bit disappointed. There was more wood than in the NCO Club and a fancy carpet at the entrance, but it was basically the same layout. Dining tables were off in a room to the left, a more open room with high tables at which they could stand was directly forward, and the bar, with lower tables and chairs and a pool table was off to the right—just like the NCO Club. Even the Enlisted Club was laid out in the same pattern. Ryck hadn't really thought about it before, but it seemed as if officers hung out, drinking beer and playing pool, just like the enlisted Marines. Officers and enlisted might not be as different as Ryck had assumed.

"Gentlemen, may I interest you in some of this '56 Chateau Latour?" a familiar French-accented voice asked from behind them, the major's hand grasping the neck of a partially drunk bottle of wine.

"Major, it's good to see you," Staff Sergeant Hecs said to Maj Gruenstein. "You kinda left us with the impression that the Legion was gonna slap your wrist some."

---

[7] Caic: rumor, scuttlebutt.

"True, I did say that. But good for me that my father is a schoolmate of our president, so after a short investigation, I was absolved of any wrongdoing. I was, how you say, whitewashed?"

He grabbed three empty glasses off a passing waiter, handed them to the three Marines, and sloppily filled the glasses.

"No disrespect, sir, but are you drunk?" Sams asked before taking a tentative sip of the wine.

"Ah, very astute of you. Yes, I most certainly am drunk. I am *bourré*. Do you say that? 'Buttered?' No, you don't," he answered for himself. "'Smashed,' yes, that is what you say. But this is very fine, very expensive wine, so it matters not."

Ryck took a sip of the wine. He had always liked wine, even the cheap stuff back on Prophesy. This was decidedly not the same. It was intense and complicated. He wasn't sure how much he liked it, but he knew he should like it, so he swirled it around in his mouth, sucking in some air, just as he'd seen on the food vids.

Sams made no pretense.

"Whew! Don't like it none. Maybe I need to try that cognac stuff instead," he said, pronouncing it "cog-nac."

"So, what's next for you, sir?" Staff Sergeant Hecs asked, talking over Sams. "You still getting your command?"

"That, my dear staff sergeant of Marines, is why I am buttered. Our dear *général* over there," he said, pointing with his glass at the Legion flag officer, "is not so much a fan of our president. And with the present situation growing between Greater France and your Federation, he seems to feel that we need a bigger liaison with you Marines and your Navy. As someone who has now performed combined operations with you, I am his logical choice. I found out this morning that I will be staying here on Alexander."

"Sorry about that, sir," Staff Sergeant Hecs said, reaching out to take the almost empty wine bottle. "But you'll get your command billet soon, I'm sure."

"*C'est la vie, mon sergeant, c'est la vie*," he replied, refusing to relinquish the bottle, tipping it up instead to drain it into his mouth.

Ryck wasn't sure how, or even if, he should respond. He looked up at the two generals on the other side of the room. Both men were watching them, and the Legion general didn't seem happy as he said something to General Praeter.

"Uh, Staff Sergeant, check your six," he said quietly, worried for the major.

Staff Sergeant Hecs casually glanced about, immediately realizing what Ryck had meant.

"Sams, why don't you take the good major and try and find that cognac you said you wanted. Ryck, grab Holleran and Groton, and let's go make nice with our honored guests."

The rest of the evening dragged on. Ryck was bored after 15 minutes, but he put up with the congratulations of the legionnaires, Marines, sailors, and civvie bigwigs. The deputy mayor wanted to drag Ryck into a discussion on whether Greater France and the Federations would ease tensions between them, but Ryck begged off commenting, saying that was for the civilian government to decide.

He finally decided that he did like the Latour, as well as several other nice vintages. The Le Bleu champagne was particularly nice. Sams, on the other hand, tried the cognac and immediately switched to beer. When Ryck spied Lips standing alone behind one of the buffet tables, he took that as an excuse to make his getaway.

"You ready to blow?" he asked as he walked up.

"Oh, cement it, sergeant! I've been ready!"

"Let me get Sergeant Samuelson, and we'll diddiho."

Sams wasn't ready, though. He was in deep conversation with and cleavage-peering at an attractive member of the governor's entourage. She seemed to be welcoming his attention.

Typical Sams, he thought as he went back to pick up Lips.

He stuffed a couple more pieces of *saucisson*, the label called it, but seemed like normal salami to him, in his mouth and grabbed a half-full bottle of wine that someone had left on a table as he took Lips and got out of there.

Chapter 3

"You coming? It's your brills-bro, after all," Sams said after sticking his head in the small squad leaders' office.

Ryck looked up from his screen to where Sams and Popo waited, both in their PT gear with their MCMA belts on.

"MacPruit's not my anything-bro, dipwad," Ryck responded sourly.

"Come on, Rycky-my-boy, you and him, you're tight, recruit buddies, and all," Sams went on as Popo laughed.

For the hundredth time, Ryck wished he hadn't told the other two squad leaders about the beasting the recruit platoon leaders had given MacPruit when the recruit had refused to acknowledge his recruit squad leader's authority. It had been Ryck's rabbit punch to the back of the neck that had knocked MacPruit to his knees, but not before he had taken down two of them. Seth MacPruit had been an MMA planetary champion before enlisting, and he was one tough customer. Against eight other recruits, though, he had taken a pretty serious beasting. It had brought him around, at least. He hadn't questioned recruit authority, and by the end of training, he had even started assisting other recruits in need.

Given his background, it wasn't surprising that he'd eventually been grabbed from a line company to coordinate the regiment's Marine Corps Martial Arts program. Ryck just wished that MacPruit hadn't gotten orders to Ninth Marines. It wasn't bad when MacPruit been in First Battalion as a regular grunt. Ryck only occasionally saw him around camp. But when he made sergeant and became the MCMA instructor, Ryck was going to have to enjoy his company once a quarter.

"OK, I'm coming. Just let me log off," Ryck said.

"You should thank your buddy, there. What Marines wants to have his nose stuck in his PA studying when he could be out kicking ass and taking names?" Popo asked, punctuating his question with a series of lame air punches and a side-kick. "Pow, pow! Take that, motherfuckers!"

"If that's the best you can do, Popo, then maybe you'd better be doing some studying, too, 'cause you aren't going to be advancing based on that weak shit," Ryck said.

He saved his notes and bookmarked the site he was reading, then powered down his screen. He'd been working on his degree in his free time, much to the delight of the other NCOs who accused him of wanting to become an officer, something he vociferously denied. He was just interested in history, something that had bloomed in him during Dr. Berber's classes back at recruit training. As long as he was studying, he figured he might as well earn a degree while he was at it.

If he could ever keep on track, that was. He had a paper on the background leading up to the War of the Lost Surrender due by 2200 that evening, and he hadn't even started writing it yet. He had started the research, but he'd gotten lost on a tangent reading about one of the true Marine heroes, First Lieutenant Ian Cannon, Jr., who was awarded the Federation Nova for taking command of the *FS Ponce* when the entire navy command had been wiped out, and instead of retreating, took the heavily damaged ship into the fray, destroying two enemy corvettes.

"Uh, forgetting something?" Sams asked, pointing down to his own waist at his blue belt.

Ryck had already changed into his skin trou and t-shirt PT gear before sitting down to study, but he hadn't put on the yellow belt that signified his MCMA level. He went back to his locker and grubbed around until he found it. He put it on.

"Satisfied?" he asked Sams

"Now we're talking! Let's diddiho. They're already out there, and Hecs and the lieutenant'll be out there soon," Sams said.

The three of them left the squadbay and made their way to the large, sawdust-filled pit where MCMA was conducted. MacPruit was already waiting, looking assured in his skin trousers, red shirt, and boots. Around his waist was a black belt, of course. He nodded at Ryck, but didn't approach the other three sergeants.

"See you two on the bounce," Popo said as they split up to join their squads ringing the outside of the pit.

Keijo and Prifit had been wrestling around, with Khouri egging them on when Ryck came up. He didn't have to say anything, though. They both stopped and started a more appropriate warm-up. Within a few minutes, the platoon commander and sergeant came out, signaling the start of the instruction.

"Marines of First Platoon, you ready to kick some ass?" MacPruit called out as he stepped into the training pit.

He was greeted by a chorus of "oo-rahs."

"As all of you know, you NEED your MCMA belt to get promoted. Iffen you don't have it, you ain't gettin' that next rank. Sose you all better pay attention. All you white belts, you ain't safe, neither. Iffen I think you don' rate that measly white belt, I can take it back right now," MacPruit yelled out as he strode back and forth in the middle of the ring.

Ryck wondered if he could take a yellow belt away, too. Not demote it to a white, but take it completely away. He decided he better keep that thought to himself. No use giving anyone any ideas.

"But you are not here jus' to qualify, jus' to get promoted. You are Marines, an' you want to close with and destroy the enemy. This is what you're made for! Am I right?"

There was another chorus of "oo-rahs," but not quite as enthusiastic. Ryck thought MacPruit might have gone a little heavy with the demotion threat. Three of his Marines--Stillwell, Peretti, and Rey--were white belts, and they had to be a little nervous. The previous regimental MCMA instructor had never mentioned demoting Marines, so for most of them, this was a new concept.

"Some of you ask why MCMA? Am I right?" MacPruit went on.

Damn skippy! Ryck agreed. Golf Company was a heavy company. They fought in PICS. All this hand-to-hand stuff was so much horseshit. Ryck knew it was to foster the warrior spirit, but in reality, just like pugil stick training, it offered nothing for a Marine in combat.

"Well, you aren't always gonna be in your PICS, you know. You could go in light, or you can lose your PICS. Your own Sergeant Lysander over there, he lost his PICS when you guys were fightin' on

Luminosity, right? Without his PICS, he even got a Silver Star, right? So you never know, you never know."

Ryck was surprised that MacPruit singled him out. He wondered what game the sergeant was playing. Yes, Ryck's PICS had been disabled, and yes, Ryck had continued the fight, but not as some kung fu master. He'd just figured out how to engage his weapons without the PICS' interface.

"So, let's get goin'. First, let's do some warm-ups. I wanna see where you all are. Give yourself a little room," MacPruit told them before leading them in some basic forms.

He wandered through class as he barked out commands, stopping to critique a few Marines. Ryck wanted to puke when MacPruit complemented the lieutenant on his form. As MacPruit moved on, the look on the lieutenant's face led Ryck to believe that the platoon commander had not been taken in by the brown-nosing.

"OK, Marines, OK," MacPruit shouted out. "Good job. But that's the boring part, am I right? You want combat, am I right? We'll get to that now, but first, I'm gonna demo it. I need a partner for that. Who's it gonna be?"

Ryck felt his heart sink. He thought he knew where this was leading. He was right.

"How about Sergeant Lysander? Me and him go back a long way, an' let me tell you, he's one tough hombre. An' he's already got combat experience without a PICS, without his skins and bones. Am I right?"

There was clapping from some of the Marines, and a "Kick some ass, Sergeant Lysander!" was shouted up from someone in Sams' squad.

Neither the reference to recruit training nor the combat was lost on Ryck. MacPruit, despite the ensuing years, had not forgotten that beasting in the showers that night. It also sounded like he resented Ryck's combat record. All MacPruit had done during his first tour with 1/9 was one show-the-flag-in-force to intimidate a case of social unrest. The unit had earned a Combat Mission medal, but Ryck doubted that MacPruit had even fired his weapon in anger.

There wasn't much Ryck could do, so he plastered a smile on his face and moved to the center of a pit. He stood in front of

MacPruit, trying to look at ease. The other sergeant reached into the cargo pocket of his skins trou and pulled out a training knife. He tossed it to Ryck, who managed to catch it.

"OK, sergeant, show me what you've got. Come at me," MacPruit told him.

This is stupid, Ryck thought. *When am I ever going to come at someone with a freaking knife?*

He couldn't hesitate, though. He raised the knife over his head and started forward with a yell.

MacPruit pulled an eGun out of his pocket and shot Ryck in the chest. Ryck looked down, staring at the slowly fading "hole" in his chest.

No shit, Sherlock. You've got a grubbing gun while you give me a freaking knife, he thought.

"That's not how you do it," MacPruit said to the platoon. "You don' need a knife. You don' need a rifle. You don' need a PICS. You, the Marine, are the weapon, whether you are naked or in a battlecruiser. But you need to know how to fight."

"Here, sergeant, give me the knife," he said, turning his attention back to Ryck. Ryck tossed it to him and caught the eGun tossed back. It was only a training aid, but it felt good in his hand. He checked the setting. I was set as a generic handgun. This was a standard training eGun, so it could be set to simulate all Marines ballistic small arms as well as several of the pulse weapons. It worked by calculating the range to a target, then sending a small electrostatic charge that simulated the effects of a specific weapon. The charge ionized at the target, leaving a glowing "impact" to show where a real round or charge would have hit. They were limited in range. The further out, the less accurate the simulation, but close in, they were a pretty fun training tool.

"OK, Sergeant Lysander. This time, I'm comin' at you."

Ryck held his eGun out. He was going to nail MacPruit and shut him up.

MacPruit turned to sweep his gaze around the pit at the Marines in the platoon before continuing, "Before I show you this, though . . ."

MacPruit suddenly spun, dropping down almost to the sawdust before springing up at Ryck. Ryck fired the eGun, but he was aiming at where the other sergeant's chest had been a moment before. The charge went right over MacPruit's head as the instructor crashed into Ryck, taking him down. Almost immediately, Ryck was stretched out, held captive by MacPruit, his right arm stretched out over his head and slightly behind him.

" . . . I should remind you never to give your enemy a warning. Hit him, and hit him hard."

MacPruit leaned back, stretching Ryck out further. Ryck tried to resist the pressure, to muscle through it, but the pain on his arm was too great. As much as he hated to do it, he tapped out with his left hand.

"Another thing. Iffen you ever get into combat with someone, neutralize him. See, this is hurtin' Sergeant Lysander's arm. See him trying to tap out, his hand flappin' like a beached salmon? But iffen I let him go now, he can still turn on me and do me damage. So I got to make sure he can't do nothing anymore."

He pulled back even further, and the pain made Ryck scream out. Something in his elbow popped, and MacPruit finally let up.

"See? Come in low, and never give an inch," he said as he got to his feet. "Let's pair up. I've got knives here in this box. Sorry, no eGuns, but we don' need them for this."

Ryck was still down in the sawdust, his arm on fire. He struggled to sit up.

"You ready to try it again?" MacPruit asked innocently. "I can be your partner."

"You mother grubber," Ryck hissed. "You broke my fucking arm!"

"Break it? Nah, I would've felt that. Maybe just sprained. Nothing a day or two in regen won't fix up, right? No harm, no foul," MacPruit said quietly.

"Doc, can you come over here?" he called out to the corpsman. "Looks like Sergeant Lysander hurt himself."

The corpsman did a quick check of Ryck's arm. MacPruit had been right. It was a sprain, and it would take two days of regen to heal it.

"Payback's a bitch," MacPruit said to Ryck as he was led off to sickbay. "Am I right?"

BHP Billiton B-19

Chapter 4

Ryck snuck another glance at Major Laurent standing across from him. The legionnaire barely fit inside the Stork, the top of his combat suit grazing the bird's overhead. It was not without a twinge of envy that he took in the legionnaire in his **Rigaudeau-3s**, the Legion's version of the Marine PICS. Ryck was proud of being a Marine, but still, every comparison between the two combat suits seemed to favor the **Rigaudeau-3s** as the better piece of gear.

It may have been a better piece of gear, but it did not marry well with a feet-in-the-wind Stork. Normally, when deploying in a PICS, Marines were lifted by an MV63-C, the Stork variant without a cargo bay. The PICS were slotted into cradle hoists which could quickly get two squads of PICS Marines onto the ground and into the fight. However, the Legion suit didn't have the coupling, so to accommodate Major Laurent, they were in an MV63-D, the latest model of the "normal" Stork. The web seats on which a Marine would normally sit were neither big enough nor strong enough for combat suits, so the seats were folded up and the pax[8] were all standing. With only the exit ramp as an egress, it would be more difficult and time-consuming to get the one embarked squad of Marines offloaded and the Delta on its way.

"What do you think of our friend, there?" Staff Sergeant Hecs asked him over the direct comms.

"I don't know. He seems OK, but his rank is screwing with me. 'Major Laurent,' but he's really an SNCO, a sergeant major?" Ryck answered back.

---

[8] Pax: Passengers.

"Yeah, and they call their gunnies '*adjudant*.' I don't mean that. I mean how are you with this guy following us, watching what we do?"

"I'm not copacetic with it, Staff Sergeant, to be honest. I still don't know why all of these observers, all of a sudden. At least we don't have the capitaine, like Sams and the lieutenant have with them. You said you were going to keep him off my ass, anyway," Ryck told his platoon sergeant.

As relations deteriorated between Greater France and the Federation, there had been a flurry of initiatives between the Marines and the Legion, fully supported by the brass. Ryck wasn't sure how the brass expected these initiatives to improve anything. The civilian politicians were going to do what they were going to do no matter what their military arms thought.

Not everyone was on board with the increased interaction, though. A plainclothes member of the Navy Office of Information, accompanied by the battalion S2 officer, had briefed the Marines prior to embarkation. The Legion observers were to be treated with respect, but care was to be taken with regards to technical information or other operations. It was pretty obvious that the Marines were supposed to keep their mouths shut while around the observers.

Still, despite the fact that he wished the legionnaire was not with them, that Legion R-3 was one sexy piece of gear. A good head taller than a PICS, it had highly advanced stealth capabilities which rendered it virtually invisible to most sensors, at least until is started firing its weapons. It supposedly used a different cooling system that didn't have to be changed out like the Marine's coldpacks. The armor, too, was supposedly better, especially against energy weapons. It was more effective and somehow more flexible at the same time. Ryck had spent a number of months in the battalion armory while a genhen, and he would have loved to get into the guts of a Legion suit and see what made it tick.

Enough of the R-fucking-3, he thought. *Eye on the prize!*

In this case, the "prize" was a command base for the Soldiers of God. BHP Billiton, the huge resource conglomerate, owned B-19. There were three major mines in operation, although exactly what they were extracting was a trade secret. The planet had never been terraformed, but it had plant life and an atmosphere, albeit one that could not support human life for long. Trace gasses would have a person coughing out his lungs within an hour after exposure.

About three months ago, the planet managing director informed their lone Federation liaison that they'd had odd fluctuations in their survey readings. He was suspicious that there could be poachers mining the other side of the planet. The Ministry of Resources looked into it before quickly turning it over to the Navy. Something was there, and it wasn't illegal mining.

A Navy Information Analysis Team, the NIS super spooks made up of ex-SEALS and techno wizards, was sent in. Within weeks, they had located the shielded station and confirmed it was SOG.

The location made sense for the criminal gang. The planet was very lightly populated and all on the other side of the globe. There was no military presence. If the MD hadn't decided to send out survey drones to see what could have been missed during the initial assessment, they could have remained undetected for years.

Ryck had a history with SOG, and when his platoon had taken down the *Robin*, an SOG-held hostage ship, Ryck's experience with them cost him over a year in regen. At least, the official report was that it was SOG. Most of the Marines involved thought it hadn't really been SOG but a copycat. Too many things didn't add up. But as the official version was that it was Soldiers of God, no one was going to go public and say anything different.

SOG was a criminal organization, nothing less. They acted under the guise of religious righteousness, but they were simply in it for the money, seeding their path with unspeakable acts of terror. Every government known to man had proclaimed them pariah, not covered by treaties of human rights. The Federation, acting hand-in-hand with the Brotherhood,[9] had thought it had cut off the head of the organization, but instead, many new heads had sprung up, far more decentralized. Wherever one of those heads showed up, it was immediately stomped.

[9] Brotherhood: The second largest confederation of planets. It has a religious basis and is a sometimes wary ally of the Federation.

This time, it was Second Battalion, Ninth Marines, with the *FS Toowoomba*, that would be doing the stomping.

Golf Company was the lead element, each platoon going in heavy. Echo was setting a perimeter, Weapons was in support, and Fox, going light, but with breathing gear, was in reserve, waiting to exploit success or move in if the complex was too tight for PICS. The attached Frog Team, with their Ratcatcher missiles, was deploying to knock down any escaping craft. The *Toowoomba*, in geosynchronous orbit above the target, with its array of weapons and Experion fighters, was more than capable of taking out a SOG ship, but if they were going to be in a fight in the first place, the Marines wanted credit, either with the Ratcatchers or their Wasp attack craft.

Ryck checked the readouts of each of his Marines, checking biostats and power levels. The upgraded command information system gave him ammo counts as well and would calculate rates of fire and depletion. It was a good add, but it was just one more thing to monitor. As a sergeant, Ryck was beginning to think he was getting to be more of a resource manager than a fighting Marine.

At five minutes out, he toggled the countdown warning. He could have passed it on over the comms, but they didn't need to continually hear his voice. A simple data message would suffice.

Like it or not, Ryck was feeling a bit nervous, and he couldn't let his Marines know that. Whether that had been SOG or a copycat on the *Robin*, memories of the misery that was regen kept creeping back into his mind. He looked at his rising pulse rate and tried to will it down. If Staff Sergeant Hecs or the lieutenant looked at their readouts, they would see his stress levels rising.

Get a hold of yourself. This isn't your first time to the party! he told himself.

He knew he just had to focus on the mission. Second Squad, with the EOD[10] team and heavy weapons team, was in a Charlie Stork, so they would be first in the zone, getting out and deployed within 15 or 20 seconds. The two Deltas, carrying First and Third, would flare in right after. Marines in PICS could actually damage a

---

[10] EOD: Explosive Ordinance Disposal

Stork if they weren't careful, so they couldn't bumrush out the back. They had rehearsed deplaning back on Alexander, like the riffle of a pack of cards shuffle in reverse, Ryck imagined it, the port aft Marine followed by the starboard aft Marine, followed by the next port Marine, and so on. It would take at least a minute to deplane. That was when they would be the most vulnerable.

There were three eyes on the target as they approached. The *Toowoomba* had her planetary sensors, battalion had a butterfly drone, and there was a recon team out there, all streaming in data. With the naked eye, their target looked like a rock face to a hill. Under different spectrums, seeds to which Ryck could switch, he could tell there was something off with it. There were odd lines visible on the display, and the rock's ambient temperature was slightly different from the rest of the rocks. The SOG had made a pretty elaborate and extensive effort, and it might confuse a casual sensor, but not the Federation's best equipment. It was SOG's bad luck that the original BHP Billiton drone was designed for deep ground analysis and not surface observation. Good luck to the Federation, though.

The go-light turned amber, indicating one minute. A matching amber icon flashed in their helmet face shields. Ryck shifted to look out the back to where the ramp was already lowering. When in skins and bones, Marines could start out of a Stork before the ramp was fully lowered: with them in PICS, this wouldn't be possible. The Stork crew was going to be over the LZ much longer than normal as it was, so they were already lowering the ramp. There was no intel on anti-air, but with the ramp lowered, the Stork's stealth capabilities would be far less effective, and if spotted, their shielding wouldn't be as strong, either.

As if to emphasize that vulnerability, a flash of light from the outside illuminated the cabin of the Stork. Ryck felt his heart drop as he tried to see out the back.

There was a surge of chatter on the comms. Ryck didn't have ears on higher headquarters circuits, but he could hear the platoon circuit. A missile, probably part of an automated defense system, had been launched at the other Stork carrying the lieutenant and Sams' squad just as they lowered their ramp. Luckily, it never hit the Stork. One of the *Toowoomba's* monitors, parked at the edge of space over the target, and taken the missile out with its ARG, the Atmospheric Rail Gun. A split second later, the jacketed round delivered its kilo-joule pulse to the missile's launch site.

Atmosphere dissipation was the bane of space-based energy weapons, requiring huge amounts of power to get that energy focused on the target on the ground. The ARG got around that by using railgun technology to send shells at amazingly high speeds through the atmosphere, each shell, a self-contained pulse generator. The jacket of the round would slough off at the target, and the pulse would initiate, focused at the target, and taking it out. A kilojoule was not as effective against hardened targets, but it should have been enough to put the launcher out of action.

Ryck hoped, at least.

Lieutenant Nidishchii' passed that one of the Wasps was coming in for a strike at the launch site, but Ryck knew the monitor's crew back on the *Toowoomba* would be watching the site closely, and at the first sign of electronic stirring from enemy weapons systems, would hit them with something a little more effective.

Worse than the scare of the missile attack was the fact that if they ever did have the element of surprise, it was gone now. Whoever was in the hidden complex had to know that they'd been discovered.

The Storks had continued their approach while the incoming missile had been destroyed. The first Stork, carrying Second Squad and the Weapons team, had already reached the LZ and was lifting back out of it. Ryck's Stork flew in fast, flaring at the last moment, its ramp slamming a little harder than normal.

Corporal Mendoza's team started the deliberate shuffle to get out of the bird. Ryck wanted to scream out to hurry, but that was just his nerves wanting to get out of the bird and to where he had more control of his situation. Peretti led, then Khouri, Mendoza, and Stillwell. Ryck was next, and he followed Stillwell out, ducking down as well as he could to make sure the helmet of his PICS didn't hit the top of the Stork's cabin at the lead edge of the ramp. He hoped his pet legionnaire wouldn't have an issue with the R-3's added height.

As soon as Ryck's feet hit the ground, he pushed forward, running a good 15 quick meters before turning to make sure everyone else debarked OK. Major Laurent was only a step or two behind him, and Ryck's abrupt stop and turn obviously took him by surprise. He nimbly dodged to his left and scooted past Ryck.

"Scooted" seemed like an odd term to Ryck to describe someone in a combat suit, but that is what it seemed to him. The legionnaire was remarkably nimble in his R-3. While the armor on an R-3 was termed "flexible" by many, it wasn't as if it was just a shirt and trou. However, there was some give to it, and the globe joints, which were small hardened spheres actually imbedded into the armor skin, offered a far more realistic range of motion than the PICS GT joints. If Ryck ignored the size and shape of the R-3, just from the movement, Ryck could almost imagine that the legionnaire was not in a combat suit at all as naturally as he was moving.

Ryck had to get his attention off the legionnaire. It was crunch time, and he had to focus on the mission. He waited until his squad had debarked, then got the Marines moving out of the zone and out of the path of any possible incoming that had targeted the LZ. He toggled up the route overlay on his display, then nudged the icons for his lead team over another 30 meters. Peretti, on point, would see where Ryck had positioned the command avatar for him and then move to the right until he was where Ryck wanted him. It was a very simple, yet effective, method of troop placement.

Ryck quickly zoomed out his display view. Echo was already forming the perimeter around the target, even placing a platoon behind the small mountain in case their targets had a rabbit hole that had not been identified. Ryck could see the Navy shuttle approaching with Fox, ready to land two platoons in the LZ Golf had just left. Golf's Second Platoon was moving forward in line with Third and First Platoon followed in trace. Things were going according to plan—so far.

The Marines moved through the five-meter tall fern-like vegetation. This was the first planet Ryck had been on that had vegetation but had not been terraformed. He'd seen alien plants before at a few botanical gardens, but never in their natural state. There was an odd homogeneity to the forest with none of the variation in height or variety found in terraformed worlds.

The two platoons moved at a fairly good clip through the fern-tree-things, simply pushing them aside. As the Marines approached the target, though, the terrain worked to pinch the two platoons together. This was the reason that only Golf was going in as the point of main effort. There simply was no room for any more units within the confined area.

As they passed one of the hillocks to their right, Ryck took a quick look with full sensors. He knew the recon team was on that 40 meter-tall rock jumble, but he couldn't pick up a thing on them. That always impressed Ryck. Going out into bad-guy territory, pooping and snooping with minimal armor seemed risky, but if the bad guys couldn't see them, then Ryck figured it was a risk worth taking. He sure appreciated having actual human eyes on a target, not just sensors. He gave the unseen team a nod of respect despite knowing they couldn't see it.

There was a surprising lack of comms chatter. As a rule, Marines were supposed to keep talking to a minimum. Even with frequency shifting and scrambling, the enemy could pick up the fact that communications were taking place, and with good AIs, could calculate potential courses of action based strictly on the amount, duration, and direction of voice comms being made. The less said over the net, the less there was to analyze. Still, voice comms were sometimes needed. So far, though, not much had been necessary during the movement to contact.

As the squad moved around another outcropping, about 300 meters from its target, a small yellow flashing number on Ryck's display caught his attention. Martin's PICS was running slightly hot. It wasn't into redline territory, but that was something that needed to be monitored. He made a mental note to have it checked.

Ryck toggled Martin's readout to the top of his display so he could keep an eye on it when the world around him erupted into a flash of flames and smoke. Ryck was thrown to the ground, banging painfully against the inside of his PICS. His display disappeared, leaving him with only a clear visor through which to see the dust cloud forming around him.

Mother grub! was all he could think as he tried to get his thoughts straight. He could taste blood where he'd bitten his tongue.

Everything was down. No comms, no data display. He couldn't even move his PICS. Ryck's immediately thought of his first mission when a squad of PICS Marines had been put out of action through a Trojan that had been wormed into the combat suit's control system. Four of the Marines had been killed. Despite this flashback, he was surprised at how calm he was as he hit the reset. To his tremendous relief, the status lights came back on, and the suit's AI began the start-up check. A set of PICS feet stepped into view, then the PICS ponderously bent over to reveal Corporal Rey's face. Ryck had no comms nor movement yet, but he winked back at his team leader. Rey gave him a thumbs up, then moved out of Ryck's narrow range of vision, probably moving to check on someone else. Yancy Sullivan had been just to Ryck's left where the blast seemed to have originated. Ryck needed to know if his PFC was OK.

Ryck was confused as to what could have hit them. Nothing was picked up by the sensors as incoming, and their sensors should have identified any mines.

The dust cleared, but Ryck couldn't see much. Marines were moving back and forth in front of him, but Ryck was facing away from the direction he wanted to face, that toward Sullivan. Two more of the squad bent down to check Ryck, turning him onto his back.

Ryck tried to take stock of himself as his PICS started coming back online. He'd banged his left arm pretty good, and he knew his tongue was bitten, but other than that, he seemed in one piece.

Lips put his face shield against Ryck's and shouted out "Are you OK?"

Ryck could hear him clearly, but muffled, through his face shield, so he shouted back "Yeah. How about Sullivan?"

As he yelled, he splattered blood across the inside of his face shield. It started to form into droplets and drip back down on his face. Instinctively, he tried to shift his body, and his PICS responded. It was coming back online. The display on his visor came to life—covered in blood splatters.

"Sullivan's out of action. Doc's got him stable though, but his leg's pretty fucked up. That blast twisted it like he was some sort of doll," Tizzard Rey said, his shout coming both through his PICS and over the comms.

"What the fuck was that?" Ryck asked. "How come we didn't pick anything up?"

"Don't know yet. Sergeant Kyle is doing a scan," Rey told him.

Frank Kyle was the EOD team leader. He would have some basic analyzing tools in his PICS-E, but Ryck knew they had to keep moving, and Frank might not have time to do a full scan. Knowing just what had exploded might have to wait for the Navy Seabees to come down and determine what had hit them.

Ryck slowly stood, checking all the readouts he could. He bent his knees and flexed his arms. He seemed to be moving OK, but he couldn't check the actual readout figures. Much of his face shield display was obscured by the blood he'd spit out. For all the advances in battle suit technology, something as simple as blood inside was a big problem. He couldn't just reach up and wipe it, after all. Not only did it block his view of some of his readouts, but it blocked some of the small micro-scans embedded in the face shield that read the eye commands used to activate the PICS' various display functions.

He turned to where PFC Sullivan had been and took his first steps to see if his PFC was OK.

"Sergeant Lysander, you back online?" the lieutenant asked over the person-to-person circuit.

"I think so, sir, but I can't really tell. My display is sort of covered in blood. I'm OK, though," he said, his words slightly slurred as his tongue was already swelling. "Can you wait one, though? I need to check on Sullivan."

The platoon commander said nothing else as Ryck arrived at where Sullivan was down, Doc Grbil working on him. The blast had wrenched the PFC's right leg, actually bending it at the knee at about a 70-degree angle. The joints were the weakest parts of a PICS, but still, that had to have been one hellacious blast. Luckily, the PICS leg had not completely detached, so Sullivan's leg had not been amputated. The angle was gruesome, but Ryck thought a couple of months in regen would make him as good as new.

"Yancy, how're you hanging?" Ryck asked as he approached the Marine.

The PFC's face shield was on clear, and Ryck could see Sullivan's face, a goofy-looking grin plastered across it.

"Oh, copacetic, Sergeant. No pain at all. Doc's hooked me up," he said as if he hadn't a care in the world.

"I've given him somamine," Doc Grbil passed to Ryck on a person-to-person. "He's not going to be feeling a thing."

Somamine was one of Pfizer's newest painkillers. It worked by changing the pain impulses into something the brain recognized as a warm feeling of contentment. The science of it was beyond Ryck, but it was a favorite among the Marines. They called it "happyland." It couldn't be used for too long as it could permanently reprogram the brain as to what was pain and what was pleasure, but it was very effective in situations such as this.

"Is he going to be OK?" Ryck asked.

"Yeah, he'll be fine. He's going to have to go through decon, though. The blast broke through his armor, and he got some of this toxic atmosphere that leaked in. I've gunked the break, and that should hold for now. As for his leg, it'll probably take some surgery to repair the damage, then regen to heal it. I think a couple of months, tops."

"Sergeant Lysander, I can see your stats even if you can't. All your readings are in the green. Are you effective? We've got to keep moving," the lieutenant asked.

"Uh, roger, sir, I'm still effective," Ryck responded.

He could hear the slight click that told him the platoon commander had switched back to the platoon net.

"PFC Sullivan has been WIA'd but is in no danger. He will be picked up by G-One for a casevac. We've still got our mission, so move it out. We don't know what ordinance was used against us, so until we identify it and devise countermeasure, watch your dispersion. Golf-Three-Six, out."

As Ryck turned to go back to his squad, he caught sight of Major Laurent standing 20 meters off to the side, clearly studying Sullivan. Ryck was suddenly washed over by a feeling of foreboding. Laurent was an observer, so he was bound to observe. Ryck couldn't help but feel, though, that he might be too interested in a weakness in the Marine PICS.

Within moments, as a team from First Platoon arrived to take charge of Sullivan, the platoon was back on the move. Ryck's PICS was moving normally. His problem, though, was visibility. Back on Prophesy, when the PCDC declared bankruptcy and pulled out, the economy had shattered with many people finding themselves out of work. A number of people took to standing at intersections and washing the windows of hovers for a few credits. Ryck would have paid 100 credits at the moment if one of those men or women was there now and could reach inside his PICS to clean off the blood.

The top of his face shield was clear. Ryck was using this section for visibility as he moved forward. This was where the anti-fogging vents were, though. In certain conditions, such as when out of direct sunlight in open space, the outside of the visor would be bitterly cold while the inside was kept warm. This could lead to fogging, so a simple vent system blew warmed air over the inside of the face shield. This was a basic, old-fashion method that worked surprisingly well.

On a whim, Ryck activated it. He didn't want to dry the blood where it was. That would make things worse. But he turned up the vent to its highest speed anyway. It worked. With the fan pumping out the air, it blew the droplets down the inside of the face shield to where it caught on the edge of where the face shield met armor. There were still streaks of blood which started to dry, but Ryck could see through his visor. More importantly, he could see his displays again.

The lieutenant had told him his numbers were good, but Ryck ran a quick check anyway. Other than a still slightly elevated pulse rate, everything was normal. Less than five minutes had passed since the explosion, so that was probably adrenalin still coursing through his body that had shot up his heart rate.

He ran a quick check on the rest of the squad. Sullivan's avatar had turned to the light blue of a Marine out of the fight, but still alive. Everyone else had normal readings.

This had been an unexpected delay, one that had cost the platoon a Marine, but the mission was still in place. Ryck forced his mind back on point, pushing the blast to the back of his mind.

He expected another blast, though, all his senses on the alert. However, they made it to Phase Line Rat without further incident. This was the final phase line before the Final Coordination Line, the FCL. Rat was in defilade to the final objective, out of any direct fire weapons. From Rat, the EOD team moved forward, supported by First Squad. The boomboom boys and Second Squad crossed the FCL and moved carefully to a point about 100 meters from the disguised entrance to the hidden depot. Ryck watched through piggybacking Popo's visuals as Sergeant Kyle unlimbered his DSD[11] and sent it trundling up to the doors. The small robot extended the first of its sensors, sending the readings back to Kyle. The EOD team leader shook his head, and then deployed the drill, trying to take a core sample. The drill easily moved through the outer, rock-like covering, but when it hit the actual door beneath, it stopped its progress. The little robot's front tracks lifted off the ground as it applied more pressure to the drill.

Sergeant Kyle stopped the drilling and deployed the laser. He had the DSD fire it where it had been drilling. Ryck remembered from his classes that the laser was not intended to penetrate but merely ablate off some of the surface so the robot's spectrometer could get an analysis.

Kyle shut down his DSD, and a moment later passed to Captain Davis on the command net "Golf-Six, these are some extremely hardened doors. They look to be a LTC variant and are around three meters thick. I don't have anything in my bag of tricks to breach this. We can look to bypass the doors and go through the rock face itself, but there's no telling yet how much rock we'll have to blast through. Waiting further instructions, over."

---

[11] Drug Sniffing Dog, slang for the E-334 EOD Remote Analytical Robot.

There was a moment of silence, probably as the company and maybe battalion leadership discussed what Frank had told them.

The nets crackled with Captain Davis' voice, "Give me a degree of assuredness on that. What's the chance that you can breach the doors."

"Uh, I'd say about zero to no chance. These things are massive. If you want me to blow our way in, we need to find a better spot to do it," the EOD sergeant replied.

"Roger that. I understand. Wait one, out," the company commander passed.

Only Ryck was able to access the command circuit, and he knew his Marines would wonder what was going on, so he passed, "There seems to be a problem. The doors at the entrance might be too big for the boomboom team. So, we're waiting for further word now."

"Shit, stand by to stand by. Typical shit," Lips said.

Lips had been a Corporal selected to sergeant when he'd been busted back down to E3 for taking a swing at an MP while drunk. He might have been Ryck's most capable Marine, but he did tend to exhibit a degree of cynicism. Ryck didn't know if he blamed him for his cynicism, given his history. And this time, Ryck agreed with Lips' sentiment.

SOG knew they were there. Delaying the assault just gave them more time to prepare whatever they had planned for the Marines. Sergeant Kyle and his team couldn't get in, but there were other resources available to them.

"Sergeant L," PFC Stillwell asked on the P2P, "Is Yancy really going to be OK?"

Ryck realized that Stillwell had never seen a Marine WIA'd. Most of his squad had never seen combat. Their operation on Soreau wasn't combat, and it hadn't prepared them for their first taste of fighting. They still hadn't fired their weapons in anger, and to see one of their own taken down was a gut-check.

Stillwell and Sullivan were also buddies, he knew. They'd gone through boot together, been assigned to Fox together, then transferred over to Golf together.

"He's barely hurt. Two months in regen, and he'll be back good as new, Jeb," he told the PFC.

"Is it going to hurt? Regen, I mean. I mean, you've been there, and they say it hurts," Stillwell went on.

"It fucking sucks, to be honest. The itch is the worse 'cause you can't scratch it. And the Navy docs can't give you anything for it. They say that can affect the healing. But Yancy's a tough mother. He'll handle it just fine."

Ryck was about to continue in that vein when the command circuit came alive.

"All hands, get your men turned around and move back to your platoon rally points. The Navy's going to drop a GD-1905," Captain Davis passed. "The ship's monitor is getting into position for the correct drop aspect. We've got four minutes, I repeat four minutes, before the drop."

Ryck looked at his display. The captain had lied. His display already read 3:47.

"I want to see heels and asses, now!" the skipper ordered.

Ryck didn't wait for the lieutenant to pass it down.

"We've got a Tungsicle coming, in 3:42 and counting. Everybody, form up now! Squad V, and move it back to Rally Point Isaacs. The captain wants heels and asses!"

The Gravity Dropped-1905, the "Tungsicle," was a simple four-meter long column of crystallized ceramic-covered tungsten. One end was pointed, the other flat. At 80 centimeters wide, it was a hefty 155,000 kg of unstoppable penetration power. It was too big for the monitor's main railgun, so a modified railgun with far less power was mounted on the exterior of the monitor to get the weapon moving. It left the monitor at "only" 2000 mps. Ryck didn't know the correct calculations for how fast it would be moving when it hit based on BHP Billiton B-19's 1.2 G gravity well and 90% atmospheric density, but with a heavy sectional density and a low ballistic coefficient, it should still be at over 1,000 mps upon impact.

That impact would be huge, in the giga-joule range. The crystallized ceramic coating not only kept the Tungsicle from burning up in the atmosphere as it fell, but it also helped internalize the KE upon impact. The weapon was designed to penetrate into a target, not expend all that energy in a surface blast. However, that much energy could not be completely contained. There was going to be a pretty big bang when it hit, the equivalent to maybe 15 tons of TNT.

Navy gunners had the motto *Velocitas Eradico*, or "I, who am speed, eradicate." The Tungsicle put fact to that motto.

The Marines were in full, if controlled flight. Ryck was proud to see that their formation was holding well, and that they were in line with the other squads. Rally Point Isaacs was the platoon rally point, some 1550 meters away from the target and back toward the LZ, just past a flat-topped rocky outcropping. The original rally point was to the side of the hill, but as he watched his display, it was shifted to the back of the hill.

The lieutenant's on the ball, Ryck thought approvingly.

The hill would give added protection to the Marines.

On open terrain and at a flat out run, a Marine in a PICS could cover that much ground in a little over a minute and a half. Over unknown terrain, Ryck thought two and a half minutes was more reasonable. That would give them a minute to take whatever cover they could get.

"Khouri, keep up," he sent on a P2P, almost automatically.

Part of his mind was focused on running, on picking the right path. Another part of his mind, the analytical part, watched the 11 blue icons that represented his men. Watching the display could tend to reduce them to pieces of a game. They were not electrons, though. They were his men, his Marines, and he was responsible for them.

His display read 1:03 when they reached the rally point. Ryck knew he had the far sector of their position, but his display helpfully highlighted just where his squad was supposed to be. His Marines fanned out, achieving good dispersion.

"Everyone, down on the deck," he told them.

Ryck activated the gyro shutdown, then had to wait the five seconds before he could actually kneel first, then fall forward onto his face. His display looked brighter with the dark dirt as a background.

Just as he was almost prone, he caught sight of his pet legionnaire. Major Laurent was kneeling, not lying flat on his face. Ryck wondered if that was by choice or if his R-3 could not switch off the aspect control of his combat suit. That was food for thought.

Flat on the deck, Ryck contemplated sending off one of his two dragonflies. He wanted to watch the target. He'd seen vids of the Tungsicle, even of the larger ship-based Doric, but he'd never witnessed the real thing. As if reading his mind, the lieutenant slaved the recon team's eyes to the entire platoon.

"The second it hits, we are up and moving," Lieutenant Nidishchii' passed on the platoon circuit. "Treat the impact the same as if EOD had blown the doors. Everything else remains the same as planned."

There was a short pause, then the lieutenant came back on the circuit with, "Staff Sergeant Phantawisangtong has reminded me that there could be significant debris flying through the air. I will coordinate with the rest, but keep your heads down and don't move until given the order."

Ryck watched the display count down: . . . four . . . three . . . two . . . one . . .

There was a brilliant flash that temporarily burned out the recon team's feed and lit the sky above the platoon. Ryck was face down, but the light made it to his face shield.

A moment later, the shock wave traveling through the ground hit beneath him, lifting him up 10 or 15 centimeters. Still another few moments later, the atmospheric shock wave rolled over them.

"Keep down," Ryck reminded his squad.

The feed from recon stabilized. It showed the rock camouflage over the doors in the rubble, the heavy metal of the doors revealing their size. A huge hole had been torn into the left side, leaving it twisted and glowing orange. Surprisingly, the right side was still up, even if canted outwards. Dust and smoke poured up into the sky while heavy pieces of debris fell between the recon team's eyes and the target.

A loud whump sounded behind Ryck as something fell from above. There was a small patter of tiny bits of debris, but only that one piece that had made the whump had been heavy enough to have posed any danger.

Ryck's action icon on his display flashed green.

"Up and at 'em," he passed to his men as he got up, reactivating his gyro stabilization system.

The overall plan had been loaded into their AIs. These worked well as an initial plan, but the AIs had only limited capability to make corrections with regards to the rest of the force as the assault progressed. This broke down the initial plan during the fog of war, and the Marines had to rely on their training and ability to react to events.

Ryck didn't need his display, though, to show him where to go. The dark column of smoke ahead of him was a beacon. This was the squad's third time over the exact same ground, so they were able to cover it quickly. It was important to reach and enter the complex as soon as possible. Intel thought the initial chamber would be a warehouse or receiving station. At least two cloaked shuttles had arrived while the target had been under direct observation, and some large pieces of equipment as well as pallets of supplies had been offloaded and muled through the doors and into the complex. Anyone directly inside the doors would probably have been killed when the Tungsicle hit, but there were tunnels and other areas that had been identified, and any SOG deeper inside the facility could have survived. If the enemy was making their way to the first chamber, it would be better for the Marines if they beat the SOG there.

Ryck monitored his squad's progress as each Marine got his PICS up to speed. The squad was moving in good order, each one keeping the proper dispersion. He felt a surge of pride. These were good men.

Ryck's squad was designated to enter the complex first. As they approached, Ryck activated one of his dragonflies, sending the small drone up and zooming it through the smoldering doors. He'd already programmed it to scout out the entire interior, and his AI took over control of the drone. Ryck could manually take control, but the AI was pretty good at this function, leaving Ryck with one less thing on his plate.

It took a lot of training to multitask in a PICS. Ryck had to move forward in a tactical method, monitor his squad, and observe what his dragonfly revealed. Watching the dragonfly's feed while reacting to what was in front of him as he moved was the most difficult part. It was as if his two eyes were looking in different directions at the same time.

The Tungsicle had blown through the big doors before penetrating the ferrocrete floor of the warehouse, a four or five-meter hole its signature. Despite the crystallized ceramic coating, this had released a huge amount of energy, and the entire deck of the warehouse had cracked and buckled. What looked to be a complete Viceroy-class fighter had been destroyed, as well as a number of ground vehicles. The warehouse had been full of supplies and equipment. Now it was full of junk.

Ryck wasn't seeing a real visual. There was too much dust and smoke inside. But the AI was taking the visual, the infrared, and the radar image from the dragonfly and compiling it into one view that made sense.

There was only one signature of a human body. At least it was half of a body. There could be more hidden in the rubble, but that was the only one evident from the scan.

The lieutenant was watching the same feed, so Ryck didn't have to report it up. Ryck tended to rely on speech too much, and it sometimes was difficult for him to step back and let the displays do their job. In many cases, a quick glance at the display could tell someone what they needed to know when trying to explain it would take four or five times as long.

Still, he couldn't resist the simple "Go" he passed to Corporal Rey to move into the complex.

Corporal Rey's team skirted the glowing edges of the destroyed portion of the door and disappeared into the warehouse. The AI noted the movement and focused the dragonfly on the team as they entered. Now, Ryck's face shield had Rey's visuals, the dragonfly's compiled display, and the actual visuals of what was in front of him. It took a lot of focus to keep things straight in his mind.

Rey signaled the all-clear, and Ryck and the rest of the squad followed inside. He closed Rey's feed and reduced the dragonfly's to a small screen on the upper right side of his face shield. This was better.

Intel had been right. This was a warehouse, a monster one. To Ryck, it looked like the preparation for a major offensive, not just the typical ship pirating for which the gang was known. This looked similar in scale to when a Marine battalion was getting ready to deploy.

Third Squad pushed to the back of the warehouse, making room for the rest of the platoon as well as First Platoon to enter.

"I've got the main passage here," Corporal Beady passed.

Ryck moved to meet him. He and Lips were standing in front of a large passage, five meters wide and three high. Down the middle was the shiny surface of a magnostrip,[12] a sure sign that supplies were floated along it to other parts of the complex.

Ryck did a quick reprogram, and the dragonfly zipped past the three Marines to enter the passage. Ryck followed the feeds as the drone flew in about 30 meters before encountering blast doors. The shock of the Tungsicle had buckled the deck even this far back, but the doors still appeared to be solid.

Ryck could see that the lieutenant was no longer on the feed, so he brought him up on a P2P.

"Sir, we've got a major passage out, but it's got a blast door barring our way. I've got my dragonfly on it now."

The small dark blue light that flashed on let Ryck know the lieutenant had slaved onto his dragonfly's feed.

"Hold your position. I'm sending Sergeant Kyle in now," he passed after a few moments.

Sergeant Kyle and his team arrived. Ryck switched over control of his dragonfly to Frank and let him fly it across the face of the door. The EOD sergeant gave the drone back, then took the DSD off its harness on his back, and sent it forward.

---

[12] Magnostrip: A positively charged strip laid down to facilitate the movement of pallets, which were also positively charged. The repelling forces elevated the pallet, making it quite easy to move up and down the strip.

"Just checking for little surprises," The EOD sergeant told Ryck.

They hadn't sensed the mine or whatever that had taken Sullivan out, so Ryck was not totally confident that the DSD could sniff out any other booby traps.

As soon as the DSD hit the door, instead of having the robot analyze it, Kyle moved his team forward. Ryck motioned Corporal Beady to move his team forward for security as well.

Staff Sergeant Hecs came up alongside of Ryck and asked, "What have we got?"

Ryck shrugged the best he could while in a PICS and ran a 10 or 15 seconds of the dragonfly's previous feed.

"Frank Kyle's in there with his team. I sent Beady's team in, too. I think I'm going to tag along," Ryck told his platoon sergeant.

"Lead on, then," Staff Sergeant Hecs said.

Both Marines walked down the passage. The overhead was low for a PICS, so low that Ryck could have jumped up and hit the top of his PICS on it. But it was plenty wide enough for two PICS Marines to walk in side-by-side.

At the corner of the door, Frank Kyle and Corporal Zhou, one of his team members, were gesturing along its breadth, obviously in deep conversation. They quickly seem to come to a course of action. The three Marines, in their PICS-Es, brought out their jack-off hands. Like corpsmen, sometimes EOD Marines needed more dexterity and control than that offered by the normal arms and hands of a PICS. When that happened, they could open their PICS' arms, then slide their real arms out the bottom, protected by a much thinner PICS "skin." The jack-off arms provided nothing other than atmospheric protection, but the Marines could use their real arms almost as if they were in a regular uniform. Ryck always thought that they looked like insects molting when they used the jack-off arms.

The three EOD Marines began placing their shaped charge limpets in a pattern. It took less than a minute to get all six charges placed. A small red light on each limpet indicated that they were ready for detonation.

"Gentlemen, I suggest we move back out of here," Kyle said matter-of-factly.

The Marines moved to the warehouse proper, stepping to the side of the passage as they reached it. Kyle reported back to the lieutenant that they were ready to blow the door.

"You holding up, Ryck?" Staff Sergeant Hecs asked him on the P2P.

"I'm fine. I might be a bit stiff tomorrow, but no problem now," he answered.

Lieutenant Nidishchii' and Captain Davis lumbered up to them. The captain took Kyle's report, then had a P2P discussion with the lieutenant, after which, the platoon commander brought up the three squad leaders, Sergeant Kyle, and Staff Sergeant Hecs on the command circuit.

"We think there's another staging area on the other side of that door. We know there's at least 20 SOG here, maybe more. We've seen only one body. That leaves no fewer than 19 others, and we know they don't meekly surrender. We've got to anticipate that at some point, they are going to fight. Captain Davis thinks the staging area might give them cover to put up a defensive position, and I agree. We've got to get in and hit them hard, but this passage is a choke point. They can Horatio at the Bridge it and make it tough for us. What we're going to do is at the moment the door comes down . . ." he paused. "You've got that covered, right Sergeant Kyle?"

"I abso-fucking-lutely guarantee it, Lieutenant," Kyle responded.

"OK. Then, as I was saying, the second the door comes down, Weapons is going to send pulse and HE down the passage. Third, you're still the tip of the spear. I want you moving right on the ass of the HE rounds. Sergeant Samuelson, you're on Sergeant Lysander's ass, and Sergeant Paul, you're next. I'm moving with Third Squad, Staff Sergeant **Phantawisangtong** will be with First. I'm loading a movement plan on where to go once we hit the room, but as always, use your judgment.

"This will be a very confined area, so watch your displays. I want no friendly fire casualties. Got it?"

The five Marines all acknowledged their orders, then split to bring their Marines up to speed. As Ryck was briefing his squad, two teams from Weapons came up with their heavy guns. Ryck raised a hand in a half salute to Sergeant Xander Kubasaki, the heavy guns section leader, who was a friend of his.

Xander's team set up two weapons just inside the start of the passage. The M232 was a small, multipurpose artillery piece. It fired a 70 mm shell and could be adjusted for mortar, artillery or direct fire. The P-996B was a self-contained pulse weapon. The gun itself was smaller than the M232, but with the power-pack attached, the system was bigger. It fired a two-joule EMP charge.

With the players in place, the lieutenant signaled Kyle to detonate the charge. Kyle took out his Marine Corps-issue Samsung PA. This being the Corps, the PA was rather obsolete, and Ryck always thought it was funny when EOD initiated huge amounts of destruction and mayhem with a 30-year-old telephone. They might as well bring back semaphore to send messages or light smoke signals.

With a simple press of this thumb, Sergeant Kyle set off the charges. There was a flash as the shaped charges, programmed for cutting, detonated. The explosion that reached the waiting Marines was subdued. Kyle was not trying to destroy the door, merely get it open.

Ryck had recovered his dragonfly to his sleeve, where it was recharging in case it was needed again. But the weapon's team had deployed another, and Ryck was slaved to it. For a moment, it looked as if Kyle had miscalculated. Then the door began to lean before falling back in a cloud of dust.

Immediately, the M232 opened up with two rounds. Those rounds impacted on the wall another 15 or 20 meters beyond the now flat door. A simple curve in the passage had defeated a modern piece of artillery. From his schoolwork, Ryck knew that even castle-makers in medieval times understood this defense and built ogees like this, as they were termed, to slow down attacks.

The P-996B had better luck. The pulse charge took off in a flash of blue, hit the far wall, and bounced past. Whether it reached the far compartment or not, Ryck didn't know. Whether it did or didn't, though, the assault was on.

Ryck followed right on Keiji's ass, two steps back and up against the left-hand wall. That made five Marines forming an interlocking front as they rushed down the passage. The weapons team's dragonfly preceded them, and Ryck tried to glance at its feed, but the Marines were already in assault mode. They passed the door, stepping on it as they ran. Moments later, they rounded the curve in the passage—and were immediately taken under fire.

A PICS relied on its armor to protect the Marine inside, and that armor was pretty effective against kinetic weapons up to a certain size and velocity. For energy weapons, the armor helped deflect the waves, but the Marines relied on small, portable shields that both repelled and absorbed the energy thrown at them.

Ryck's shield took on the blue glow which indicated it was activated by incoming fire. With the dried blood still on his face shield, the light blue glow took on a darker more sinister tone.

Ryck's display flashed with the warning, and the intake gauge began to rise. Whatever was being fired at them was pretty powerful, and he could see the numbers flash as he approached critical. If he redlined, he was done for. The suit, at best, would shut down. At worse, the situation would go critical with potentially fatal consequences. At the rate at which the gauge was climbing, that point could come as soon as ten seconds.

Ryck let loose a string of his 8mm high-velocity darts. He wanted to send in his shoulder rockets as well, but with Keiji bobbing just in front of him, it was too risky. Keiji let loose with his rockets, though, four salvos of three each, one after the other. Then he let loose with his 20mm cannon. He had a full combat load of 104 shells, and he looked bound and determined to expend them all by the time they closed with the enemy.

The little dragonfly had been knocked out of action by the first pulse fired. Ryck's AI tried to make sense of just where their targets were, but with the huge amount of energy flying around the confined area, the sensors were struggling to gather any meaningful data.

It didn't matter. Ahead of him, behind a barricade of some sort, the faint green flashes of pulses being fired at the Marines pinpointed their adversary. The green flash was indicative of a Confederation[13] weapon system, something Ryck noted despite the urgency of their situation.

Ryck shifted his darts to the green flashes. At immense speeds, the darts could actually penetrate armor given lucky circumstances. They could also mess up the circuits of EMP weapons if they hit right.

Ryck was almost redlined. The Marines had to get out of the kill zone, but the only way out was forward.

His exterior sensors failed, burnt out. Those gave him atmospheric readings, so they wouldn't stop him from fighting, but the rest of his sensors couldn't be far behind.

"You mother grubbing toad suckers!" he shouted as he pushed to the end of the passage and his system alarm went to a single, ominous tone. He was in the red, past the manufacturer's tolerances.

To his right, another salvo of rockets went off while Keiji kept pumping 20 mike-mike grenades. Explosions filled the 30 x 30-meter room, and suddenly, the incoming blasts of energy stopped. What had taken the weapon out, Ryck didn't know nor care at the moment. He was still redlined—how far into the red, he didn't know. It was beyond the gauge's ability to measure it.

He rushed with the other four Marines to where the incoming had originated. Two shattered, armored bodies, hung down over the barricade they had been using while firing the pulse cannon, which was now canted upwards. Another man was still alive. He was getting to his feet and unlimbering, amazingly enough, an honest-to-goodness sword. Technically, a mono-molecular edged blade could do damage to even a Marine in a PICS, but with five PICS Marines bearing down on him, he had no chance. Whether he died as a result of the 8mm darts fired into his chest or when Lips simply ran him over, Ryck couldn't tell. He was <u>definitely, 100% dead, though</u>, Ryck knew that.

[13] Confederation: The Confederation of Free States, a small loosely-aligned group of planets.

The rest of the platoon was there in seconds. Ryck stood there, heart pounding. He didn't need his readouts to know he was hyperventilating, which was good, as all his readouts had flickered, then failed. He forced himself to calm down, to center himself.

The lieutenant barely looked at the three dead SOG before going on his exterior speaker and asking for status checks. That puzzled Ryck for a moment before he realized that his comms were out, too. With First Platoon entering the room, it was getting crowded, but they took up positions while Third took stock of themselves. Without comms and displays, it was pretty confusing. It shouldn't be, Ryck knew, but they were pretty much married to their electronics. Ryck would have to think on that later. War should not be so reliant on electrons.

It took about five minutes to tally the damage. Of the squad, only Peretti hadn't redlined. Ryck and the lieutenant and three Marines from First Platoon were also redlined. Once redlined, a PICS was combat ineffective until the armory gave it a full check and repair. Somehow, no combat suits had suffered catastrophic failures, and no Marines were WIA. All five of the first Marines in the assault had taken their suits well past their tolerances, which would interest the brass back at the head shed.

Captain Davis arrived and took over, but not for long. He told Staff Sergeant Hecs, who still had comms, to take over the platoon, which must have galled the lieutenant. A quick look at the passages leading off from the scene, though, made it obvious that the PICS Marines had done all they could do. The passages were just too small for combat suits. Fox Company was called forward, to take the fight on to the remaining enemy.

As Ryck waited to move out, he thought that his squad had fought well, especially given the fact that this was the first combat for a good chunk of his platoon.

Corporals Rey and Mendoza, Lance Corporals Keiji and Martin, and Private Peretti were the only Marines who had faced combat before. Caesar Peretti was the only one who even had a bronze star on his Combat Mission Medal, earned before a drunken spree out in the ville had gotten him busted back down to private. Yet the squad had faced an armed, determined enemy and had not blinked. Ryck felt honored to be a part of the squad, part of this group of men.

His reverie was broken as they started to form up. The platoon, using the hand and arm signals Ryck had thought were obsolete back at Camp Charles when the recruits had to learn them, rallied up and started moving back down the main passage to get out of the complex and where they could get picked-up for their ride to the ship. They filed past Fox as the light company made its way in. They would be fighting in their skins and bones against a foe that had managed to take out one Marine in a PICS and almost disabled an entire platoon of PICS Marines.

Ryck had been in Fox when he first joined the battalion, and he had friends there. When he saw his old running mate T-Rex filing in with his squad, Ryck gave him a thumbs up. Even if his squad had led the initial assault, he felt guilty about leaving the field of battle before the battle was won. Now his friends, his fellow Marines, would have to go in and finish the job.

Fair winds and following seas, brothers, he sent his thoughts out to them as his fight was done.

Prophesy

Chapter 5

Ryck looked in the mirror. His medals hung straight, his dress blues sharp and creased. Everything looked right with his uniform. Today, everything *had* to be right.

"Looking good, little brother, looking good. You're going to make the ladies fall hard," Lysa said from the bathroom doorway.

"None will be as good looking as you, sis," he said.

"Ha! Like this?" she asked, pointing at her very pregnant belly.

"Men on Prophesy like their women fertile. You know that," he said with a laugh.

After seeing the look on her face, he protested, "Just joking, just joking!"

"Well, that's me, fertile, despite the misogyny inherent in your statement," she said, punching Ryck in the arm. "When your new nephew arrives on the scene, I'll be up on you three to zero, so maybe you can use this opportunity to find your own wife? Women get the nesting instinct at weddings, after all, and you, little brother, more than most, need someone. And speaking of weddings, Barret and the girls are already in the hover waiting. You about ready?"

"Yeah, just trying to make sure I look OK," he answered.

He followed his twin down the stairs and out the front door to where Barret had the Lexus idling.

"Uncle Ryck, sit with me!" Camyle called out from the back seat.

"No, your Uncle Ryck is going to sit in the front seat. He has to keep his uniform nice and clean," Lysa told her four-year-old.

"But he never sits with me!" she cried out.

"Yes, he did. This morning, to go to the store," Kylee told her.

"That doesn't count!"

"Should I?" Ryck whispered to his sister.

"You kidding? You may be a Marine, but you'd stand no chance with those two. No, you get in front. We've got an hour before we get there."

As soon as they got in, Barret lifted the big hover off the pavement and pulled out of the development. This was the fourth Lexus Barret had since Ryck had known him. The water reclamation business was very kind to him. Ryck knew he could have the same kind of life. Barret had offered him the position of vice president of the company, but Ryck had decided that he wanted to re-enlist in the Corps. He didn't regret his decision, but still, this was one sweet ride.

The hour drive flew by quickly with Camyle teaching Ryck *The Popcorn Song.* Kylee, with her 6-year-old sense of maturity, didn't join in.

Ryck had only been to the Hope-of-Life family compound once, and he had thought it crowded then with his friend Joshua's large family. This time, it was a zoo. A teenager was directing traffic, and he waved Barret to park the Lexus right up against a cornfield along with what had to be 30 or 35 other vehicles.

They got out of the Lexus and walked over to the barn, each of his nieces taking one of his hands in hers. Joshua's mother was in the yard in front of the barn, giving instructions. She saw Ryck and waved him over.

"Do you know my Uncle Ryck is a Marine?" Camyle asked Joshua's mom.

"Of course she does," Kylee said in an exasperated tone. "Uncle Ryck and Mr. Joshua are Marines together, and Mrs. Hope-of-Life is Mr. Joshua's mom."

"Ryck, it be good to see you again," Joshua's mother said, giving him a hug and a kiss on the cheek. "Joshua be in the house in the guest bedroom. Why don't you go in and see what he be needing. Tabitha here will take care of your family."

Before Ryck could reply, she shouted out "No, no! Those are to go under the tent!" to some unseen worker.

"Sorry, Ryck, I must be going," she said before hurrying off to take care of whatever emergency she had discovered.

Ryck left Lysa, Barret, and the girls and walked over to the main house. People were streaming in and out of the main doors on various missions. Most of the women and men were wearing the plainly-colored clothes typical of a Torritite, but there were a few splashes of color, and more than a little cleavage and leg exhibited by some of the women. Not all the guests were part of the Torritite community.

Ryck walked into the foyer, barely getting out of the way of a young girl rushing out carrying a pitcher of some sort of drink. He spied the stairs and started to them when a familiar face caught his eye. Hannah, Joshua's sister, had come out of the large kitchen, wiping her hands on the little white apron that most single Torritite women wore. Ryck made a beeline to her.

"Hi Hannah. You busy?" he said as he came up, immediately regretting his choice of an opening line.

Busy? Really? That was the best he could do?

Hannah's eyes lit up when she saw him.

"Ryck, welcome! Joshua's going to be happy to see you. He be afraid all week that you weren't going to make it, and he be so happy afta you called last night," she said, giving him a hug and a kiss on the cheek. "Oh, it be good to see you!"

She reached up and flicked his Silver Star.

"Joshua, you know, he be always talking about you. 'Ryck be a hero, Ryck be going to make sergeant major.' But if you don't be showing up here, I think I be tracking you down and let you have some."

"Have some what?" Ryck said, trying to inject a playfully suggestive quality to his voice.

"Oh, don't you be trying that stuff with me, Ryck Lysander," she said with a laugh. "No way I be getting with a soldier boy, no sir. Not like poor Hope, the dear girl."

Hope was Joshua's soon-to-be bride.

"What do you mean? She's marrying your brother," Ryck asked.

"Well, aside from her new name, Hope Hope-of-Life, she be marrying a Marine. A Marine be like any soldier. He be gone from home. And the wife be worrying, waiting while her husband fights, waiting for the chaplain to come a'knocking on the door to tell her that her man won't be coming home. No, not for me, thank you very much. Not for me."

Ryck felt deflated. He didn't know Hannah well enough to have any serious intentions with her, but to be knocked out of the race before even leaving the gate was a little rough.

"Oh, listen to me, rattling on. This be a joyous day," she said, reaching out to take one of Ryck's hands in hers. "You go on upstairs and see Joshua. He probably be about ready to pass out by now. And after the ceremony, come see me. Mayhaps we can get together some evening while you are here."

"You and me? Like on a date?" he asked stupidly. "I thought you didn't want to date a Marine."

"I don't want to be with a Marine, as in marry one. But I want to see if men in uniform be really as fun as the other girls say, and you be cutting a rather fine figure, if I do say so."

That was fine with Ryck. More than fine.

"OK, then. It's a date. I'll catch up with you later," he said, reluctantly pulling away and rushing up the stairs.

He should have known better by now. The Torritites dressed conservatively, and they followed the teachings of the Bible as they understood them, but they were not prudes. Joshua liked to lift a pint or two, and he was no stranger to the ladies. Why would Hannah be any different?

Never having been upstairs in the Hope-of-Life household, he didn't know which was the guest bedroom. He opened one door to see the bride, in her long white gown, getting help with her veil. A dozen female voices screamed at him to get out.

He did.

The next room was empty, but he felt a sense of relief when he saw Joshua in the third room he tried. He was leaning up against a dresser, talking to several other men both in uniform and out. As soon as he saw Ryck, he broke out into a huge smile.

"'Bout time you showed up, bro," he said as he strode over to Ryck and gave him a bear hug.

They pounded each other's back a few times, then tried to disengage. Ryck's medals, though, hung up on Joshua's shooting badges, hooking them together.

"Oh, snark. You hero shit's trying to mess me up. A little help here!" he called out.

Another Marine stood up and reached between them to unhook the two.

"Kellen Krupt. You must be Ryck Lysander," the Marine said. "Josh's told us all about you since we left Tarawa."

"I swear I'm innocent. Don't believe all his BS," Ryck said as the others broke out into laughter.

There were eight men in uniform, all wearing sword belts. Six were Marines, Joshua's friends from Camp Charles where he was a DI. One was a Navy corpsman, also one of Joshua's drill field friends. The eighth was a legionnaire. That had to be Joshua's older brother, Ezekiel. The eight were to form the sword arch to welcome the new bride into the military family. The last man in the arch would swat Hope on the butt as they passed through the arch.

"Hey, come help me with my SGA,[14]" Joshua told Ryck, leading him to the guest bath off the main room.

Ryck made a show of checking the alignment of the Marine Corps emblem on Joshua's collar, but he realized that had just been an excuse to talk to him.

"You OK?" Ryck asked.

"I be stressed but good," Joshua said, momentarily reverting to his Tortie speech patterns.

"Seems normal to me. I'd be stressing, too, if I be getting married," Ryck replied, mimicking Tortie speech.

"But, I'm glad you're here, bro. You and I go back. Remember when we were sitting there, ready to enlist in the Legion? Then your friend, what was his name?" Joshua asked.

[14] SGA: the Star, Globe, and Anchor, the emblem of the Federation Marines

"Proctor. Proctor Miller."

"Yeah, that's the guy. He convinced us to go see the Marine recruiter, and that sly cat hooked us. Your buddy didn't even make it. DOR'd[15]. But we did. Now we're Sergeants of Marines."

"And why the history lesson, bro?" Ryck asked.

"I don't know. Just been thinking. About life, you know. I had my tour with 1stMarDiv as a grunt, then re-upped and went to the drill field. Never saw any action, though, not like you. I don't know how I would have reacted," Joshua said matter-of-factly.

"You would have been fine, kicking ass and taking names," Ryck assured him.

"Maybe, but I was single then. Now, I'm gonna have me a wife and kid, and they're gonna need me."

"No hurry on the kid, there, big boy. Take it a step at a time," Ryck told him.

"Already took that step," Joshua admitted.

"You mean you knocked her up," Ryck asked, surprised.

"You'll see in about seven-and-a-half months," Joshua told him. "Hope came out to visit me on Tarawa, and well, you know how that goes."

"Yeah, I guess I do now!" Ryck exclaimed.

"So, what I mean is, I still gotta prove myself in combat. You've been there. You've proven the temper of your steel. We've never talked about it, but I gotta know if I can do the same. But now, I'm going to be a husband and a father. Hope thinks she's gonna like the military life, but only if I redesignate into a pogue billet."

"You want to do that?" Ryck asked his friend.

"Fuck no. I need to prove myself first. Maybe after, but not now."

"Well, you're just going to have to tell her," Ryck said.

"Hey, you two done making out in there? They're calling for the groom!" a voice shouted, accompanied by a pounding on the door.

"Just a freaking minute!" Joshua shouted back.

---

[15] DOR: Dropped on Request. Quit the training program.

"Hey, don't stress out now. This is your happy day. We'll talk later, OK?" Ryck said.

"OK, OK. We'll talk," Joshua said, taking a deep breath. "Thanks, bro, though, for coming."

"Wouldn't miss it for the world. And I am honored to be your best man. Surprised, though. Your brother is out in the next room, and you've got your Camp Charles buds."

"What, Ezekiel? Nope. He's married, and Kellen, he's married, too. According to tradition, a best man has to be single. The other guys, I just needed eight for the sword arch."

"So I'm your third choice? Suddenly, I'm not feeling so honored," Ryck said with a chuckle.

"Hey, at least you made the list, bro!"

"Before we go, here," Joshua said, taking a slim package from his trouser pocket. "I think it's traditional, right, for the Best Man?"

Ryck took it, admiring the clean packing for a moment, then tried to slide off the ribbon without breaking it."

"For goodness sakes, just open the grubbing thing!"

Ryck broke the ribbon and slit the paper. His heart caught when he saw the name on the box. He opened it, and yes, there was a Rolex Adventurer, shiny and beckoning.

"Shit, Joshua, that's amazing, but it's what, a month's pay?"

"A month-and-a-half, but who's counting?"

"I can't take this!" Ryck protested.

"Yeah, you can. This is from me to you, brother."

"I don't know what to say."

"You can say thanks. And you can make sure I don't grubbing faint out there. No viral vids making the circuit of me passing out, OK?"

"Sure thing, and well, thanks. I think your blushing bride is waiting for her prince." Ryck told him.

They hugged one more time before opening the door and stepping out to where the others were waiting.

"Enjoy your last few minutes of freedom, there, Sergeant of Marines. Let's go get this thing done," Ryck said as he escorted his friend to change his life.

Pannington

Chapter 6

The Stork flared above the LZ, the ramp coming down to half a meter above the grass. Ryck was up as the light turned green, pushing forward to debark and deploy into a defensive position.

Ryck was nervous despite his previous combat experience. Over the last five years, he'd gotten used to his PICS. He hadn't gone into a hot zone in skins and bones since Atacama, his very first operation. Still, he was a Marine, and every Marine was a rifleman. It was the man inside the PICS that wreaked havoc amongst his enemies, not the hardware itself.

He kept telling himself that.

He rushed out, immediately moved to his nine o'clock, and took a knee at the edge of the zone. Glancing down at his forearm, he saw avatars that told him the rest of the squad and the automatic weapons team from Weapons Platoon had deployed in textbook fashion. The LZ was not that big, maybe 40 meters across, so he could have just lifted his eyes, but old habits died hard, and even if the display was on his sleeve and not on his visor, he now trusted the electronics more than actual visuals.

For the zillionth time, he wished the Corps had not moved away from the combat face shield he'd first used in recruit training. He didn't' believe the tests that concluded that having a face shield made each Marine ever-so-slightly less efficient and reactive. As a squad leader, having the displays in front of his eyes seemed more natural than having to look down at his forearm.

Ryck felt somewhat naked, but with only a squad of mercenaries guarding the complex, this was not expected to be a serious action. Navy intel had told them Luminosity was going to be a cakewalk, too, though, and Ryck remembered how that had turned out.

The wind kicked up by the departing Stork died down, so Ryck told the squad to move out. They were to marry up with Second Squad 200 meters to the northwest, clearing the zone for First. Sams' squad would be in their PICS, but they would be acting as the heavy reserve. The point of main effort was Third and Second.

The squad formed into a wedge just inside the treeline, then moved through the low canopy. Pannington had only been terraformed for 50 years, so the forest didn't have any old growth. The tallest trees were perhaps 20 meters. A newly populated planet or not, there was a myriad of animal life, mostly birds, flitting about them as they moved to the link-up.

Popo and the Lieutenant met him as they took position off Third's right flank.

"Nothing new from the company," Lieutenant Nidishchii' told him. "Third Platoon has met up with the NIS agent, and they'll be moving to the cargo bays on schedule. Second Platoon has landed at Parkerville and has deployed, making its presence known by inspecting the legitimate warehouses. We don't have an exact location for the mercenaries, but intel thinks they will be deployed around the main entrance. Our guide is about five minutes out, and we've got 45 minutes to get to the emergency exit, breach it, and take the escape tunnels. No one, and that means *no one*, is to get through us."

Ryck tried to catch any flicker of uncertainty in the lieutenant's voice. The wiry Marine had been with the platoon for over a year now, and he'd been promoted to first lieutenant. This was their second real action as platoon commander and squad leader.

Ryck didn't know what to make of the lieutenant. He didn't seem to have much of a personality one way or the other, but his reputation was stellar. Evidently, as an enlisted Marine, he'd built up quite a name for himself, earning two Silver Stars and a Purple Heart. He'd gotten an appointment to the Naval Academy, and came out a new second lieutenant. During the last year, though,

Ryck hadn't seen anything noteworthy in his platoon commander. Nothing bad about him, but nothing noteworthy. He done OK on BHP Billiton B-19, but hadn't really stepped out to match his rep, in Ryck's humble opinion. Maybe Ryck would see something now that they were in the real deal.

The platoon commander's voice was steady, no hint of uncertainty. Ryck hoped his own voice didn't reveal the uncertainty in his mind, though, uncertainty rooted not only because the squad was going in light and not in their PICS, but in the mission itself.

Golf Company's mission was to take out an illegal warehouse complex, a hub of black-market trading. At the same time, Fox would be taking out another complex located deep underground on the larger of Pannington's two moons. Echo would "occupy" Robbinsville, the planetary capital, showing the flag with PICS Marines.

The assault on the SOG warehouse made sense. SOG was a terrorist gang who attacked and killed Federation citizens. This mission was different, though. As far as he knew, the people running this operation were not terrorists. They did not kidnap and kill. Ryck knew that black-marketing was illegal. He'd downloaded a few vids without paying, of course, but didn't everyone do that? That wasn't wholesale commerce. He understood the need for the government to regulate commerce, to collect taxes. Some of those taxes paid for his salary, after all.

But why the Marines? Since when had they become Commerce Cops? The Marine Corps' mission was defense, not being policemen. The Federation Charter forbade armed Marines from even stepping foot on Earth, so strong was the concept that the Marine Corps was not an instrument to use against the general populace. Yet here they were, being cops.

All that was above Ryck's pay grade—way above. He had a mission to accomplish, and he was going to get all his Marines through it and back home. That was a mission that he understood.

This was Ryck's sixth combat op, seven if he counted the NEO[16] on Soreau. Of the six, this would be the third time he was

---

[16] NEO: Non-combatant Evacuation Operation

going underground. He'd done a paper on the war in Vietnam back in the 20th Century, old time, and he'd been fascinated by the tunnel rats of the US, Australian, and Korean forces. It looked like he was turning into a modern version of them, though, and he wasn't sure he really wanted to be. He wasn't claustrophobic, but fighting underground could give anyone the jeebies.

Their guide, a local whose name was withheld, contacted the lieutenant. Three Marines from Second went out to meet him, then escorted him back. He was wearing a ski-mask, which had to be hot in the muggy, late morning heat. With no name and a mask, Ryck did not get a warm and fuzzy about the man. Supposedly, he worked in the complex, but NIS had turned him (for what had to be a tidy sum.) He could just as well be leading them into a trap, though.

The two squads broke into columns. With Ryck's squad 50 meters to the left of Second, they made their way through the forest. A column was not a secure formation for a movement to contact, but it did allow for a smaller front to any observers. There were sensors guarding the exit and surrounding area, of course, but the Marines had been assured that they had been deactivated.

First Squad, in their PICS, would follow in trace, staying out of the complex itself while securing their rear. Any belligerent who somehow made it past the other two squads would be picked up by them.

There was not much undergrowth, which surprised Ryck. Normally, with younger forests, thickets and other vegetation made movement difficult. Here, it was pretty clear. Evidently, many of the different kinds of plant life which could fill the forest floor had either never been introduced, or more likely, given the biogenesis teams penchant for a full bio-diversity, they just hadn't established themselves yet. Terraforming was not like engineering. Nature had a way of asserting itself despite centuries of mankind's experience.

The two squads stopped 150 meters short of their objective to wait out the final 10 minutes. Ryck pulled up the map of the complex one more time on his display. His mission was to follow Third through the exit, then take the right-branching tunnel. They would move forward to the next intersection, secure it, then sit and wait for the ants to come scurrying out.

There was no telling how accurate the map was, though. The best ground penetration sensors, both from space and from atmosphere drones, had only been able to discern the larger passages. NIS had acquired some hand-drawn maps as well, but who knew how accurate they were?

At five minutes to go-time, the boomboom team from Weapons Platoon crept forward, covered by one of Second's fire teams. Sergeant Kyle led them as they placed their charge on the door. Ryck half-expected someone to come out shooting, but all remained quiet.

Second Squad crept closer while the boomboom team retreated back. They would not be detonating the charge. It was slaved to the charges that Third Platoon would be placing on the cargo bays. Once armed, the charge would detonate at the same time as Third's.

"Get ready," Ryck sent on the squad circuit needlessly.

His Marines would be watching the same timer as he was. When it got to 10 seconds, he gathered his legs under him and got into a crouch, ready to move. At exactly zero, a muffled explosion sounded in front of him.

Second Squad was up and moving before the smoke and dust had cleared. Ryck gave them ten seconds, then sent off Corporal Rey's team. He followed next with the other two fire teams and the automatic weapons team behind him.

Ryck should have waited another ten seconds. Rey's team ran into the tail end of Popo's squad, and they had to stop. Within a few heartbeats, though, the last Marine in Third was in, and Lance Corporal Keiji led the way for Second.

Sweat was already pouring down Ryck's back, faster than his skins could wick it away. His PICS was temperature controlled. Skins were not, unless a heavy environmental pack was carried.

He scooted past the big steel door that hung ajar. The boomboom boys knew their stuff. Just enough explosives had been used to breach the door, but not enough to destroy it.

The lieutenant had stopped at the Y in the main corridor. He was playing traffic cop, motioning Ryck's squad off to the right. With Keiji on point, they moved quickly down their assigned corridor. A small room on the left slowed them down. The room was not on the map, but it had to be cleared. The room had a half-dozen drums, and each one had to be checked to make sure it was empty. That took time, at least 30 seconds. They still had another 50 meters to go before they reached their objective. Ryck had Mendoza's team cover Rey's as First sprinted the last interval.

"We're at Blue Whiskey," Rey passed as he set his team.

Ryck jumped up and moved forward. The intersection was too small for his entire squad. The main corridor was about three meters across, the side corridor two. He had 15 Marines, the 13 in his squad and the two in the heavy machine gun team attached to him. He sent the machine gun team to join with Rey's team, told Mendoza to cover the side corridor, and told Corporal Beady to cover their rear.

"We've got movement to our front," Keiji passed before the machine gun team could get their M449 deployed.

Ryck could see their renewed efforts to get the gun ready as other Marines took whatever cover they could find.

"Halt! Put your hands up!" someone, probably Prifit, shouted in front of Ryck.

A three-round burst sounded, at least one round winging past Ryck's head as it ricocheted along the wall of the corridor. Ahead of him, Ryck could see shapes hitting the deck as the M449 opened up.

"Cease fire! Cease Fire! We surrender!" a panicked voice called out.

"Push your weapon away from you, slowly. If you make one move, so help me, I'll ghost you right there," Prifit called out.

Ryck was already moving. He slid past the M449 team, leaving them a field of fire in case they had to open up again. Prifit and Keiji were standing in the middle of the corridor. Corporal Rey and Hartono were hugging the wall, but covering the 10 or so people lying on the ground 10 meters in front of them. One man was on his back, leg twisted under him, one hand still grasping his Lancet. His dead eyes stared at the ceiling while blood pooled rapidly to his side. Two more men in military-looking utilities were slowly, ever so slowly, pushing their own Lancets away from them.

Ryck touched Keiji's shoulder and motioned him to move to the side. They had to leave the middle of the corridor open in case the gun team needed to engage again.

"John, get your team up here," he passed to Corporal Beady.

"That's far enough, you two. Hands behind your head," Prifit told the two living gunmen.

It took only seconds before Third Team was there. Ryck had Beady send two men, Holleran and Ling, to pick up the three Lancets, then slap zips on each of the prisoners. Once the last man had his hands secured behind his back, Ryck could finally turn down the stress a notch.

Shots rang out, momentarily bringing the stress back until Ryck realized they were sounding from off to the left of his Marines, out of their area. Second Squad sounded like they were in it, but within 20 or 30 seconds, the firing died away. The last shots sounded like M99 reports, not Lancets, though it was hard to tell with all the echoing.

Ryck had reported their catch to the lieutenant and was ordered to sit tight. One of the prisoners asked to have his zips adjusted. Ryck ignored him.

It only took about 30 minutes for the all-clear to sound. The lieutenant told Ryck to move back, taking the prisoners out of the complex. A few of them had to be helped to their feet. Two had pissed in their pants, and the smell was getting ripe. That was another advantage to PICS that Ryck missed: filtered air.

He released the zips on two of the men in overalls, then refastened them with their hands in front. They had to drag the body of the dead merc. The younger of the two, a heavyset man, looked like he wanted to throw up as they picked up the merc's arms. The blood trail, which looked dark brown under the fluorescent lights, seemed to mesmerize him for a moment of time before the gag reflex took over him. Ryck heard Holleran bet Martin that the guy would lose it before they made it out. Ryck pushed to the front, and he never did find out who won the bet.

Two Marines in PICS stood outside at either side of the exit, looking like ancient statues guarding a temple. Several of the prisoners tried to crowd the center, trying to keep as far away from the motionless Marines as possible. The two surviving mercs didn't give the Marines a second glance.

For once, Navy intel seemed to have been right. This had been an easy mission, all things considered. A Marine in Third Platoon had been slightly wounded, but that was the only WIA from Golf. Two Marines in Second Squad had been hit, as had Hartono, but their bones had hardened as they were designed to do, and none of the three had been hurt. Ryck looked over at Hartono who was showing the boot, PFC Ling, where he had been hit.

Ryck thought Ling didn't show enough gumption as a member of the squad. He wasn't sure how the PFC had even made it through boot camp. To Ryck, this mission was barely worth mentioning, but to PFC Jeb Ling, this was a pivotal moment in his career. He had been blooded. Maybe that would stiffen up his backbone.

The mercs and workers had not fared as well as the Marines. Ryck didn't know how many had fallen before Third Platoon, but a three had died facing Second. There was the merc killed by the M449 with Ryck, and Third squad had killed two of the workers. A merc with them had been gut-shot. Doc Steuber was working on him, and he didn't seem too concerned, so the merc was probably going to pull through.

"Good job, Sergeant Lysander. Your Marines did well. We'll wait for recall instructions, but meanwhile, work on your after-action report. I'd like it by 2200," the lieutenant told him, cool as could be.

This was the lieutenant's second combat action as an officer, discounting the rescue of the Legion officers on Soreau, and he acted like this was simply another training exercise. With two Silver Stars, he'd been in the shit before, and this was nothing to compare with that, but still, Ryck expected a little more emotion.

"Aye-aye, sir," Ryck responded. At first, he'd hated the after-action reports he'd had to draft up after every training evolution. When he started treating them like homework for his academic classes, though, they became less of a burden, just one of those routine things he had to do.

"Hey, what unit are you guys?" one of the mercs asked from where he was sitting.

Ryck caught his eye, then looked away.

"Come one, what harm is there? Let's see, one heavy squad, two light. From where we are, you're, what Third Marine Division? Ninth Marines maybe? So not a heavy company. I'm guessing Alpha, 1/9," he went on.

"Shut the fuck up," Holleran told him, stepping up and bending over to address the merc.

"Calm down there, Joe. Just making conversation," the merc said, seemingly nonplussed by Holleran's aggressive stance over him.

"Name's not Joe, worm, and I said shut up," Holleran said, leaning over further to put his face right in the merc's.

"Remember Paragraph 2002. You don't want an international incident, do you?"

"Lips, stand down," Ryck said, putting his hand on the lance corporal's shoulder and turning him around. "Go wait by Doc and bring him here when he's done. This guy's been hit, too."

"But what about what he said?" Lips protested.

"Go," Ryck told him, giving him a light shove.

"Lips? That's precious," the merc said as Lips strode off.

"What do you know about Paragraph 2002?" Ryck asked.

Paragraph 2002 was part of the Harbin Accords, the agreement in which the interplanetary rules of combat were delineated. That paragraph specifically prohibited any maltreatment of civilian prisoners.

"I used to be a Marine. Lance Corporal Jerry Damien, at your service," he said with a smile. "I'd offer you my hand, but I'm kind of tied up at the moment."

Ryck just stared at him, mouth falling open.

"Yep, thought that might surprise you," the merc said.

"You, what, you deserted to become a mercenary?" Ryck asked, still stunned.

"What? No, of course not. I did my time. Didn't get recommended for re-enlistment, though, so I got out. Thought about the Legion, but got picked up by Phoenix Security, instead. They sent me here."

"But you're a mercenary," Ryck protested.

"And you are . . .?" the man asked, waiting for Ryck to reply.

"I'm not a grubbing mercenary, that's for sure!" Ryck answered.

"Really? So what mission of 'defense' are you on right now? Who are you saving? At least I know what my job was. I was hired to protect a legitimate business enterprise. You, on the other hand, were sent to close it down. Sounds like a corporate mercenary to me," he said.

Ryck had noted this very point to himself earlier, so the merc's statement hit him hard. He could not admit that, though.

"Sorry, you're all fucked up. I'm a Federation Marine," he stated with conviction. "and this 'business,' as you call it, is not legitimate. It's a smuggling operation."

"Smuggling? Because it doesn't pay Federation protection money--excuse me--tariffs? Who do you think runs this operation?"

Ryck shrugged.

"Greater France, that's who. They're not part of your vaunted Federation."

"But the Mutual Defense Treaty. They have to kick in for that, right?" Ryck asked.

"Do you know your history, Sergeant? The American Revolution? 'No taxation without representation?'" the merc asked, continuing before Ryck could reply. "Well, Greater France doesn't feel that they have to kowtow to the great Federation. I know you've been following the news. You've seen the goings on back on Earth. Things are coming to a head, and I wouldn't be surprised to see war break out."

War, with France? No, it'll never happen, Ryck thought. *What am I doing arguing with him?*

"Enjoy your time in prison, asshole," he said.

"Prison? Won't happen."

"Yeah, right. You attacked a Federation military force. You're going to a POW camp somewhere in the far reaches of space. Enjoy the rest of your life," Ryck told him.

"Attacked? No, as bonded security guards, we reacted to what we thought was a criminal action taken against our clients. When we realized that you were Marines, we laid down our weapons. No, I'll be back out on the street within a week," he said confidently.

Ryck went over the events in his mind. With a sinking feeling, he realized that this merc was probably right. The lawyers would get them all freed.

"On the other hand," he said, looking around to see if anyone else was listening in, "I don't really want to spend a week as a guest of the Federation, so if you could see to let me walk, I could get a cool 10k to you, more if you walked with me. When you and the Legion go head-to-head, no one's going to win, so you might as well look out for yourself, and we pay much, much better."

Ryck just stared at him for a moment, not believing what he'd heard, before answering, "Are you freaking high? You think you can offer me anything at all? Look at you. You've been shot in the arm. Your buddy over there, he's dead!"

"He was an asshole anyway. Good riddance. But this is about you. What's it going to be?"

"Fuck you," Ryck said as he turned away and walked off.

"What was did that guy want?" Popo asked as Ryck joined him.

"He wanted someone to put a round through his grubbing brain, and I came close to granting him that," Ryck said. "Forget it."

But Ryck couldn't forget what the guy had said. He was afraid it might be true.

Alexander

Chapter 7

With one simple click, Ryck closed his exam—his last exam. What had started as a means to combat boredom while going through his first regen had somehow grown into a full student status. With this exam, Ryck had completed the requirements for a degree—if he passed, that was. The school was pretty quick on letting students know their grades, so Ryck should know within a couple of days.

He got up from the testing station and walked up to the proctor. This was McBored, the proctor who always seemed to wish he was somewhere else. The identities of the two proctors for Camp Kolesnikov were guarded, as per SOP. Ryck thought that was pretty funny, as if this was some top-secret spy mission. Someone had to know who they were just to give them base access, after all. Instead, they were anonymous figures who were supposedly above corruption and who monitored both military and civilian testing on the base. McBored and Goat, two nameless cogs in the Federation bureaucracy.

Ryck smiled as he handed McBored his ID and put his thumb on the reader. Unlike Goat, who at least made a show of checking the pic to the face, McBored simply waited for the green light over the thumb reader before leaning in for his own retinal scan. Once that was done, the outgoing was unlocked, and Ryck's exam was off to the University of Phoenix for grading.

Getting a degree would mean nothing to Ryck as a Marine, but in the civil service, any certified education meant an increase in salary, and after several grand corruption schemes were uncovered, the exam processes had been changed. The military had been caught up in those changes as well. It didn't really matter to Ryck one way or the other, but he usually had to withhold a laugh at the super-spy-like procedures. It was just an exam, not the plans for a new bubble space projector.

He left the testing center feeling pretty good. A degree! He'd never really considered any schooling after high school. Glancing at his watch, he picked up the pace back to his IBC. As an NCO, he rated an Individual Berthing Compartment rather than the Dual Berthing Compartment of a non-rate. He had to get ready for the Camerone Day reception and had less than an hour before the bus left.

The Legion only had a small detachment of about 30 legionnaires on Alexander, including the embassy staff. They handled liaison with both the Navy and Marines. But no matter the size, every Legion post celebrated April 30. Larger units had parades, but all units read the story of the battle where *faire camerone* became embossed in the Legion psyche. After the ceremonies, "receptions," or authorized excuses to get drunk, were usually the order of the day, and it was to the reception that Ryck was invited. All the members of the two platoons who had been on Soreau were honored guests, along with the military and civilian bigwigs. Last year's reception, which had been the first to which the Golf Marines had been invited, had started slow, but by the early hours of the morning, had turned into something the Marines only blurredly remembered, but remembered as a smashing good time.

He checked his watch. It wasn't Camerone Day back in Paris yet, but by the time they got to the Westin in St. Petersburg, it would be.

He got into his room and gave his underarm a sniff. Unfortunately, pit juice wasn't going to cut it. He jumped into the shower, ignoring the autocycle in order to manually zip through it. He used his old t-shirt to dry off as he took his blues out of the closet. Luckily, he'd prepared them the night before. He gave them a once over, but they looked fine. He dressed and was about to leave when his PA chimed. He looked at the desk screen to see if he could ignore it. He couldn't.

He hit the accept, and Hannah's face appeared. She had a big smile which morphed into a look of grudging admiration.

"Wow, you be looking smart, there, Ryck. Very impressive! Makes a poor girl's heart flutter!" she said with a laugh.

"Right. I know you can hardly contain yourself," Ryck said, pleased to see her, but knowing he had to cut the cam short.

"What girl can resist a handsome wolf in uniform?" she asked.

"Well, as much as I'm happy you cammed, I need to leave. I've got a reception I have to get to," Ryck told her.

She looked puzzled as she asked, "Reception? What time be it there? I installed the app like you told me, and it says it be 3:15 your time."

With all the planets in the Federation, each rotating at different speeds, each with different landmasses, keeping track of local time could be confusing. All Federation planets and countries, as well as many independents, kept Greenwich Mean Time as the official time and date. But night and day, not to mention planetary years, varied, and Hannah, for all her scholastic achievements, continually got confused on what local time it was for Ryck. The app Ryck had her download was so she wouldn't keep waking him up in the middle of the night.

"No, you're right, it's after three here, but I have to take a bus into St. Petersburg, and we're leaving in 15 minutes."

"Oh, too bad. I tried to get a hold of you a few hours ago to wish you luck on your test, but it's been hard getting a line out. How did you do? Did you take it?"

Hannah was working on her masters and had been a big supporter of Ryck's attempt to earn his own degree.

"Yeah, I took it. All good, I think. I'll find out in a day or two," he told her.

"OK, that's copacetic. Well, that be all I wanted to know. You have fun at the reception. Don't let those local girls snare you, though," she said.

"Nah, all they want are officers, not a lowly sergeant like me," he said. "I don't make enough to keep them in the lifestyle they want."

"A handsome wolf like you? You'll have your pick."

"Hah. I think you need to get your eyes adjusted again, young lady. They seem to be failing you," he said. "Uh, I . . . I really have to go. Thanks for camming. Tell your family hello, OK?"

"Oh, sure. Don't let me be keeping you," she said.

"OK, well, goodbye!"

Ryck turned off the cam and looked at his watch. He needed to move it. He grabbed his cover and rushed out of his IBC, then hurried to the battalion CP. He didn't want to run and start sweating under his blues, so he kept it to a speed walk.

Staff Sergeant Hecs was standing at the door to the bus, his PA out.

"Glad you decided to join us, sergeant. We keeping you from anything important?" he asked, checking Ryck off the list on his screen.

"Sorry, Staff Sergeant," Ryck told him, climbing up into the bus and sitting down in the seat Sams had saved.

Staff Sergeant Hecs followed him and told the gunny everyone was aboard. Gunny Smith told the driver to take off. The big bus rose on its air cushion, then eased out of the camp before opening up on the highway.

Ryck dozed off during the three-and-a-half-hour ride to the capital city. He woke up when Sams punched his arm as they pulled into the Westin.

"Some company you've been," Sams said sourly.

"Sorry, I was up late studying for my exam," he said.

"I still don't know why you've been putting in the time for that," Sams said. "Popo and Brett swear you're gonna be putting in to be an O."

"An officer? No, I work for a living," Ryck said with the time-honored reply. "I just like history, and Hannah thinks it's a good idea?"

"Crispus! It always 'Hannah this' and 'Hannah' that lately. You getting serious?"

"Oh, good God, no. She doesn't like the military. She's just a friend," Ryck protested.

"Yeah, that's what everyone says before they're hitched."

As the officers got off, Gunny Smith stood up and said, "This is our second time here as guests. We want no liberty incidents. Enjoy yourselves, but remember, this is not just a drinking binge. You are representing the Federation Marine Corps. General Praeter is there, the governor is there, Admiral Yost is there, the French ambassador is there. I don't have to tell you what's going to happen to the negat who spills some of that fancy French wine over one of those esteemed gentlemen."

"Won't be me, Gunny. I'll be drinking beer!" Staff Sergeant Gordon, the First platoon sergeant said amidst the laughter.

"I'll be watching you most of all, Gordon!" the Gunny replied as the laughter intensified.

"OK, OK! We're all in a good mood. Last year was brills, so have fun. One more thing. The CO, that's the battalion CO, says no politics. No matter what, no matter who asks you, especially some civvie who's probably a reporter looking for a tag line, you say nothing about what's happening back on Earth. This is a social gathering, so keep it social. Any questions? OK, no? Then let's go have some fun!"

The Marines trooped off the bus and wound their way into the huge lobby of the Westin. Ryck had been there a year ago, but it was still pretty impressive. About 50 meters across, it reached up to the hotel's roof, some 20 stories above them. Hanging from the roof was a sculpture that had to be 40 meters tall, given that it covered eight stories of rooms. Ryck wasn't sure what it was supposed to be, but he liked it.

A Legion lieutenant was standing to the right of the lobby, and when the Marines came in, he started ushering them to the ballroom. It would have been hard to miss even without their guide. A French flag was beside the doorway, and a huge bunting of the same blue, white and red was hung over the door. Not many people were there yet: Marines being Marines, they had gotten there early. Major Gruenstein, though, was there, and he hurried over.

"Welcome, sir," he said to Lieutenant Colonel Adeyemi, the battalion CO, as he shook his hand. "As always, the Marines of Golf, 2/9 are eternally welcome. I hope you enjoy our hospitality."

He looked behind him, then turned back around and continued, "I see the receiving line hasn't started yet, but if you and Captain Davis would follow me, I'd like to introduce you to Colonel Giraud, our new head of mission. I don't believe you have met him yet, no?"

Sams nudged Ryck as the CO and company commander were led off, gesturing at the two bars in the back of the ballroom. Unfortunately, Gunny Smith put the kibosh on any immediate libation.

"No drinking until after we make pleasant with the brass. Just hold steady for now," he told the gathered Marines.

"Well, might as well check out the chow," Sams said. "The gunny said nuttin' about that."

Ryck and Rey followed Sams to the buffet line. There was a huge ice sculpture of a hand in the middle of the line, between a huge ice bowl of peeled shrimp and an equally huge bowl of small cracked crab claws. Ryck knew that had to represent Captain Danjou's wooden hand. The real wooden hand, recovered from the battlefield at Camerone and then bought by the Legion a few years later, was probably the Legion's most sacred relic.

The spread was pretty impressive. It was mostly finger food, some on crackers, some in little glasses. Sams grabbed a puffball of some sort and popped it into his mouth.

"Hey, you heard the gunny!" Ryck said.

"Yeah, no drinking he said. Last time I checked this was eating, not drinking you Alice," Sams replied, speaking around the puffball still in his mouth. "Hey, not bad!"

"What is it?" Ryck asked, inching closer to snatch one for himself.

"Hell if I know. Where's Henri?" Sams asked, referring to Corporal Henri, a Marine in Second Platoon. "Rey, go get him, OK?"

Sams grabbed another and popped it into his mouth. Ryck glanced about, only to see Gunny at the other buffet table, filching something for himself. That was good enough for Ryck, so he took one of the same fried balls and bit in. It was pretty good; a little fishy, but light.

Corporal Rey returned with Henri in tow.

"What are these?" Sams asked the corporal.

"Hors d'oeuvres. Appetizers," Henri answered.

"No shit, Sherlock. I mean what kind?"

Henri looked over the spread, then said "I don't know. Just hors d'oevers," before taking a small glass with what looked to be a bite-sized piece of chicken and avocado inside. "Tastes good, though."

"What do you mean, you don't know. You're French, right?" Sams asked.

"French-Ergat, yeah, but I don't know shit about cooking. I'm a fucking Marine, not a chef. We're BBQ people, anyway, big hunks of meat."

Ergat was one of the French worlds, out there in Second Quadrant. France populated all or the bulk of nine different planets. Three, like Ergat, were technically part of the Federation."

"You might try Lance Corporal Paddyfoote. He's from Clercy," Henri said, scanning the waiting Marines. "There he is," he said before waving the Marine over.

"What's cracking, *mon corporel*? You feeling your blood here?" asked gesturing at the French-themed decorations.

Paddyfoote was one of the darkest Marines Ryck had seen, his skin almost black. Ryck didn't know much about him other than he was one of the strongest Marines in the company. He knew Henri was ethnically French, but he hadn't realized Paddyfoote was, too.

"Sure, *oui* and *liberté, égalité, fraternité* and all of that. But Sergeant Samuelson here is asking me about these hors d'oevers, and I can't answer him. You know what this shit is?"

"Shit? You wound me, *mon corporel*. This should be your lifeblood," he said with a laugh. "Let me see . . ." he said as he looked around the table.

"Theese eeze *a ballotin*," he said with a comically exaggerated French accent, pointing at pieces of asparagus wrapped in some kind of ham. "And theese, theese eeze *accras*, what you say feesh balls, from lovelee 'aiti," he told them, pointing at the puffball Sams had just taken.

"In zee glass, we call theese *verrines*, but for 'eaven, you must try zee *beignets*," he said, bringing his fingers to his lips and kissing them before pushing them out while making a popping sound, then grabbing what looked to be a fried doughnut ball.

Several other Marines had gathered and were laughing at Paddyfoote's over-the-top performance. Six or seven did grab the beignets, though, at his suggestion.

"Gents, the receiving line is about to start. I would suggest we all get in line and pay our respects before it gets too long," Staff Sergeant Hecs said, pointing back to where the French Ambassador, the Legion colonel, and some other men and women were lining up.

The quicker through the line, the quicker to the bar, so the platoon sergeant didn't have to tell them that twice. It wasn't actually a rush, but still, no one took their time as they got into position.

The line started moving as each guest was introduced, shook hands with the ambassador and her husband, then the Legion colonel and his wife. Each person was asked his or her name by a resplendent legion lieutenant, who then repeated it to the ambassador.

Staff Sergeant Hecs followed Lieutenant Nidishchii' and was right in front of Ryck. The poor Legion lieutenant had a hard enough time with Nidishchii', but he completely mangled "Phantawisangtong." He seemed relieved when Ryck told him his last name.

The receiving line was, well, a receiving line. The ambassador smiled and thanked the Marines for coming. The ambassador's husband seemed friendly, but a strong smell of mouthwash did not completely hide the aroma of alcohol in his breath. Evidently, his celebration had already started. The Marines filed past the colonel and his wife, then most made a beeline for one of the two bars. The few teetotalers headed back to the buffet line to start loading up on food.

Ryck headed for the bar. It was well-stocked, but Ryck thought it was only fitting that he try some wine, first. The bartender gave him a glass of *beaujolais nouveau*, something Ryck had never heard of much less tried. It meant "new beaujolais," and it was light and a bit sweet, OK, but not great. Ryck thought Hannah might like it, though.

Sams was drinking single-malt scotch from New Halifax, pleased to see not only Greater French booze, while Popo, Rey, and Corporals Henri and Stenski from Second Platoon were drinking beer while they munched on the various appetizers. It wasn't too long before Sams drifted over to chat up a young lady in a long, blue gown.

Their little core group shifted with the three corporals drifting off, Staff Sergeant Groton drifting in, PFC Ling coming over and trying to impress his NCOs with some sort of questions on tactics. The boot was a certified butt-kisser. Several of the legionnaires came over to make them feel welcome, but mostly, it was Marines mixing with Marines, which was fine with Ryck and the rest. The booze and food were good, and that was what mattered.

Shortly after it turned April 30 back in France, the ambassador gave a speech full of praise for French history and brotherhood between France and the Federation. Everyone dutifully applauded, then got back to his or her drinks.

"Fucking Sams," Popo said, pointing to where the young lady, obviously in her cups, was now leaning against the tall Marines, laughing at something he had said. "How does he always manage to pull a dove wherever we go?"

"Yeah, it got him busted to private once, back on Atacama. He'd be a staff sergeant now, maybe a gunny if not for that. He says it was worth it, though," Ryck told him.

"Looking at the ass on that girl, yeah, it might be worth it," Popo said.

When the busybody Legion lieutenant came and whispered into Colonel Giraud's ear, no one seemed to notice. The two legionnaires left, then the lieutenant came back a few moments later to fetch the ambassador, who stopped socializing with the governor and hurried out of the room.

"Wonder what's up with that," Staff Sergeant Hecs said. "Hope nothing cuts this party short. I'm just catching my stride."

"Shit, don't worry. You ever see a froggie leave with booze still in the bar?" Staff Sergeant Groton said before lifting up his glass in a wordless toast before downing the rest of his beer. "Time to get recharged," he added before staggering ever-so-slightly, off to get more beer.

Talk drifted back to Sams and his magic touch with women when Ryck noticed General Prater getting a call. He didn't think much about it until the Division commander's posture changed and he held up his hand to get the officers around him to stop talking. When the Legion lieutenant came back into the ballroom one more time and evidently asked both the CG and Admiral Yost to follow him, Ryck knew something was up. The CG said something to Colonel Pierre and the others, then followed the legionnaire out of the room.

The regimental sergeant major waved over the gunny as the officers put down their drinks. Gunny Smith listened, then nodded. Ryck felt the tension build as the gunny came back to them first.

"The bar is closed. Quietly and calmly, get everyone to dump whatever drink they have. I want everyone to move to where Captain Davis and First Sergeant Peale are heading. Be ready for an order to move out," he quietly told them.

Most of the Marines and other party-goers hadn't noticed anything, and a few Marines thought it was all a joke. One look at the company staff, though, brought it into focus. Something was going on, something big.

Staff Sergeant Groton tried to ask what was happening as the company gathered, but Captain Davis motioned him to be quiet. Ryck thought the captain was in the dark as much as the rest of them.

With the Marines in one corner of the room and the small Legion detachment gathering back near the bar, the civilians slowly coalesced across from the Marines. The governor started walking over, and Colonel Pierre met him, whispering in the politician's ear. The two of them stood there for a few moments, discussing what was happening, before the CO came back to the rest of the Marines.

A long 15 minutes later, Admiral Yost, the Legion colonel, and General Praeter, came back into the ballroom, somberly marching to the center of it.

The admiral cleared his throat and began, "Ladies and gentlemen, please listen up. Colonel Giraud, General Praeter, and I have something to say. At 0100 Paris time, the Greater French president formally revoked the Mutual Defense Treaty with the Federation, declaring themselves divorced from all Federation laws and agreements. At 0115, FCDC troops began to move into France and the French Lunar base."

Fifteen fucking minutes to invade? This was no surprise, thought Ryck.

"At 0120, Greater France declared an opening of adversarial relations and appealed to the independent states as well as the Brotherhood for support. For those of you who are not familiar with the legalese, this is not a declaration of war, but one step below. What this means, we don't know yet. Can the politicians fix this? Will war be declared? We don't know. We are now on Class 1 Alert, and all military hands are to return to their bases for further orders.

"I have given Colonel Giraud my assurances that he and his detachment, that all French embassy personnel, will be allowed to depart Alexander unmolested. Ambassador Basel is already making preparations. All Legion personnel in this room are requested to follow your colonel. Transport off Alexander is now being procured."

There was a stunned silence as everyone digested the news. Things had been dicey back on Earth, but very few people could have imagined the situation could disintegrate so thoroughly.

Ryck thought back to the ex-Marine merc back on Pannington. He had said it would come to this, so clearly, some people, though, had been aware of the oncoming storm.

Colonel Giraud stepped forward and said, "Admiral Yost, I want to thank you for your chivalrous gesture. You have my respect," before switching over to French.

Ryck couldn't follow what was said, but there was obviously a lot of emotion in the telling of it. When he finished, the legionnaires in the back of the ballroom slowly started moving forward, eyes to the front. Not only the legionnaires started moving, though.

From the corner of his eye, Ryck caught movement from within the Marines. He turned his head to see Lance Corporal Paddyfoote making his way out of the mass of Marines. He made it to the front of the crowd and then marched up to join the legionnaires.

Ryck stared at him in shock. It was obvious that he was deserting the Corps for the Legion. Ryck looked around to see who was going to stop him, to arrest him. When someone else started moving, he thought that was the person who was going to grab Paddyfoote.

"What the fuck you doing, Marc?" Sergeant Temper from Second Platoon was shouting, grabbing Corporal Henri by the arm.

"Those are my people, Devin. I gotta go," Henri said with tears welling in his eyes.

"No, Marc, we're your people. Think about it. What about Hermone, saving your ass at the mine? What about that?" Devin Temper shouted as the other Marines around them moved back a step, giving the two friends a buffer.

Marc Henri looked up at the retreating legionnaires, then back at Devin, before saying, "You, all of you, have been there for me, and I'm proud to be a Marine. But if this is war, do you expect me to fight my family? The family who welcomed you, Devin, when you came to visit, the family who fed you. What about Giselle? You met her, took her out for dinner, for God's sake? I've known her family for all my life. You really expect me to fight them?" he asked, a tear making a track down his cheek.

"But you can't! This is desertion! I won't let you do—" he started before Lieutenant Colonel Adeyemi stepped up to them. He took Devin's hand and gently pulled it away from Henri's arm.

The CO simply shook his head, effectively telling the Marine to leave it be, and Devin slumped back, defeated. Lance Corporal Marc Henri, UFMC, shook his head, then turned and marched forward to join the last of the legionnaires leaving the room.

What had just transpired was beyond Ryck's comprehension. War with France? Marines deserting? It didn't make sense. He scanned the Marines to see if anyone else was going to leave. Colonel Pierre, the regimental commander, was French, wasn't he?

His brother was a Legion colonel. Ryck had seen him at the change of command when Colonel Pierre had taken over the regiment.

Colonel Pierre stood emotionless in with Captain Davis. He wasn't moving.

With the last legionnaire gone, the room broke into a hubbub of chatter. The civilians went right for their PAs, some as they hurried out of the ballroom, their devices glued to their ears. The Marines were no different, bringing out their PAs and connecting until the sergeant major yelled out that they were in a Security Status 2, which meant no unauthorized communications.

Within moments, the SNCOs had taken charge and were forming the Marines up. The General and his aides left first, his staff car whisking him back to division headquarters. Colonel Pierre and Lieutenant Colonel Adeyemi took Captain Davis and the sergeant's major with them in their van, leaving Lieutenant Patrick, the company XO, in charge of the movement to camp. The two buses arrived, and the Marines were quickly embarked.

Within minutes, the buses were on the way back, but back to what, Ryck just didn't know.

PART 2

Jonathan P. Brazee

FS Ark Royal

Chapter 8

Ryck settled into his cradle in the 14-man PVS-14, or Personnel Vacuum Sled 14. The "reki" looked more like a roller-coaster car instead of the old-time Finnish reindeer sleigh from which it took its nickname, and Ryck had the temptation to lift his arms roller-coaster-style if they did, in fact, deploy out of the *Ark Royal*. This was the fourth time the Marines had been loaded into the rekis since the beginning of the interdiction, but each previous time, the target vessel had turned back, and the Marines stood down without any action.

A state of war between Greater France and the Federation did not technically exist, at least for the moment. The FDCD officers (always referred to as "officers," never "soldiers") had moved into France shortly after the Mutual Defense Treaty had been abrogated. They stopped well short of Paris, though, leaving the city itself in the hands of the French government. The FCDC had moved in to "protect the integrity of the Federation borders." The six planetary republics in Greater France filed grievances, as had governments of seven other worlds. Three of those worlds had been colonized by French companies but were members of the Federation; the other four were independents. The Federation responded by employing exclusion zones around each of those 13 planets. The only exception was a narrow "elevator" over the nation of Guildenhaus, a Federation member-state located on the otherwise independent planet of First Strike.

The *Ark Royal* was the flagship for the small task force enforcing the exclusion zone around Tel Aviv. Tel Aviv had never been a member of the Federation but had generally worked within the Federation sphere, which made sense as the Federation bought the bulk of its exports. Upon the incursion of the FCDC into France, though, Tel Aviv quickly sided with Greater France and pledged its support. The planet was immediately slapped with the exclusion zone by the Federation.

The *Ark Royal* task force was small with only three ships. But the *Ark Royal* itself would have been enough to enforce the blockade. The ship was, in a word, huge.

Bubble ships, by design, were spherical, so from the outside, the *Ark Royal*'s primary difference from other bubble ships was its size. In this case, that size difference was immense. A full 800 meters in diameter, the ship was not a dreadnought in the sense of an offensive weapons platform like the Prion Class Battle Cruisers. It was a more direct descendant of the old wet-water Navy aircraft carriers. The ship's huge hangars housed three full squadrons of Experion fighters, a squadron of Griffyn monitors, four orbit-to-ground assault craft, each capable of carrying a company of PICS Marines or 400 pax, and all the assorted support, ECM, recon, and comms craft necessary to support any mission given to the ship. The embarked Marine battalion, complete with the attached Wasp flight and Stork squadron, was easily lost among the 16,000 sailors onboard the ship.

With all the sailors, the Marines almost seemed an afterthought, shunted aside. They were in Ancillary Hangar 3A, a small (in comparison) hangar located off of B Deck. At 30 meters across, there was more than enough room for the 12 rekis in it, all loaded with Marines. The rekis were in two ranks, six abreast. Ryck's squad was in the third reki, ready to deploy in the first rank if the call came through. Squeezed in beside the first reki was a PVS-2, the small two-man version of the larger 14-man reki. Two Recon Marines, in their slicks, stood by, leaning up against the PVS-2's nose.

Ryck took a quick look behind him. Two of the rekis in the second rank had four PICS Marines each, ready to act as heavy hitters if needed. Ryck wasn't too confident on how the two fire teams from Second Platoon would fare if anything happened to them on an EVA. Each PICS had been outfitted with both an external oxygen tank and a small auxiliary thrust pack. The thrust packs, though, were really not very effective. "Space farts" was the commonly used term for them, able to nudge a PICS Marine in a vacuum, but not really move the combat suit with any degree of authority. If anything happened and one of the Marines separated from his reki, then he could easily be lost for good. PICS were just not designed for EVA work.

Ryck never felt completely comfortable in his Marine Corps EVA suit, but at least they were designed for the mission of open-space operations. He went through his checks again, and all lights were green. He would have already known, though, if anything was wrong, given that the hangar doors were open and he was sitting in the vacuum of open space.

The small, dull blue numbers in the lower right corner of his helmet face shield counted out the seconds as time passed. They'd been in the suits for almost 45 minutes so far. The mission would probably be another scratch. What commercial carrier was going to risk destruction at the hands of the *Ark Royal*?

Since the interdiction was declared, military action was primarily Navy. As on Alexander, Legion troops had been generally given free passage off Federation worlds, and the small Federation attachments on the Greater French worlds had been accorded the same courtesy. It was only on Pallidyne IV, an unincorporated planet in the Third Quadrant, that fighting had broken out. A Marine expeditionary company and a Legion light battalion had gone into battle with the Legion emerging victorious. This surprised no one given the much smaller numbers of the Marines and the superiority of the Legion weaponry.

The Legion had reported to the press that the Marines had attacked, and the Legion post was forced to defend itself. No Marine believed that. There was no logical reason why an expeditionary company, only lightly armed and there to provide security for a Navy scientific team, would take on a Legion combat battalion, even one with only two companies. Even in the best of times, the Legion had better war-fighting equipment and weapons. The Legion always bought the most advanced gear available while the Marines relied on old technology, preferring half-assed upgrades than a full acquisition of the next generation gear. It wasn't actually that the

Marines didn't want the newest and best—it was the Federation that didn't want to pay for it. Military funds in the Federation went to the Navy first and foremost with the Marines and, to an extent, the FCDC, sucking hind tit.

"Heads up," the lieutenant passed on the command circuit. "The target is making a run for it."

The target had been identified as the New Chilean-registered freighter *Marie's Best*. It was an old hull, laid down over 120 years ago. It had gone through a full retrofit some 40 years earlier, but this was still old techno. How its captain thought it would be able to evade the *Ark Royal*, a frigate, and a destroyer was beyond Ryck. It had been trying to sneak in, approaching Tel Aviv directly from the system's sun. That plan had little to no chance in succeeding against the Navy ships, so it was no surprise that the attempt failed. What was a surprise was that the ship didn't surrender when the captain realized they had been compromised.

"Listen up," Ryck passed on the squad circuit. "The target ship is making a run for it. There still won't be much for us to do if the Navy blasts it out of space, but . . . hold on, I'm getting something else."

"The target has been hit by one of the *Ark Royal's* monitors. Scans indicate that it has not, I repeat, has not been destroyed. There are life readings on board. We are a go," the lieutenant passed before remembering to open the platoon circuit and repeat the message for all hands.

Ryck looked to his right where the two recon Marines were scrambling to board their coffin, the nickname given to the PVS-2. It didn't really look like a coffin but more like a large cigar. Like the reki, it was basically a simple powered platform open to space, but where Marines in a reki were sitting side-by-side, in the coffin, one man lay on top of the other. Their slicks were a dark, slate grey rather than the lighter-colored EVA suits of the grunt Marines, and they allowed a wearer to remain in space for longer, but many of the other differences were classified.

Within moments, the two recon Marines had launched, moving out to provide eyes on the target. It took a bit longer for the rest of the Marines to launch. The lead reki had a Navy cybo on board to provide navigation. The rekis could be put on automatic nav, but for the distance to be covered, the Navy felt better with one of their own in control.

In this case, the lead reki was #2. The other 11 of them would move out to a pre-determined distance from #2, then move to the target in tandem with the lead sled. Only as they approached the target would the connection be broken and a Marine, acting as a coxswain, would navigate to the appropriate spot on the target.

Ryck keyed in his three fire team leaders, "We've trained for this. There shouldn't be any surprises, but if there are, just keep your heads and react. Any action is better than inaction. Any questions?"

When there were none, he isolated Corporal Beady, his Third Fire Team leader, and asked, "John, how's Ling?"

PFC Ling was the second junior man in the squad and Ryck's headache. Even after their last op, he still seemed to be more bark than bite, somewhat of a kiss-ass, but he had been uncharacteristically quiet while they were forming for the possible mission. Ling had been with the squad on Pannington and so was technically blooded, but for all intents and purposes, he was still a combat virgin, and there was no telling how he would react under fire. Ryck didn't want to have to worry that one of his Marines would be ineffective.

"He's nervous, but not too bad. I think he'll be fine," Corporal Beady answered.

If they were in their PICS, Ryck could be monitoring the vitals of all the Marines in the squad. The EVA suits didn't have that capability, so Ryck had to rely on his unit leaders.

"Ok, but keep an eye on him," he said.

Ryck looked back at the *Ark Royal* as his reki moved into position. The ship was even more impressive from the outside. The Marines had boarded the ship from an enclosed shuttle, where the lack of portholes had kept them from seeing the ship. Here, in the openness of space, the big ship glistened in the harsh sunlight.

Too quickly, though, all the rekis had been launched, and they were moving away. The *Ark Royal* dwindled and vanished behind them as the small reki fleet picked up speed.

Dashing through the space, on a one-horse open sleigh . . . Ryck couldn't help but sing to himself as they accelerated at five g's, the vast openness of space surrounding them.

Without the compensators, Ryck knew they would be pulled against the harnesses, struggling to breathe. As it was, they only felt a slight tug as they zipped over to their target.

The EVA suits did not compile as much combat-related information as a PICS or even a sleeve display on skins, but it did provide better data in other areas. Ryck had a location of the target, approximately 10,000 klicks away. At 5 g's, accelerating halfway before beginning deceleration, they should arrive at the target in about 26 minutes. The cybo navigating #2 would have more exact data, taking into consideration that the target, even if hit, would still be moving, but the Ryck's guesstimate was good enough for government work.

"Settle in for the ride. We've got about 25 more minutes until we arrive on the scene," he passed to the squad, keying in the lieutenant and Staff Sergeant Hecs as well and hoping he entered the correct input.

When the lieutenant didn't correct him, he figured he had done the math right.

Ten-thousand klicks was more than most EVAs, but the rekis could handle the distance, and EVA suits were generally good for up to 18 hours. In the back of his mind, Ryck also knew that the Marines were far more expendable than the *Ark Royal* or the other two ships in the task force. Years ago, the *FS Mumbai* had been destroyed when it moved in to facilitate the rescue of a damaged Western Alliance frigate. It had never been proven that the frigate had suicided to take out the *Mumbai*, but that was the general consensus. Consequently, losing a few Marines and EVA sleds was a risk the admiral would feel far more comfortable taking than putting any of the capital ships in harm's way.

The recon team arrived at the target within 11 minutes of leaving the *Ark Royal*. That was smoking fast, and the best compensators couldn't completely neutralize the g's it would have taken to get there that quickly. The two recon Marines would have had to fight the g's the best they could.

The team started with passive surveillance, and the feed they sent back was forwarded to each Marine's face shield. The *Marie's Best* had the characteristics cigar shape of an ion-tube ship. The side facing the recon Marine's cameras was dark, the edges of the ship framed in the sunlight. The damage to the front of the ship was evident, but looked to be isolated to that small section. Ryck had to admire the Navy gunnery skills. The monitor that had taken down the *Marie's Best* was unmanned, controlled by a team on the *Ark Royal*. This had been a surgical strike, not the wholesale destruction Ryck had expected. The skill of the gunnery team, to take down a ship while basically leaving it whole, really impressed him.

Instinctively, Ryck peered ahead of the reki, but they were still way too far to be able to pick out the target. He paid more attention to his data stream on his face shield. More input was coming from the team as they employed a fairly impressive array of passive gathering processes. The ship was essentially dead. A cloud of gasses surrounded it, indicating that the ship's atmosphere had been vented. There were no sustained emissions in any of the normal spectrums, only flickers as the ship's emergency systems tried to come back online.

Captain Davis was in command of the operation, and he ordered the recon team to move to active surveillance. This was a moment of truth. The stealth capabilities of the PVS-2 would have kept the team invisible to anyone on the *Marie's Best*. As soon as they went active, though, their position would be revealed. There wasn't much a coffin could do against incoming missiles or energy weapons.

A few moments later, new data started streaming in. It was too much for Ryck to grasp, so he blinked his AI to make some sense of it. The AI put those results in what it determined to be in order of importance to a combat Marine. Foremost among this was that none of the ship's weapons systems were operational. Second was that there were 133 living humans aboard. Third, there were working, active personnel weapons on the ship.

The scans couldn't determine if the survivors were armed with any of the active weapons. It couldn't tell the intent of the survivors. But the mere fact that there were people alive on the ship, a ship that had tried to run the interdiction, and that there were functioning small arms on the ship, was something Captain Davis had to take under consideration.

Captain Davis, the two platoon commanders, the gunny, and the Navy engineer were massaging the plan as the small flotilla approached the *Marie's Best*. The engineer had no command authority, but he was the Navy rep, answering directly back to the admiral, and his mission to secure the integrity of the ship was second only to the overall security of the task force. Ryck listened in as the company commander made the adjustments. Several times, the captain's local command circuit was cut, probably when the battalion CO or even the admiral stuck their noses into things.

As a young private, Ryck thought captains, if not gods, were at least saints, doing what they pleased. It took him a while to realize that they had the same pressures and "input" from above. Private or captain, all Marines answered to someone else.

At five minutes out, the plan had gelled. Of course, no plan survived the first few moments of combat, but at least Ryck knew where his squad would be breaching and what their task would be. That was a start.

Ryck took a minute to relay the word to his squad. Only three Marines in the squad had ever done any actual ship takedown ops. For the rest of the squad, their only experience had been in Phase IV of recruit training. Since embarking on the *Ark Royal*, the OpsO[17] had scheduled an immediate action drill, but without actually going EVA, that was only moderately useful. It would have to be enough, though.

The entire platoon was going to breach the *Marie's Best* amidships, close to the galley where the bulk of the survivors were gathered. Each squad was going to breach at about a 120-degree angle from each other so that they would be essentially encircling the galley and coming in from different directions. With no artificial gravity working on the ship, there would be no up or down, so the Marines could not think in a two-planed battlespace.

[17] OpsO: Operations Officer. This is the individual who creates and runs an operational plan.

At two minutes out, the company got a "good luck" from the recon team. The Marines couldn't pick out the team, but the team could pick them up as they approached the *Marie's Best*. Ryck wondered about the recon Marines for a moment. When Ryck went into battle, he had his Marines around him. The two recon Marines just had each other as they drifted out there in space somewhere.

The *Marie's Best* registered on their sensors before they could actually see her, but finally, Ryck could pick her out with his zoom panel. Technically, he wasn't seeing her but rather an image captured by his shoulder cam and displayed on his face shield, but for all intents and purposes, she was in view.

The Navy cybo released control of the rekis, and Lance Corporal Keiji, the squad coxswain, took over, "diving" below the x-axis to come up on the other side of the ship. They passed under it, "under" only because their orientation within the reki made them crane their heads up to see the ship as they went past. "Under" and "over" had little real meaning in space, so the terms were used within a personal perspective connotation. Marines on the other side of the ship would also be passing "under" the ship as well.

Ryck half-expected fire to reach out from the ship to rake the reki, but the *Marie's Best* remained quiet and unresponsive.

Something did hit the reki, though, as they moved in. They couldn't hear it, of course, but all the Marines could feel the vibration. Some of the debris from the monitor strike had not been blown away. With no atmosphere to slow it down, the debris kept alongside the ship as it continued through space. The reki didn't seem damaged, but whatever hit the sled might have been able to put a serious hurt on the unprotected Marines.

"Slow it down, Keiji," Ryck ordered. "Let them wait up for us, if they have to. No use getting one of us zeroed by pieces of dead ship."

He started to report their speed change when he heard Sams pass the same thing. The debris field surrounded a good portion of the ship. Ryck could see some of the larger pieces closer to the bow of the ship, but even around the center, glints of reflected sunlight caught his eyes as pieces and shards tumbled. It was as if space fireflies had gathered around the ship.

Keiji slowed them down to a crawl. They were a good 200 meters away when they passed a piece of cloth, probably part of a blanket. Ryck had to push it out of the way. At their relative speed, it wouldn't have done any damage, and Ryck was glad they'd slowed down instead of coming in blazing.

The reki had a very simple console. An image of the ship was displayed on it, with their breach-location highlighted with a narrowing yellow square. Lance Corporal Keiji was using it to guide the sled to the correct spot. He brought the reki to a stop just 20 meters from the skin of the *Marie's Best*.

That was a relative stop, Ryck reminded himself. It was a little hard to grasp that they were still hurtling through space at a pretty good clip. If the Navy engineer team couldn't get the ship under its own power, or if task force couldn't get a tug on the ship, it would probably plunge into the planet's atmosphere and burn up, at least most of it. Some pieces would undoubtedly make it to the ground.

At his signal, the squad released their harnesses. Third Fire Team flew to the back of the reki where their breaching chamber had been loaded. In space it didn't weigh anything, but it still had mass, and once moving, its momentum could make it dangerous. The other Marines and Doc Grbil gave way, leaving the team plenty of maneuver space to get the chamber up against the skin of the ship.

It took almost five minutes of slow maneuvering to get the chamber emplaced and locked. This would be a simple breach. With no atmosphere inside the ship, there was no need to create an airlock. If the damaged area could be sealed off after the ship was under Navy control, the breach could be sealed once again.

"Golf-three-six, we are in position and waiting to execute," Ryck passed on the platoon circuit.

Ryck used the lieutenant's call sign to indicate he was speaking to the platoon commander. He could have gone on a direct P2P circuit with him, but he wanted everyone else to know their status. Third Squad itself was "Golf-three-three," but as his identity was indicated as soon as he keyed his mic, passing that merely took up unnecessary time.

"Roger that. Wait for my command," the lieutenant passed.

Ryck checked the feed from the recon team. The blobs that indicated living people were still grouped inside. There was nothing to indicate a marshaling of forces. The recon team was at the wrong angle to give a clear indication of what was right inside Third Squad's planned breach, but it looked like the area might be empty of life.

First Platoon would be entering the ship through the damaged nose. Ryck didn't envy them that task. There was much more debris up there, and inside, maneuvering around wreckage in an EVA suit could be a stressful undertaking. The suits were tough, but not indestructible. However, the Navy engineer needed to check that area first. Only if it was totally destroyed would he take his team to the aft control center.

It took longer than expected, but First Platoon finally picked their way through the debris. Captain Davis gave the command, and the Third Platoon started breaching. Sparks flew from the end of the chamber as the LTC blades bit into the ship's skin.

Breaches could be made by either blowing their way into a breach or by cutting. Given the age of the Marie's Best and her hallo aluminum skin, cutting was the least catastrophic method of breaching. Within twenty seconds, the breach was made, and the Marines poured into the ship.

The ship was dark where they breached. Each EVA's AI recognized that and turned on the infrared lamps located around the face shield. Ryck didn't like having to rely on them. He could see with them on, but the EVA's night vision capability left him with a flat, almost two-dimensional view that left him feeling out of sorts.

The EVA suit displays, while not as detailed at those in a PICS, did display ID avatars, so when one Marine lost control and slammed into another, sending the second one cart wheeling to the far side of the room, Ryck could see it was Ling who slammed into Beady. Null-G movement had to be controlled. Being too hyped made it difficult to gain that steady control. Ryck wanted to remind Corporal Beady that he had to keep an eye on Ling, but he knew that Beady knew that, too. No use harping on it.

"First, move it out. Second, cover them," Ryck passed.

He hooked a strut with his M99 and pulled himself forward. Outside or inside a ship, the EVA suit's thrusters would work. But in the confines of a ship, the exhaust of the thruster could impact other nearby Marines. So, movement became a series of jumps with tiny adjustments from the microjets to keep steady. Controlling the footpads to grip when needed, but to let go when jumping was an exercise in timing that did not come easily. The six-centimeter hooks that some Marine had designed to slip over the muzzle of their M99s was a godsend. With them, a Marine could reach out and pull himself along without having to ground his feet.

Greg Prifit had his usual assignment as the fire team's heavy gunner. Instead of a 20mm grenade launcher, though, he was armed with an M51 plasma gun. Set on full dispersion, he could fill a ship's passage with blue death, sending it out over 20 meters before its effectiveness started to diminish. He cautiously pushed out of the compartment, peering down the passage. The retrans from the recon team indicated there were no life forms in the passage, but there were a number of ways to counteract or spoof sensors. He paused only a moment before pulling himself through the hatch and down the passage, the rest of his team on his ass. Ryck followed, and behind him were the other two teams.

First Team was hugging the sides of the passage, one Marine on the deck, the overhead, and each bulkhead. All were oriented with their feet toward the outside of the passage, their heads toward the middle. This allowed for better fields of fire, and would allow for easier support from the rest of the squad. Realistically, if they hit the shit, only two or three of the other Marines would be able to support with fire without too great of a risk of friendly fire casualties.

The squad moved like a disjointed snake down the passage, making its way to the galley. There were compartments along the way, but there was no time to clear each one, so Hartono used the weldmaster, a small gun that "flowed" a small area of the metal hatches, bridging the seam between the door and the jamb and sealing them shut until an engineer could come by and opened them.

First Fire Team had only moved about 30 meters through the curved corridor when they saw their first person. Ex-person, that was. The young man was in the grey overalls popular with many fabrication factories. He was floating a few centimeters off of the outer bulkhead. His eyes were glassy and bulging, his mouth open. Around his nose and mouth were bubbles. Ryck knew they would be red under normal lighting. He'd obviously been without access to an EVA suit, and when the ship was breached, he would have had only 20 or 30 seconds until the air was expelled, leaving the ship in a vacuum. Clearly, he had tried to hold his breath while he struggled to reach safety.

Back at boot, one of the things drilled into recruits was that holding the breath in a vacuum was tantamount to a death sentence. The air in their lungs would quickly expand, causing embolisms that would kill within seconds. This could be avoided by immediately expelling all the air from the lungs and keeping the mouth open. A human could remain conscious for up to 15 seconds in a vacuum and could remain alive for up to a minute or more. People could be revived even after longer than that. A Brotherhood sailor had supposedly been brought back after six minutes in a vacuum with no signs of permanent damage.

This young man undoubtedly never had that type of training, though. He was probably the factory worker he seemed to be. What he was doing in a ship trying to run a Federation blockade was a mystery to Ryck. Whatever the reason, it ended up killing him.

The man was drifting in front of Keiji, and the lance corporal tried to avoid the body. He just nudged it, though, as he passed, sending the body slowly tumbling. Ryck tried to scoot past the dead man, but the body's tumbling took up a lot of space, and it rotated into him. This could slow down the squad it every Marine was trying to avoid the corpse. Ryck took a hold of it and planted his feet on the corridor's overhead. Slowly turning, he steadied himself, and with a sure push, sent the body down the very center of the passage. With the Marines around the corridor's periphery, the body floated past them, making it beyond the last Marine before hitting the far overhead as the corridor curved.

"The passage to the next deck isn't here," Corporal Rey passed. "It's supposed to be here."

Ryck turned back and moved forward, switching to the ship's plan on his readout. Every ship moving through Federated space was required to have complete ship's blueprints registered. Rey was correct. He was right at the spot where the passage to the inner decks was supposed to be, and the galley was two decks in. There was a fine seam in the bulkhead where the entrance to the ladder should have been. The ship had been modified, and the new plans had never been submitted.

"There has to be a way," Ryck said, checking his readout.

"Sams, is your access to Bravo and Charlie decks there?" he asked the First Squad leader.

There was a pause until Sams came on the circuit and said, "Roger that. We're just passing Bravo. What's up?"

"They've modified the ship. Our ladder is sealed off. There's not another passage on the plans until we reach yours, but there is a compartment, Alpha-One-Six, between us, and it looks like it opens on both decks. If it's sealed, though, or doesn't open to Bravo, then we're going to have to move on and use your route in," Ryck said.

"OK, just give me a heads up if you are going to be coming up our butt," Sams said.

Ryck reported the issue to the lieutenant, who told Ryck to keep moving and try that compartment as a passage to the inner decks.

"Rey, do you see Alpha-One-Six on your plans?" he asked.

"Not really. How far down is it?" Corporal Rey asked.

With a PICS' more advanced display capability, Ryck could have highlighted the compartment and activated that highlight on Rey's display. With the EVA suits' less-capable displays, that wasn't possible.

"Thirty meters ahead, proximal," Ryck told him.

"Oh, proximal. I was looking at the regular compartments. Yeah, I see it," Rey said.

The *Marie's Best* had artificial gravity, and that oriented the ship so that down was proximal, toward the center of the ship. The overhead was distal. For ships that used rotation to simulate gravity, this was reversed. With both methods, the larger compartments tended to be medial, on the horizontal axis, surrounding the corridors. In between decks, though, there was space, valuable space. This was primarily used for conduits, air tubes, and the like, but wherever small compartments could be jigsawed in, they provided extra storage space, control rooms, or even hydroponic farms.

"Head for that. Let's see if we can get through to Bravo. According to this ship's diagram, it should," Ryck said.

"Yeah, but it also showed this ladder going though, and this is one of the main ones," Corporal Rey said.

Ryck snorted, then replied, "Got that right. Well, let's see if it's right on this."

Corporal Rey led his team down the passage, pushing with the grip-tight toes of his EVA for forward momentum and the hook on his weapon to keep him close along the bulkhead.

Ryck liked to use the hook more than anything else. If someone hit them while the hook was latched onto something, he knew the split second it took to release that and bring his weapon to bear could be the difference between getting shot and shooting the enemy. But First Team was in front of him, so he felt simply using the hook kept his eyes steady and gave him a better picture of what was going on. The grip-tight that was on the toes of the EVA suit did as advertised, gripping most any surface and giving traction, but the push and dolphin motion it took to move forward without drifting out interfered with his line of sight.

It only took a few minutes before First Team reached the round door on the deck that led to the compartment. Ryck pulled Second Team up to flank him, then gave Corporal Rey the signal to open it up.

Hartono slid the M99 into the magholster on his thigh and grabbed the door's wheel, bringing his legs under him and flat on the deck. Braced by holding the small, recessed wheel, he could exert as much force on the door as his hands could maintain their grip. He spun the wheel, and the door immediately opened without resistance. With his right hand, he grabbed his weapon; with his left, he pulled himself into a dive down through the door and into the compartment. Keiji and Prifit were on his ass.

Corporal Rey was about to follow when Keiji told him to stop. Ryck crowded up, ready for anything, but Keiji's head appeared through the open door.

"It's kinda tight here. This is some kinda bunkroom. Harts is ready to open up the door to Bravo Deck, so me and Tip are gonna cover. That's all the room there is."

"Wait one," Ryck said, pulling himself over to the door so he could see inside.

Keiji was right. Inside the cramped space were six racks, three on a side. This had to be crew's quarters. Ryck had heard that some lines were tight-ass stingy, using all bigger compartments for cargo or paying passengers, but this was the first time he'd ever run across this shoehorning in crew wherever they could.

Ryck called up Corporal Mendoza's team, arraying the Marines the best he could around the small round door. It would be extremely difficult to provide supporting fire if there was anyone right there at Bravo Deck as First Team would be in the way, but at least they were closer and could get down there quicker if need be.

"OK, hit it," Ryck told PFC Hartono.

Hartono spun the wheel on the door, and it silently opened into Bravo Deck. Ryck could just see the overhead past him as Hartono's infrared torch lit up the area.

"Oh God!" the PFC exclaimed as he pushed into the corridor.

"Go, go!" Corporal Rey shouted at his other two Marines who quickly pulled through the door to join Hartono.

Ryck was already diving through, right on Rey's ass. In front of the two NCOs, Keiji was motionless just inside the door.

He held up a hand and quietly said, "All clear."

Letting Rey go first, Ryck followed through the door and into the Bravo Deck corridor. He twisted and landed feet-first on the deck. He immediately saw what elicited Hartono's exclamation. In front of him, illuminated in the infrared, were six people, all dead. Two adults, four children. The man looked to be in his early 30's. All he had on was a pair of dark shorts. The man was facing the others, one arm reached out toward them. Facing the man was a woman. Ryck couldn't see her face, so only her close-cropped hair and unitard registered. With one arm, she was reaching out for the man. Her other arm was crooked, holding the baby. In death, her arm was still positioned to hold the little one, but her grip had slackened, and the infant's legs could be seen protruding from the side of the woman. Ryck was suddenly glad he couldn't see the baby's face.

He could see the other three children's faces, though. The closest victim to the Marines was a young boy, possibly 10 or 11 years old. He had on a Thunder Bluster t-shirt, the band's skull logo catching the infrared beams and looking as if it was lit. He would have looked like any other kid scoping the mall after school—if it weren't for the look of utter agony frozen on his face. His eyes were protruding and dark with petechiae, his mouth opened in a silent scream. One arm was obviously broken, probably from being slammed against something as the air rushed out of the ship. The kid had not gone easily into the night.

In front of him and up against the overhead were the two girls. They looked like twins, around five or six years old. Each was locked in the other's embrace, faces against each other's. At least their eyes were closed, and while they had to have suffered, they seemed more peaceful.

In a complete vacuum, a person would lose consciousness in less than 15 seconds. However, when the ship this size was breached with the degree of destruction the *Marie's Best* suffered, it would have taken 20 or even 30 seconds for the ship's atmosphere to be vented. That meant this family would have known what was happening. They would have suffered as the air pressure dropped toward zero.

Airtight bulkheads could have kept pockets of air inside, but for some reason, they had not been activated. The crew had probably felt the AI would take care of that, but the AI could have been destroyed in the initial strike. That was why on all military ships, at least, the AIs had several secondary "brains" located throughout the ship, and all ships going into battle had airtight bulkheads sealed.

The family was stretched out over about 20 meters. They must have been bounced through the corridor as the air evacuated, with them trying to stay together. With the artificial gravity fading, it would have been even harder. Ryck tried not to imagine what it must have been like.

He swallowed trying to keep the bile from rising in his throat. Vomiting in an EVA suit was not a good idea, but this scene hit him hard. He tried to block it, but images of Lysa and his two nieces floating in the cold vacuum of space flooded his imagination

The rest of the squad slowly made their way into Bravo Deck. Everyone was silent as they took in the scene.

Why hadn't the family been in evac suits? They had to have known they were running a blockade. And why run a blockade in the first place? These were not combatants. They were just people. Why was it that important to get them to the planet's surface?

Ryck knew that warfare was dirty, that civilians got killed. He'd been on ops where he knew that had happened. This was the first time, though, that he'd really seen the effects right before his eyes. This was the first time he'd really seen "collateral damage." He'd cheered when he'd heard the *Ark Royal's* monitors had scored the hit. He'd felt pride when he'd seen the damage to the *Marie's Best*. He wasn't feeling so enthused now.

"Three-six, this is three-three" he passed on the platoon circuit, "we've got six dead civilians here. Looks like a family."

"There's quite a number of bodies throughout the ship," Lieutenant Nidishchii' passed back. "They'll be taken care of later. What's your progress now? I can't get a good fix on you."

"We're on Bravo, heading back to see if we can make it to Charlie," Ryck replied.

"Three-two is already at the objective. We will be there momentarily. You need to get a move on."

"Roger that. If we have a ladder, it shouldn't be more than five mikes," Ryck said.

"Understood. If you have any problems, keep me informed. Three-six, out."

"Let's move it. We're behind schedule," Ryck passed through the squad circuit.

"Which way?" Corporal Rey asked.

Trying to see if the original ladder connected Bravo and Charlie meant passing through the family, and Ryck could hear the strain in Rey's voice as he asked. Going the other way, though, meant they would be using the same ladder as First Squad. Ryck didn't want to disturb the family as they floated in the corridor, but that was the direction they had to take.

"Forward," was all he passed.

Ryck tried to keep his gaze forward as they moved between the bodies. The twin girls were blocking his route, so he jumped across the corridor to use one of the bulkheads. He also made pretty heavy use of his microjets to not only maintain attitude, as they were designed for, but to bend him around the bodies. He determinedly refused to even glance at the woman's face or the infant still in her arm as he passed her.

Thankfully, they reached the clear corridor ahead. A few moments later, Corporal Rey passed that the ladder between Bravo and Charlie was in fact there. Whatever modification had been done to the ship had only affected the space between Alpha and Bravo.

They went down the ladder, one at a time, to emerge in a cleared Charlie Deck. No bodies rose to greet them. From there, it was only about 25 meters to their assigned entrance to the galley. Ryck let the rest of the platoon know the squad was entering, then when given the all-clear, the squad filed inside.

Emergency lights lit the galley, bringing color back to their view. The four lights in each corner cast harsh, but sufficient illumination. The galley was about 20 meters across, and there were probably close to 100 people from the ship there. With the 40 Marines there as well, it was somewhat packed. However, with no gravity, groups had drifted in all three axes, making it a little less crowded.

Doc Grbil, with the red cross illuminated on his shoulder, was easy to spot as he worked on one of the civilians. The much taller Doc Francis, one of the battalion aid station corpsmen attached to the platoon for the mission, was there assisting. From the civilians waiting, it looked like many of them needed help.

The civilians were in "walmarts," the cheaply made but effective emergency suits that were never intended to be worn for long. By Federation law, there had to be at least one temporary emergency evacuation suit for each and every soul on board. Ryck wondered why the first man they'd seen and the family hadn't gotten into their walmarts. The recon team had reported 133 people alive on the ship. Take away those killed in the bridge and close to it, and there still would only have been a little over 200 people. A ship this size would be able to provide emergency suits to that number and more.

Unless more were killed, Ryck thought soberly.

There were a few commercial evac suits being worn, so it looked like some of the crew had survived. They were sized for each wearer, not like the one-size-fits-all walmarts. Ryck could see at least two baby bubbles, so at least some infants had made it.

This was a deflated group, and they didn't look to be offering any resistance. Only one crewman, in the far corner of the gallery, had a defiant posture that suggested different. He had stationed himself in front of three bodies, all in walmarts, but obviously dead. The walmarts were actually a pretty good piece of gear, but they seemed to have failed with the three dead people in front of the man. In the maelstrom of the air rushing out of the ship, they could have been breached when the three had been pushed up against something hard or sharp.

The crewman reminded Ryck of the vids of dogs, guarding over their dead masters. None of the Marines were bothering him.

Ryck made his way to the lieutenant and Staff Sergeant Hecs, who were with the Navy chief from the engineer division as they discussed what could be done to make conditions better for the civvies. Most of the work was being done by Captain Davis and the head engineer up in the destroyed bow as they evaluated the damage done to the ship.

"Sergeant Lysander, spread your teams out. There doesn't seem to be a threat here now, but keep alert. We're awaiting orders at the moment. If we get them, I'm going to want you to escort Senior Chief Han here to aft engineering. But for now, just spread out, keeping it low key. I want eyes open, but no aggressive posture," the platoon commander said as Ryck came up.

"Aye-aye, sir," Ryck acknowledged as he turned and went back to where the squad waited.

He'd wanted to get more of the scoop as to what was going on, but orders were orders, and he figured that whatever he needed to know, he would be told. Keeping the "no aggressive posture" part of his orders, he broke the squad into teams, sending each team to a position toward the back of the galley. He put each team on a different plane, one on the overhead, one on the deck, and one on the bulkhead. This would give them a better view of the people. This was right out of the training pubs, as people tended to process things better when what they were observing was on the same plane as they were.

Ryck decided to move around his little claimed sector of the galley. There were around 20 or 25 people crowded in the back. Most seemed to be ignoring him, but that could be just shock. They'd been through a lot.

Doc Grbil popped a zip-lock out of his med-pack and deployed it. Normal zip-locks were simply clear bags that could hold a person and maintain an atmosphere for a number of hours while people were transported to safety. The corpsmen had special zip-locks that had small stasis units that could slow down the metabolism of whoever was inside. These were not the same stasis units as those which were in a ship's sickbay. They were portable units that slowly lowered the metabolism, never reaching full stasis. Still, the time they gave a patient could make all the difference between life and death.

The civvie was unresponsive, and he was probably fading, but Doc must have thought the zip-lock could help. He and Doc Francis maneuvered the civvie inside, and then partially closed the zip-lock. Doc Grbil reached in with a scalpel, and with a quick slash, slit the man's walmart before pulling his arm out and sealing the zip-lock. Almost immediately, the zip-lock puffed out.

Ryck wondered why he'd compromised the walmart. Maybe it would have interfered with the stasis? He'd have to ask Doc later.

Ryck turned back and pulled himself along, using the galley tables as anchor points. Three civvies, a man and two women, were sitting at one of the tables, their legs under the tabletops and keeping them in place. These walmarts were the basic ones, without comms, so they weren't talking but just keeping each other company. As Ryck pulled himself past, he gave them a thumbs-up. The man and one woman stared at him blankly, but there was a flicker in the eyes in the second woman as she inadvertently glanced over to the recessed fabrication nook of the galley.

Ryck looked over in that direction but didn't see anything out of the ordinary. There were three fabricators, a double sink for clean-up, and cupboards for plates and utensils. He glanced back at the woman, but she was once again staring blankly ahead.

Ryck pushed off toward the nook, pulling his legs under and thrusting them in front so he hit the sink area feet-first. He couldn't see anything that caught his attention. He felt eyes on him, though, that weird, tingling feeling that he could not explain. Casually glancing back into the galley seating, he could see one of the crewmen carefully avoiding looking at Ryck, in a way that told Ryck the man had seen Ryck's interest in the nook. Ryck moved to his right, and he thought the crewman relaxed slightly. He then reversed and moved back to his left. He could swear the crewman tensed up again.

There was nothing there, though. The nook ended. There was the small access hatch through which the bases for that meal's recipes came. But that was only a passage leading up from storage. It wasn't a compartment. But that small compartment they'd taken from Alpha to Bravo deck hadn't been designed for people, either. On the *Marie's Best*, it had been crew berthing. Ryck casually left the nook and approached Corporal Beady.

"John, bring your team and follow me. There's something fishy about the fabrication nook. I don't know what it is, but at least two people out there seem to be very interested in it. Could be something there. All I can see, though, is the feed tunnel for the food bases, but let's take a look."

Corporal Beady motioned for his team to follow. All five Marines looked over the nook, which was only about five meters long and two meters deep. Ryck pointed at the small hatch, about one-meter square, though which supplies were delivered. If this were like any other delivery chute, when the hatch was opened, a small tray would slide out on which the supplies would be loaded. As one carton was lifted up, another would slide in to take its place.

Ryck took a look back. The crewman who'd been so studiously ignoring him before had abandoned all pretense now. He had moved closer and was staring at them.

Ryck pointed at the access hatch with the muzzle of his M99. Corporal Beady motioned Ling to the overhead, where he would be looking down at the hatch. He positioned Lance Corporal Martin to the sink, just to the side of the access hatch. Martin put his feet in the sink, his grip-tights keeping him in place. He motioned Lips Holleran to get ready to open the hatch.

"First and Second, it may be nothing, but we're checking out the supply access hatch here. Keep an eye on anyone who might not want us to take a look," Ryck passed on the squad circuit.

He joined Corporal Beady, oriented on the deck, facing the hatch. They had three of the four directions around the hatch covered. The fourth was the nook bulkhead, and there wasn't room for anyone to fit in given the half-meter between the edge of the hatch and the bulkhead.

"OK, Lips, let's see what we've got," Ryck passed.

Just as Lance Corporal Holleran started opening the hatch, Ryck couldn't help but turn slightly to see what their crewman friend was doing. The crewman had edged forward, but had stopped and was simply watching. Ryck knew he should have put one of the other Marines on him.

Holleran had opened the hatch, which opened outwards to the rest of the nook. Ryck turned his head just as the hatch was forced open quicker, pushing Lips back. A small blue light flashed in the dark recesses of the tunnel, followed by a shape erupting out of it. Ryck felt more than saw Corporal Beady getting hit.

In front of Ryck, coming out was a man in a white, military EVA suit. It was Legion design, Ryck realized, and the Legion Sallie Gun that had hit Beady was swinging right at him, the hypervelocity darts making a stream that could easily puncture his EVA suit.

In null-G, it is impossible to quickly turn and dodge. Ryck had shifted his attention to the *Marie's Best* crewman, moving him out of position. Martin was out of position, too, on the other side of the open hatch and with Lips tumbling between him and the legionnaire. Ryck started the kip-around to get his own M99 deployed, but he knew he wasn't going to make it in time.

Just as he expected to feel darts impacting on him, something big and heavy hit him from above, sending him flying. He started spinning, bouncing him off the deck and back up. He tried to get a grip with his toe, but his momentum was too high.

As he spun, though, his M99 was out, ready to fire. In null-G, the M99 automatically shifted from the Roeniger Display scope to old-style "iron" sights. The Roeniger scope inputted drop from gravity, coriolis, wind, and any other influences that could affect the trajectory of a dart. In null-G, those forces did not exist, so what you saw is what was hit. As he bounced off the deck, Ryck caught a flash of white through his peep sight. It wasn't a good sight picture, but at a meter-and-a-half, it was good enough. He depressed his trigger, sending three or four darts into the legionnaire before he spun past. Martin was clear by that time, and he also fired a burst into the man.

Corporal Mendoza and Lance Corporal Khouri bounded in just then.

"Cease fire!" someone shouted, but Ryck was too busy regaining control to pay attention to just who passed that. He kipped his legs under and absorbed the shock as he hit the overhead. His grip-tights kept him in place.

"Doc, get over here. Man down!" he shouted into his mic.

Above him, he could see Corporal Beady, arms barely moving as he drifted slowly backward. A small pink mist was coalescing in front of his chest. It looked like he'd taken two hits, through and through, but his suit had already sealed the holes, the bright blue sealing patches very visible.

Ryck's helmet speakers exploded into a cacophony of talk. That suddenly quit as the lieutenant over-rode the circuit, switching Ryck to the command circuit.

"Report!" he commanded.

Ryck could see the lieutenant pulling himself over the tables, rushing to the scene.

"We've got one man down. There was what looks to be a legionnaire hiding in the supply tube, and he came out firing. We took him out," he said, glancing to where the legionnaire floated lifelessly.

Oddly, for a moment, all Ryck could notice was that legionnaire EVA suit patches were red, not the blue of Federation suits. Ryck could see half a dozen or more red patches on the front of the man's suit.

It was only then that Ryck noticed the blue patch on Ling's arm. Suddenly, he realized that it was Ling who had hit him. Ling had seen that he was out of position, and he'd launched himself at Ryck, knocking him out of the line of fire. Ling had taken at least one round as a result. This was the brown-noser who Ryck thought might be a liability. The kid had saved Ryck's life.

"Correction, two down. Beady and Ling," he sent to the platoon commander.

By then, the lieutenant, Staff Sergeant Hecs, and the two corpsmen had gotten there. More Marines would have come, but the lieutenant had ordered them to maintain total security. Hecs immediately checked the access tunnel for anyone else, something Ryck should have done, he realized.

Doc Grbil went right to Corporal Beady, checking his vitals on the readout. The EVA suits recorded O2 consumption, pulse, and perspiration, less than what a PICS monitored, but things that were valuable to a corpsman. Doc Francis went to check Ling, but after a cursory inspection, came back to Beady. That was not a good sign.

Ryck pushed off the overhead, spun around, and came down to where the two corpsmen were working on John. The fire team leader was not doing well; even Ryck could see that. Blood had frothed up against his EVA suit face shield.

Grbil and Francis were pretty obviously on a medical circuit, one Ryck could not listen in on. By their gestures, Ryck could tell they were arguing. Ryck was getting frantic.

Quit arguing and save him! he shouted in his mind.

Doc Francis reached out and put his hand on Doc Grbil's shoulder, only to have the platoon corpsman knock it away. Francis seemed to deflate, and Ryck could swear he saw the moment when he capitulated to Grbil. What that meant for Beady, Ryck didn't know.

"OK, this is what's going to happen," Doc Grbil passed on the platoon circuit while Doc Francis got out another zip-lock and started preparing it. "Corporal Beady is bleeding out. There is no way he will make it back to the *Ark Royal*, and I don't think the portable stasis will be effective enough, fast enough. I need to stop the bleeding, first."

How could he do that? If this was on solid ground or in a pressurized ship, it would be easy. Doc could take Beady out of his suit, close off any arteries, and give him a spray of skin-in-a-can. But in this situation, it was the same as in open space. If Doc was going to take him out of his suit, Beady would die anyway.

"The only thing I can do is go in there with him, stop the bleeding, then start stasis," Doc passed.

The zip-locks were not that big, Ryck knew. Two men in EVA suits just weren't going to fit. If they did manage to squeeze in, there would be no room for Doc to work. And even if he did, once sealed, the zip-locks could only be opened in a sickbay, so how was Doc going to get out once the stasis generator was turned on?

"What I need is for two Marines to hold the zip-lock opening, half-closed. I'm going to have Doug here cut off my suit, and I've got to get inside immediately. I need the opening closed and air pumped in right then if I'm going to remain conscious. If— " he started.

"No way!" Lieutenant Nidishchii' shouted over the net. "That's too dangerous. I'm going to canc that plan right now!"

"Sorry sir, but you can't," Doc Grbil told him.

"The hell I can't! I'm your commanding officer, and I say no!"

"You know better than that, lieutenant. You are in tactical command of me, true. But in medical matters, my authority trumps yours. We can argue this. We can send back to the *Ark Royal* for confirmation, but time is wasting. I need to do this right now if

Corporal Beady is to have a chance," he said, looking at the lieutenant.

The platoon commander stared back for a moment before passing, "All right. Two Marines, up here now."

Ryck was right there, so he took the edge of the zip-lock that Doc Francis held. Lips and Keiji started to join him, but as Lips was in Beady's fire team, Keiji backed off. Doc Francis gave them a 15-second brief on what to do. It wasn't difficult. They'd all been in zip-locks back at recruit training, and Ryck had been in one in an actual medical situation, even if he was unconscious at the time. The seal was a simple groove-in-slot, just like the old-style zip-lock bags from which they got their nickname.

The two docs maneuvered Beady into the zip-lock, pushing him toward the back. Ryck saw no movement from the Corporal and hoped he was still alive, still hanging on. With Doc Francis assisting, they closed the opening half-way, leaving the top half unsealed. Doc threw in a medical kit, then stood in front of the opening. Doc Francis stood behind him with a scalpel in his hand.

Ryck could see Doc Grbil's EVA suit expand as he took several deep breaths. Doc wanted to get as much O2 into his system as possible before he tried the transfer. He held up one hand, then exhaled as much as he could, bringing down the hand as a signal to Doc Francis.

The battalion aid station corpsman quickly sliced down the side of his fellow corpsman's suit, from shoulder to calf. With a quick reverse, he slit Doc Grbil's left sleeve.

With several shakes, Doc Grbil tried to free himself from the suit. He was already in a vacuum, and time was ticking. His hand seemed to be sticking, so Ryck reached out with one hand and gave the glove of the suit a jerk. That seemed to work, and Doc Grbil was diving forward into the zip-lock, blood globes spinning off from where Doc Francis had cut him while slicing the suit. Doc went in head first, but his feet hung up on the opening, and Lips and Ryck had to grab them and push them in.

Doc Francis had hit the switch that started the air flowing into the zip-lock even before the two Marines had sealed the opening. Staff Sergeant Hecs and the lieutenant jumped up to help, pulling the seam out straight so Lips and Ryck could get it sealed.

It took a few long seconds before the zip-lock began to puff out. Doc Grbil was crumbled in the bottom of the lock, not moving.

Had it taken them too long? Ryck wondered.

If Doc was unconscious, the increase in pressure brought him around. He shook his head once or twice, then squirmed around to face Corporal Beady. He checked Beady's breathing. Ryck could not see his corporal's chest rising, but he must have been breathing as Doc Grbil went on to the second B in triage, "bleeding."[18] Reaching into his kit, he took out a fabric cutter, which was nothing more than a scalpel with a curved guard that kept it from slicing into the person whose clothing was being removed. He inserted it into the suit at Beady's waist, then ran it up, cutting the fabric away from his torso. Underneath the suit, Beady's white cottons were soaked red with blood. Doc Grbil cut the cottons away, exposing the wounds to the torso.

Ryck wanted to turn away, but he had to watch as Doc quickly inserted the cauterizer into the holes made into Beady's body when the darts burst through him. The little tool sought out major arteries and veins, automatically sealing them off. Quickly, but with a sure hand, Doc Grbil took out the *siliderma*, the skin-in-a can, and closed off all the outside wounds. Turning Beady around, he slit off the rest of the corporal's EVA suit, then repeated the process.

Ryck watched the entire process, willing Doc to hurry. He knew his team leader had to get into stasis quick. Field expedient first aid was great, but Beady needed surgery.

Doc gave Beady the once over, sealing shut another wound in his arm and checked Beady's breathing again. He didn't seem satisfied, so he intubated the corporal, then started oxygen. He looked out through the clear sides of the zip-lock to his fellow corpsman. Doc Francis pointed at his wrist as it to a watch. Doc Grbil nodded, and Doc Francis started the stasis generator.

---

[18] Triage's Three B's: A simple way to triage patients with "breathing" the highest priority, then "bleeding," and finally "breaks."

Ryck felt a surge of gratitude toward the corpsman. He put his life on the line to try and save John. Even going into stasis had a degree of danger. On occasion, people in stasis were damaged in the process, and some even died. Doc Grbil was putting himself at risk.

While waiting for stasis to take over, Doc Francis went back to work on PFC Ling. He looked at the readings, then applied a broad, low-pressure bandage to the area. Blood would still flow, but at a reduced rate, thereby slowing any bleeding.

The portable stasis generator was slow, and it took several minutes for it to take effect on Beady and the doc. Ryck could see no change in Beady, but Doc's head began to loll, and his mouth opened. Within moments after that, he was out. It still took another ten minutes for Doc Francis to be satisfied that full stasis, at least as full as the portable generator could reach, had been attained.

"Corporal Beady was still alive when stasis took over. Harris is fine, too. We need to get them back to the *Ark Royal* ASAP, though," Doc Francis said.

"Captain Davis has a reki waiting right outside Finland," the lieutenant said, referring to the operational name of the breach where Second Squad had entered the *Marie's Best*. "If he's ready, let's get them there. PFC Ling goes, too. Sergeant Lysander, get a team together and get it done."

"Aye-aye, sir," he replied, then to his team, "First, take point and clear the way. Just because it was cleared on the way in does not mean someone else hasn't moved in afterward. Stillwell, you help Ling, Peretti, you've got our rear. The rest of you, you've got Corporal Beady and the doc. I shouldn't have to say it, but be careful!"

He switched to a direct circuit and asked, "Joab, how are you doing?"

"I'm fine, sergeant. No problem," Ling answered.

His voice did not sound fine, though. It sounded shocky.

"If you feel nauseous, if you are having any problems, let me know. Corporal Beady and Doc Grbil are in stasis, so a few more minutes won't matter much. One more thing, though," Ryck said as they moved out to take Beady, Grbil, and Ling to the reki and then back to the ship.

"What's that, sergeant?"

"Thanks. You saved my ass back there," he told his PFC.

Chapter 9

Ryck entered the lieutenant's stateroom. He shared it with four other lieutenants, but it did have a small table and four chairs that he could use as a workspace.

The platoon commander motioned for Ryck to take a seat. Staff Sergeant Hecs was sitting there, but none of the other squad leaders had been summoned.

"You about done with your after-action report?" the lieutenant asked.

"Uh, not quite yet, sir. I've been in sickbay to check on Corporal Beady and PFC Ling, then getting the squad back in the squadbay," he answered.

They had only been back to the *Ark Royal* for a couple of hours. What did the lieutenant expect? He knew the platoon commander had to get his own report up to Captain Davis, but still, Ryck needed more time, and unless the lieutenant could read gibberish, he really needed some shut-eye before writing it.

"No problem, just get it up to me when you can. I just wanted to ask a few questions so I have it straight in my mind and give you some intel. First, the man you killed was in fact a legionnaire, a Lieutenant Colonel Tolbert. He had his full ID with him, and in his stateroom, his full compliment of uniforms. We don't know why he was attempting to land on Tel Aviv, but N2 thinks he was the reason the *Marie's Best* was trying to run our blockade," he told Ryck.

Ryck sat back in surprise. A man was a man, a kill a kill, but still, it was a shock that the man he'd shot was so high-ranking.

"But why did he fight? He had to know he couldn't win." Ryck asked.

"Have you ever heard of the old phrase, suicide-by-cop?" the platoon commander asked.

"Well, yeah, when a guy wants the cops to kill him, and he goes after them. I've seen it in some old flicks."

"Well, N2 is pretty sure this was suicide-by-Marines. Whatever Colonel Tolbert was doing, it was pretty important, and he did not want to be interrogated by us, so he went out fighting."

"And almost took Corporal Beady with him," Ryck said sourly.

The lieutenant seemed almost to admire the guy's actions. Ryck was still pissed that two of his Marines had been hurt, and now to find out it was just so the guy couldn't talk, well, that torqued him even more. *Grub the guy!*

"Well, yes, there is that. But you took care of him, so I would say it evens out."

No, it never evens out, Ryck thought. *Not when you hurt one of mine.*

"Yes sir," he said instead.

"Speaking of which, I've already spoken to Captain Davis. I want to put you in for another BC3 and Doc Grbil for a BC1. Congratulations," he told Ryck.

"Uh, sir, if you wouldn't mind, I mean, if you could withdraw that, I would appreciate it," Ryck said. "Not Doc's, but mine."

The lieutenant's eyes seemed to cloud over just the slightest and a steely tone took over his voice as he asked, "What, with your Silver Star, a BC3 isn't worthy?"

"Oh no, sir, that's not it at all. It's just that, well, I made a mistake, and I almost paid for it. I was looking the wrong way, and if it weren't for PFC Ling, I don't think I'd be here, or at the least, either Corporal Beady or I wouldn't have made it. Ling saw I was in trouble, then launched himself to get me out of the way. He took a round for that. I just think he deserves it more than me," Ryck said.

The lieutenant turned to Staff Sergeant Hecs and asked, "Had you heard this?"

"No, sir. This is the first time I've had to talk with Sergeant Lysander," the staff sergeant replied.

"Well, that puts a different light on it. And others will back that up?" the lieutenant asked.

No, I'm grubbing lying, Ryck thought. *Geez!*

"Yes, sir. Lance Corporals Martin and Holleran were there," he said.

"But you shot Lieutenant Colonel Tolbert, right? I am sure I saw that," the lieutenant went on.

"Yes, sir, but only because PFC Ling had already knocked me out of the way of the legionnaire's fire," Ryck answered.

"PFC Ling, the kind of, well, squirrely Marine? One-point-six meters? Maybe 65 kg?" he asked Ryck.

"Yes, sir, that PFC Ling. Joab Ling."

"Wow, I would never have guessed that," Staff Sergeant Hecs said. "Pretty fantasmagorical, if you ask me."

"So, sir, my point is that if anyone is going to get a medal, I think it should be Ling," Ryck said.

"Well, OK. I guess it would be deserved. I wish you had told me before I went to the Captain, though. It's going to make me look bad, but there's no getting around that," Lieutenant Nidishchii' said.

Well, wait until you talk to me, or wait until you get my after-action before you go run to the captain, he thought.

That probably wasn't fair, he knew. He was tired, dead tired, and stressed with two hurt Marines. Ling was going to be fine, nothing a week in regen wouldn't cure. John was more seriously hurt, and he had some rehab coming, maybe a month or so in regen. The lieutenant was running on even less sleep than Ryck, and he had his own stressors. The fact that he would even go up to the captain and admit he had been wrong about something was a big point in his favor.

"Thank you, sir. I appreciate it," Ryck said.

"Look, I was going to ask you how you knew there was someone in that stores access, but I can see you're dragging. Your squad is racked out?" he asked.

"Yes, sir, about an hour ago."

"You look like you need a clear head. I'll go see the captain now, but I want you to go get showered and hit the rack. Don't get up until, say, 0430 GMT," he said after looking at his watch. "You, too, staff sergeant. We can't do our jobs if we are falling asleep on our feet."

"And you too, lieutenant," Staff Sergeant Hecs told him.

"I will, after I get a few more things done."

"No, sir, as soon as you speak to the skipper. Nothing more than that. You're not superman, and you need your sleep, too." Staff Sergeant Hecs told him.

Ryck was surprised at Hec's tone. This was not just to get his platoon commander out of his hair. He sounded like he really cared for the lieutenant, the man himself, not the platoon commander. Ryck filed that away for when he was more alert to figure out what that really meant.

"OK, OK, I promise. Fifteen minutes with the captain, then I'm hitting the rack."

"And not getting up until when?" Staff Sergeant Hecs asked.

"Zero-four-thirty," Lieutenant Nidishchii' said with a laugh. "No putting anything past you."

"And that's why I'm a Marine staff NCO," Hecs said.

"Yeah, I guess it is. OK, both of you, get out of here. Get some sleep, and that's an order!"

That was one order Ryck would be very, very happy to obey.

Chapter 10

Ryck was in the mess decks, eating breakfast, when the world was passed over the 1MC.[19]

It was War.

---

[19] 1MC: The generic term for the ship-wide speaker system over which word can be passed.

Chapter 11

Hannah looked worried as she tried to go on, "I just want to know . . . I mean . . . well, Joshua be still at his, you know, and you?"

Hannah was being careful. All comms were being monitored by the censor bots, and if they picked up any security breach, the line would be cut, and the military side of the conversation could face punishment.

Ryck thought it was amazing that the Federation even allowed personal comms in time of war. But the powers that be thought a happy sailor or Marine was a good sailor or Marine. Self-serving or not, Ryck appreciated it.

Ryck knew what Hannah was saying even if she couldn't be too direct. Joshua had expected to be sent to a line unit, but all DI positions were frozen as draftees started arriving en masse at the recruit depot. He was out of any fighting, and she wanted some assurance that Ryck would also be safe. He couldn't say that, and not just because of the censor bots. He didn't know if he would be safe. He was on a capital ship of the Navy, going into harm's way. The Federation Navy was far stronger than the coalition Greater France had gathered, and would still be even if the Confederation decided to join with the French.

Thankfully, The Brotherhood had declared its neutrality. Their Navy could match the Federation's, and their Army was much larger than the Federation's Marines.

"This will all be over soon, and I'll be back for I-Day, just like I promised," he told her.

She looked at him with a small frown causing her forehead to wrinkle up.

"How do you know that? I be wanting that more than you can imagine, and I've prayed for your safety, but the news is . . ."

Ryck held up a finger to silence her. He didn't want the conversation cut off.

"So, Lysa says you've been accepted for the Ph.D. program? I thought you said you didn't have a chance," he said, trying to change the subject.

She sighed, then took the hint.

"I guess I just wowed them with my proposal. You know me, Miss Sunshine," she said, her demeanor anything but sunshiny.

"I knew you would. You are the most capable woman I've ever met. No, the most capable person," he said.

It was true, he realized. The two of them had gotten quite close since Joshua's wedding, and despite his protestations to his friends, he was thinking about a future together with her. If she would take him, he constantly reminded himself. He was proud of being a Marine, but he was hardly in her class. Extremely intelligent, athletic, and very personable, she could have whomever she wanted. It amazed him that she seemed attached to a dumb grunt.

"Quit the sugar-mouth, Ryck, always thinking you can sweet-talk me," she said, but Ryck could see her soften up.

She always protested his compliments, but Ryck thought she secretly liked them.

"OK, then get this. I'm getting better at Five. I challenge you to a best two out of three as soon as I get back."

"Hah! You be dreaming if you think you can beat me. I accept, and I be spotting you five points per game. Deal?" she asked, her smile making a return.

Ryck, the big tough Marine, had suffered a humiliating defeat to Hannah on the Five court. She didn't have his strength, but she had a knack for putting the small ball to where he had to lunge and struggle just to reach it. It was all in good fun, but Ryck's competitive nature had risen, and he had kept playing whenever he could, trying to get better. Truthfully, he still might not be able to beat her, but at least he could make a better showing at it.

"I don't need your points — " he began when the connection was cut.

What? I didn't say anything, he thought.

"All hands, report to your stations. This is not a drill," came over the 1MC.

"Stations" was not "battle stations." For Marines, that meant going to their berthing decks and staying there, out of the way of the sailors. "Battle stations" meant going to their ancillary hangar and combat up as ordered.

Ryck joined the 20 or so sailors and Marines who had been camming as they made their way out and started back to their respective assigned stations. This was the smallest cam center with only 25 consoles, but because it was smaller, not as many people used it, and the wait to get on was usually not as lengthy. It was a long way to the Marine berthing, though, so Ryck and two other Marines had to dodge sailors rushing to their stations as they made their way slowly across the bulk of the ship. The Marines always gave way—the sailors had jobs to do, while the Marines' job was to stay out of the way.

Ryck was the last one to reach their compartment. He hit his thumb on the register, and the report went up. Golf Company, Third Platoon, was present and accounted for.

The entire platoon, minus the lieutenant and Staff Sergeant Hecs, was berthed in the compartment. The NCOs had partitioned off the far end of the space, but with bunks four high, it was rather crowded.

Ryck made his way down through the other Marines, pulling back the curtain to the NCO's quarters.

"Son of Cain, Sams, you stink like rotten ass!" he exclaimed as he pulled himself into his rack.

"Can't help it none if we get stations while I'm in the gym. Which reminds me, where were you? You promised to meet us there."

"Got held up. There wasn't a line at the cam shop, so I took advantage of it . . ."

". . . to call your Hannah, yeah, we figured," Sams interrupted. "You are seriously PW'd[20], my man, seriously."

Ryck was about to retort when the vid screens lit up. While there were real holos in the ship's lounges, space in berthing was

---

[20] PW'd: Pussy-whipped. A man controlled by a wife or girlfriend.

limited, and there were only two-dimensional screens installed for the Marines.

Admiral Starling, over on the *Bismarck*, was whistled onto the screen first. It sounded like a real boatswain did the whistling, maybe even the *Bismarck's* bos'un. Ryck guessed admirals didn't use recordings.

"All hands, we have located the rebel fleet," he began.

French fleet, Ryck thought. *Isn't "rebel" a bit dramatic?*

"We are now on a course to intercept it. We have superiority, both in numbers and in the moral righteousness of our cause. If we all do our duty, we can end this war before it ever really starts, saving countless lives. I trust every single sailor on every ship, and every Marine, to perform his mission with utter devotion."

He went on in that vein, mostly a pep talk. He gave no details, which Ryck wanted. How many ships were opposing them? Which kind? More of this would make its way down the pipeline, but Ryck hated being in the dark.

The admiral signed off after only five minutes, something of a record as he tended to be a bit longwinded. It made sense, though, as planning the mission should take priority.

Col Petrakis came on next, at least on the Marine vids. Other Navy staff would be addressing different Navy divisions. The colonel was Colonel Pierre's replacement as regimental commander. The official word was that Col Pierre had been promoted to a higher staff billet, but even the newest boot private smelled the shit emanating from that line of bull. No one was "promoted" from a command to a staff billet before his command tour was over. "Pierre" was just a bit too French for the current climate.

Col Petrakis had a good rep, but Ryck disliked him on principle. It wasn't fair, but Ryck thought Col Pierre hadn't been treated fairly, either, and Ryck was loyal to the man.

Col Petrakis didn't add much in the way of more specific info, just to stay ready for any call. Ship-to-ship was the Navy's game, though, and the Marines didn't expect much except possibly to take damaged vessels. If that happened, though, it would be long after any battle. He did mention the *Jean d'Arc*, though, and that caught Ryck's attention.

It caught everyone's attention.

"Admiral DeMornay," Corporal Revis, one of First Squad's team leaders, said in a hushed tone.

As the colonel signed off and the vid screen went black, most of the NCO's swung about so they were facing the center.

"Who the fuck is Admiral DeMornee?" Teller Simms, Corporal Revis' squad leader asked.

"DeMornAY," Ryck answered. "Celeste DeMornay. You mean to say you've never heard of her?"

"'Celeste?' Like in a woman's name?" Simms continued. "No, never heard of her. Why should I have?"

"Only because she's the most famous French admiral. She was awarded the Légion d'honneur *and* the Federation Nova during the War of the Far Reaches," Popo added.

"Shit, a woman? And in the War? She's got to be an old biddy now. So what?" Sams asked.

"You too? Don't any of you negats read any history?" Popo asked.

"I'll read the history of your dick," Simms said. "Better yet, I'll give her mine," he added, grabbing his crotch.

Simms' attitude was somewhat typical, Ryck knew. For over 150 years, women had not been allowed to serve in the Federation armed forces. The original proclamation came after the devastating Tenner War, when a huge percentage of the population was either killed or suffered extreme chromosomal damage. Women were deemed "too vital" to be put in physical danger and were relegated to breeding up a new generation. That was what the history accounts said, at least. Whatever the reason, women effectively became second-class citizens and had been so ever since. There wasn't any regulated second class status; it was just that many paths were closed to them.

Ryck wasn't about to start a revolution to bring about social change, but thought that if there ever was a need to "protect" women, that time was long gone. It was ironic that one of the heroes of the Tenner War, and of the Marine Corps, was Major Melissa "Missy" Walters, one of only two people to have been awarded two Federation Novas. The second one was awarded posthumously.

Ryck didn't know many women well, but he thought either his sister, or especially Hannah, could serve admirably in the military. The Brotherhood, the Confederation, and most other planets had women serving in all walks of life. Gender equality was a fact of life. And if it was Admiral DeMornay facing them, and if her abilities were only half that of her reputation, then Admiral Starling might be facing much more than he expected.

Corporal Revis tried to give his squad leader a short history lesson on the admiral, but Simms was making light of it. Ryck just sighed, lay back down on his bunk, and did what all good Marines did when given the chance. He caught some z's.

Chapter 12

Every Marine's eyes were glued to the holo display in the lounge. With the Navy at Battle Stations Bravo, the lounge was empty, and the battalion CO had gotten permission for the Marines to watch the feed in the lounges rather than in their berthing spaces. Trying to watch on the 2D screens in berthing did not convey the true breadth and depth of a battle in space.

Battle Stations Bravo meant the Marines were in longjohns or cottons, as their mission required, but not in full battle gear, be that PICS, or EVAs. That would be Battle Stations Alpha.

The *Ark Royal* was on the periphery of the probable battlespace, providing security along the Z-axis, several million kilometers from the *Bismarck*. That was why the crew was only in Battle Stations Bravo. If she was with the main force, they would already be at Alpha.

The Y-axis was always parallel to an arbitrary line running through Earth and along the galactic center. During fleet ops, one ship, in this case the *Bismarck*, was the reference point, with the X, Y, and Z axes radiating from it.

The display had the 41 Navy ships in the task force identified, 29 in the main assault force, the remainder in peripheral security. A few platoons of Marines had been cross-decked to other ships, but the bulk were on three ships: the regimental headquarters and 1/9 were on the *Bismarck*, 2/9 was on the *Ark Royal*, and 3/9 on the *Chakri Naruebet*, which was on the other side of the Z-axis as the *Ark Royal*. If things continued as was being announced, only 1/9 might see any action, much to the dismay of most of Ryck's fellow 2/9 Marines.

This was history in the making. TF-207, with Admiral Starling in command, was the first Federation fleet to locate a French task force, and the upcoming engagement would be the first naval full-fledged action since the War of the Far Reaches. If things went as forecasted, a quick defeat would force the French to capitulate and be absorbed into the Federation. Careers would be made in this battle, and it could even pave the way for Starling to assume the Federation chairmanship.

"This sucks the big one," Sams muttered beside Ryck as they watched the slowly shifting display. "1/9's going to get all the glory."

"You've got that right," Ryck whispered back.

Ryck had nothing against the French, and truth be told, he thought Greater France might have had a legitimate beef with the Federation, although he knew better than to ever express that opinion. He'd even almost joined the Legion before enlisting in the Marines. But he was not involved with the politics—he just did his duty as ordered.

Ryck doubted that 1/9 would really get any glory, anyway. This was going to be a Navy fight. But still, to be there in the thick of things in what would be a pivotal moment in history, that would be something special.

"Sergeant L, why is everything moving so slow?" asked Tipper Prifit.

Keeping his voice down, Ryck answered the lance corporal, "What you see there covers millions of cubic kilometers of space. The ships aren't moving slowly. They've just got to cover a long ways."

Prifit seemed to consider that for a moment. "But I can see the French ships right there. Why doesn't the admiral just go get them?"

"Well, first, we don't exactly know where they are or even how many there are," Ryck said as a few other Marines sitting close by turned to listen.

"But we can see them. Right there!" Keiji said, pointing at the display.

"No, we can see where we *project* some of them to be. It is a calculated position, not a real-time position," PFC Ling put in.

"What?" several Marines asked in unison.

"Ling's right," Ryck said. "We don't really know exactly where they are. We've caught some signatures as we keep trying to pierce their cloaking, just little hints, and the AI's on the *Bismarck* use those to calculate probable positions. Those . . ." he paused, counting the small red icons, ". . . 11 ships might actually be all of the

French fleet. There might be more, there might be fewer. And their positions might be close or pretty far from what we see represented here. As far as what specific ships, their names, all we know for sure is that that one," he said, pointing at the only red icon with a designator, "is the *Jean d'Arc*."

"Sergeant Lysander, for all those still confused, why don't you come up front and repeat what you've been saying," Lt Nidishchii' said from the other side of the lounge.

Ryck hadn't known the platoon commander was listening in to him. Ryck stood up and moved to the holo. Both Third and Weapons Platoon were in the lounge. He knew all the Marines in the two platoons, and they knew him. He glanced up at the two platoon commanders, his own and 1stLt Baca, the Weapons Platoon commander. Both of them looked at him expectantly.

Ryck cleared his throat to buy him a few seconds of time. He'd taken a class in Naval Strategy while earning his degree, so the constant battle for supremacy in cloaking and spoofing and piercing the enemy efforts at the same was something he'd studied. The rest of his knowledge, though, came from a class at boot camp, a class every single Marine had taken, so they should have known all of this. Looking out at the Marines, though, a good half of them looked confused.

Ryck glanced back at the display. Not much had changed, which didn't surprise him. The distances covered were just too great for the scale to show anything in greater detail.

"OK, well, as I was saying back there, to put this into perspective, first, you gotta keep in mind that this small display is set to represent a huge pocket of space. I can't see the legend . . ."

"Down on the base, that second button," Lieutenant Nidishchii' said.

"Sir? Oh, OK," Ryck said, reaching down to push the button.

Immediately, a scale popped up along with the three axes, oriented on the *Bismarck*. It took Ryck a moment to orient the scale in his mind.

"OK, this is the flagship," he said, pointing to the largest blue icon. "This, is us," he added, pointing to another blue icon, this one slightly down and a good distance toward the bulk of the Marines in the lounge.

"Right now, we're about 6,200,000 klicks from the *Bismarck*. Up here," he continued, this time pointing to the red icons above the *Bismarck*, "are the calculated positions of the French ships. That's at about 10,000,000 klicks away from us. If we were in bubble space, that would be nothing, but we're combat deployed, in real space, so even at top speed, it would take us, I don't know, maybe an hour to close the gap? So, forget that we look close to them now on the holo. We're really a long ways apart.

"The second thing is that really, what you see is not what's really there. These are all calculations," he said, waving an arm at the red icons. "You have to remember that all the time, both fleets are cloaking and spoofing each other."

Several of the Marines had blank looks on their faces.

"OK, the difference is that cloaking means hiding where you are, like what we do with our comms, when we shield our transmission so the bad guys don't know we're there. Spoofing is telling the enemy that you are somewhere else, like when you activate the Fractured Array in a PICS. Given enough time, we can penetrate both of those, so all the time, they are changing frequencies and methods, bouncing back and forth and hoping we don't catch up to them. We do catch up to them, though, even if only for a split second, and that is enough to grab a data point. Given enough grabs, and our AI's can start predicting where the ship actually is."

He looked over at the lieutenant, who had a slightly pleased look on his face. Ryck figured he hadn't made a mistake yet.

"During all of this, ships try to disguise themselves, so when we get a data point, we still don't know exactly what we face."

"Then how do we know that's the *Jean d'Arc*?" one of the Marines from Weapons asked.

"Well, I'm not sure in this case. Maybe the Navy scout that spotted them got that before the fleets came together and managed to paint her specs. Or, maybe she just screwed up," Ryck answered.

"Screwing up" did not sound like something Admiral DeMornay would have allowed to happen, given her rep. It was more likely something in line with his first guess.

"So, we don't know their positions, but they know ours?" Corporal Johnson, from Sams' squad asked.

"What do you mean?" Ryck asked.

"There, all our ships are there, so the froggies know where each of our Navy ships are."

Most of the Marines groaned, and the Corporal sitting next to him reached up, grabbed the back of his head, and pushed Johnson down.

"We know where we are 'cause we don't spoof ourselves, you dumb negat," the Corporal told his buddy.

Johnson looked suitably sheepish when he was let back up.

Ryck tried to think of anything else. He wasn't an expert, but he hoped he'd explained things correctly. Then something else hit him, a pet peeve of his.

"One last thing. Forget about every war flick you've seen. When our ships actually start shooting, they are not going to be firing from a few kilometers away. They won't be able to see each other with the naked eye. They'll still be tens of thousands, probably hundreds of thousands of kilometers apart. When we boarded the *Marie's Best,* remember, the *Ark* was over 15,000 km away, and it was only that close so we wouldn't take forever getting there on rekis.

"Lieutenant, that's all I've got, I think. Is there anything else I should say?"

"No, good job, Sergeant. I think that was helpful," he replied.

As Ryck move back to his seat, he realized that the platoon commander hadn't only been looking for a field expedient class in naval warfare. He'd wanted to break the tension that had been building since the Marines had gathered around the slowly evolving display.

Sams had his hand in a fist, and was slowly rotating in back and forth around his nose as Ryck walked up.

"Fuck you, too, Sams. It ain't brown-nosing unless you volunteer. I was just following orders."

"If you say so," Sams said as he and Popo laughed.

Even Corporal Rey was smirking.

"I can't do anything about these negats," Ryck said, pointing at his two fellow sergeants, "but I've got power over you, Corporal of Marines. I've seen corporals stand fire watch, and who knows, that might be a good idea."

At that, more Marines broke out into laughter. If the lieutenant really had been trying to break the tension, then the trash talk and laughter showed he had succeeded.

It was a temporary respite, though. There was a battle building, and after a few more jabs back and forth, the Marines slowly settled down and focused their attention back on the display.

After about twenty minutes during which the blue and red icons inched together, a voice came over the feed.

"Sailors and Marines, this is Lieutenant Commander Huang, the task force PAO.[21] As we close in with the rebel fleet, Admiral Starling has given me permission to narrate what is happening, so even those on ships not actively engaged will be able to follow the battle to our inevitable victory."

That perked Ryck up. He was cynical enough to think that the "narration" was more aimed at furthering the admiral's ambitions after the battle, but that didn't mean he couldn't enjoy being more in the know.

The PAO started with more comments on history in the making without giving out very many details. Ryck started to tune the officer out, instead watching as the *Bismarck* and the two frigates *Monty* and *Decatur* adjusted their track to close in on the *Jean d'Arc*.

The *Bismarck* was one of the most capable ships in the Navy, but Ryck thought it slightly odd that it looked to be the admiral's tip of the spear. Both the *Ark Royal* and the *Chakri Naruebet* were, on paper, at least, more than a match for the *Jean d'Arc*, and the task force's three cruisers were at about par with the French flagship.

---

[21] PAO: Public Affairs Officer

Jonathan P. Brazee

Sending in two cruisers would put fewer men at risk while still projecting enough firepower for a victory. Sending in two cruisers and a couple of frigates or destroyers would be extra insurance in case Admiral DeMornay had a few tricks up her sleeve. It probably wouldn't make any difference, though, as the *Bismarck* could handle herself. The cynic in Ryck rose once again as he realized that a personal victory would stand the admiral in much better stead than if he'd just ordered other ships into the fray.

Technically, he wasn't the captain of the *Bismarck* and wouldn't actually be fighting her. The *Bismarck's* captain would be giving the tactical orders. Admiral Starling was the task force commander, in charge of the overall picture. But the public wouldn't make that distinction.

The PAO's voice rose in excitement, bringing Ryck back to the battle. First blood had been drawn, and not by the *Bismarck*. Two frigates, the *Madras* and the *Tehran*, had fixed a French corvette's position and fired their big plasma guns. The corvette's shields had collapsed within seconds, imploding the ship.

The Marines in the lounge cheered, drowning out the excited PAO. Ryck cheered, too. In the back of his mind, he knew over 200 men and women had just been wiped out, but on the holo display, they were just electrons.

One concern had been whether energy or kinetic weapons would be more effective. Ship defenses had improved dramatically since the War of the Far Reaches, and while tests and calculations had been continuously made, things could be different in real combat.

Kinetic weapons were harder to bring on target, being slower than energy weapons, smaller ships could carry only so many of them, and the rounds or missiles could be shot down or deflected. They packed a big punch, though, much bigger than an energy weapon. There were also a very wide array of kinetic weapons from which to choose, ranging from point defense auto-cannons to huge megaton warhead missiles.

Energy weapons acquired targets easier, and in the vacuum of space, had very long effective ranges. However, they were easier to shield against and usually took a while to break through defenses.

The speed at which the French corvette was destroyed, though, boded well for the use of Federation energy weapons, especially as the frigates used plasma guns. Several of the ships in the task force, to include each of the cruisers, had the more effective hadron cannons, and the *Bismarck* had the Navy's newest energy weapon, the terajoule P2-Meson Cannon.

All three energy weapons had about the same degree of effectiveness in knocking out a target once they hit it. The plasma, which fired in near-continuous pulses, was bulkier and more of an energy hog as it required an electromagnetic "jacket" to keep the plasma charge from dispersing as it traveled through space. Hadron cannons bypassed the inverse square law, so they didn't need a jacket. They focused an unbroken beam on the target. The cannon itself, which was actually a type of projector, was smaller and more efficient than a plasma gun, but it built up charges on the hull of the ship firing it, which interfered with cloaking and sensors. The new meson cannon, never before fired in actual combat, was the most efficient and could theoretically be fired without pause, as long as the ship's engines could supply the juice.

During their class on ship-borne weapons systems, Ryck thought it bass-'ackwards that the smaller ships had the larger, energy-hogging weapons while the huge capital ships tended to have the smaller, more efficient guns. He thought a small corvette, maybe only 50 meters long, armed with one meson cannon, would be one über-nasty weapon.

Within minutes, the *FS Pretoria*, one of the cruisers, launched two SCAT missiles. They passed through where the display indicated a large French ship of some kind was, but there were no detonations. The *Pretoria's* target acquisition AI had been spoofed.

Things in the battlespace were quiet for a few moments as the red and blue icons did a slow ballet in the display. Then the *Pretoria's* sister ship, the *Cairo*, launched another SCAT. The SCAT flew at over 20,000 km per second, so the Marines on the *Ark Royal* could actually see its icon move. Three, four, five seconds. Then the display flashed to represent an explosion. The Marines cheered again, but the SCAT had not detonated on a French ship. It had been destroyed by a French anti-missile battery.

The French ship had knocked out the SCAT, but by firing its weapons, the ship had given up its position. Within moments, three Navy ships concentrated their weapons, two firing plasma guns and one firing a hadron cannon, on where their AIs calculated the French ship to be. After ten seconds of intense fire, the French ship went up.

The PAO was going crazy, announcing the battle as if it was a football game.

"Did you see that? Did you see it? Oh my God, we're kicking ass!" he shouted, forgetting his officer-like decorum.

They all had seen it. Actually, they had seen a representation of it. Humans could not see energy weapon beams, could not watch a SCAT fly across space. The display AI created representations of the beams, missiles, and explosions so human viewers could make sense of what was happening.

The excitement level in the lounge was high, but then for almost 20 minutes, nothing much happened. The blue icons maneuvered smoothly in the display; the red icons jumped here and there as the AIs calculate new probable positions.

From a spot without a red icon, a beam of light flashed to envelop the *Madras,* one of the two frigates that had drawn first blood. Firing had given up data points to the French, and the cloaked ship had opened up on the Federation frigate from less than 50,000 kilometers away, almost spitting distance in space battles.

The AIs calculated with a 76% probability that the French ship was the *Giraud*, a cruiser. This ship was more than a match for the *Madras*, and as the fire locked on the frigate, Marines in the lounge stood up yelling for another ship to come help.

The *Madras* couldn't even escape to bubble space. The enveloping energy being thrown at it made generating the bubble space field impossible.

In the same way that the *Madras* had given away its positional data by firing, the *Giraud's* firing pinpointed its position as well. Beams of energy and at least two SCATs reached out to the French ship. It was a race to see whose shields would last the longest. The *Giraud* had the stronger shields, but it had at least four Federation ships focused on it. Just as the *Madras'* shields started to redline, the French ship imploded.

Another cheer rang out in the lounge. It had been a close thing, though. The *Madras'* icon shifted to a light blue. She was alive, but no longer effective.

Three French ships destroyed, one Federation ship out-of-action. Ryck wondered how many French ships were actually out there. The French Navy had 98 capital ships—only 95 now—and another 20 from their allies, bringing their total fleet to 115. The Federation had almost 600. TF-207 had 41 ships, and there were seven other task forces aggressively patrolling Federation space at the moment. How many of the French fleet were opposing the task force? The display showed nine ships left, but it had shown eleven prior to the first engagement. The *Giraud* had never registered on the display. What other ships were there lurking, unseen?

The Federation had the numbers, but when the French-allied forces made the strategic decision not to protect any French or allied planets, their Navy had the initiative. The Federation was forced to protect all Federation territory. The French could consolidate their forces and engage when and where at their choosing.

"Now they're gonna pay," Sams said as the *Bismarck* maneuvered closer to the *Jean d'Arc*, which looked to be swinging up to engage. The *Monty* and *Decatur* were pulling back, leaving the field of battle to the two flagships, which had closed to just under a million klicks.

This is medieval, Ryck thought. *Since when do flagships square off like jousting knights? It just isn't done this way.*

He was fascinated, though. It may not have been what was taught in any military tactics book, but two giants lumbering at each other was something of note.

Of course, "lumbering" was not an apt description. They were closing at extremely high rates of speed. Ryck kept watching for the *Monty* and *Decatur* to pounce, thinking that made the most sense. They kept station, though.

The PAO was excited, obviously thrilled to be part of an epic clash. He started speaking quicker, trying to describe what he was feeling. What he wasn't doing was offering any concrete info that the Marines couldn't already see from the display.

At 800,000 klicks, the *Bismarck* reached out with its meson cannon. It splashed the *Jean d'Arc*, which kept coming at the Federation battleship. The display didn't show the soft orange glow it gave to active enemy shields, but the French ship kept coming, so she was still in the fight.

Ryck would have thrown in a few missiles, maybe the huge HYNA-3's that battleships and dreadnaughts carried, but he thought the ship's commander might want to register the first-ever kill with a meson cannon. It might be a footnote in history, but Ryck was more in the better-safe-than-sorry camp.

"How come the froggie isn't firing back?" Corporal Mendoza asked.

Good question, Ryck thought.

The two ships kept closing, and the *Jean d'Arc* had yet to fire anything.

She couldn't have already been crippled, could she?

The seconds ticked away as the ships came closer together.

Was she going to try and ram the Bismarck? Ryck wondered.

That didn't make any sense. If she tried, the *Bismarck* had the kinetic weapons that would not only stop her, but also blow her apart into tiny little pieces.

And then it was over.

The energy signature of the French ship disappeared. She was dead.

It was easier for Ryck to think in terms of the entire ship. "She" was dead. Not that over 8,000 men and women were dead. They were the enemy, but the sheer numbers of casualties were staggering. That was the same as two full regiments of Marines, gone, just like that.

The lounge erupted into cheers as LCDR Huang shouted himself hoarse over the comms. It hadn't been the epic battle that it might have been, but from both a tactical and strategic standpoint, it had been a major victory.

Something caught his attention, and he listened into the PAO.

" . . . so, with that in mind, Admiral Starling has ordered the *Bismarck* to match trajectories with the rebel flagship. If in fact our sensors are correct and the ship was not totally destroyed, we will rescue any survivors and stabilize the wreck for salvage."

That was a new wrinkle. The "survivor" comment was a throwaway for public consumption. Unless someone was in a heavily shielded, self-contained capsule, they could not have survived the bombardment of the meson beam. However, energy weapons did not in and of themselves destroy ships. When a ship imploded or exploded, it was because of the rupture of its own fields, weapons, and energy supply. A ship could actually shut completely down to avoid that, but, of course, that would kill the crew and leave the crewless ship defenseless against a KE weapon. More than a few times, though, ships "killed" were left basically intact and could be salvaged. At least 14 Federation ships had once been acquired that way, either in the War of the Far Reaches or through anti-piracy actions.

"Shit, those 1/9 mothers are going to cash in!" Staff Sergeant Groton shouted out.

IF the *Jean d'Arc* was intact, or partially intact, and IF she was salvageable, not only would that be a huge propaganda victory, but each member of the *Ark Royal* crew would get a prize bonus, and that included the onboard Marines.

The Marines erupted into chatter, mostly expressing disgust at their lack of luck. Not only was 2/9 out of the action, the battalion's Marines would not share any prize money their 1/9 brethren would receive.

The battle was not over, but there was a subtle shift in the disposition of the icons in the display as the remaining red icons began to leave the battlespace. The *Chakri Naruebet* moved to intercept one French ship, opening fire as the *Bismarck* was still matching trajectory with the carcass of the *Jean d'Arc*. Even 3/9 was getting in on the action, despite the fact that the AIs could not confirm the kill to give the Federation cruiser.

On the *Bismarck*, 1/9 would be getting ready for an EVA. Additional readings had indicated that the *Jean d'Arc* was probably in small pieces. There just wasn't enough there to indicate an intact ship. But it had not exploded, so there could still be good intel to be gathered. The Marines and a Navy boarding team were still on. Dreams of huge prize money were shattered, but there was still the potential for a nice bonus.

The "battle" such as it was, was on the far side of the battlespace from the Ark Royal. After an hour, the ship downgraded to Battle Stations Charlie. A few of the Marines trickled out to get some chow, but most stayed, watching the display.

The *Bismarck* positioned itself 40,000 km off the *Jean d'Arc*. The two ships were motionless in relative terms, but like the entire task force, were hurtling through space at tremendous speeds. LCDR Huang signed off, giving way to a JG, as the 1/9 Marines loaded their rekis, and with a Gryphon monitor and several Experion fighters in support, started the long journey to the French ship. Forty-thousand klicks were nothing to a warship, but to a reki, that was an hour-long journey. Forty-thousand klicks was also the by-the-manual minimum safe distance for a warship to maintain when approaching another. The *Ark Royal* had gotten closer to the *Marie's Best*, but that had been a civilian ship. The *Jean d'Arc* was a warship, and if she somehow blew, either by design or by accident, the stand-off safe distance was greater.

The *Jean d'Arc* didn't blow. What it actually did, though, was confusing. Just as the Marines started their journey, there was a flicker on the display as sensors detected some sort of energy emissions.

A warning icon flashed, and the JG stopped mid-sentence. Ryck knew the meson cannon, as well as other weapons, would be trained on the *Jean d'Arc*, but he knew the meson cannon would need approximately five seconds to activate the electron and positron collisions that resulted in the mesons. More importantly to him, the Marines were outside the ship, now almost 500 km away, between the *Bismarck* with its meson cannon and the French ship.

Time seemed to slow down, but it was actually fewer than the five seconds needed to fire the meson cannon when a number of yellow streaks took off from the *Jean d'Arc*.

Immediately after that, the *Bismarck* opened up.

Ryck jumped up, his heart in his throat as the small blue icons for the rekis immediately faded to grey. The embarked Marines had no chance. The meson beam had swept through them. A battalion of his fellow Marines had just been killed, something that seemed unimaginable.

Ryck was numb as he watched the yellow icons rushing to the *Bismarck* at a blazing speed, undeterred by the meson cannon. The icons switched from the yellow of an unknown object to the orange of a KE weapon of some sort a second after the *Bismarck* fired, but the meson beam had no effect on them. Another two seconds, and the battleship's point-defense auto-cannons opened up, their stream of rail-gun projected depleted uranium rounds making a ribbon on the display as the rounds rushed out to meet the incoming weapons. The orange icons split up into nine separate— rounds? Missiles?—as the AIs analyzed the readings. Six of the French weapons were knocked off their course by the intense fire, but three made it through the *Bismarck's* defenses and pierced the shields, slamming into the battleship.

The anonymous JG's voice was cut off, then and the display went out.

Each Marine was on his feet, staring at the dead display in shock.

What the fuck had happened?

The display flickered, then came back on as the *Ark Royal's* AIs took over from the *Bismarck's* feed. The *Bismarck* was still there, but the icon was light blue. Then a new red icon appeared about 500,000 km to the *Bismarck's* upper right, an icon with full identification.

The *Jean d'Arc*.

It fired its own weapons at the *Bismarck*, more kinetic rounds. Almost immediately, the *Decatur* opened up on her, followed by the *Monty*. Neither ship alone was the match for the

Jean d'Arc, but that didn't stop either one. They started rushing to attack, to protect what was left of the *Bismarck*.

Battle Stations Alpha sounded on the *Ark Royal*.

"To your stations, now!" Lieutenant Nidishchii' shouted, the first Marine to utter a word since everything unfolded only 15 seconds ago.

As Ryck rushed to leave the lounge, he glanced back to see the *Chakri Naruebet* and several other ships converge on the French flagship when the icon for the *Jean d'Arc* disappeared from the display.

Chapter 13

Twenty-two hours after the battle, Ryck was with the rest of the battalion NCOs and Marines in Hangar B while the senior chief briefed them. All over the ship, all hands were getting their first explanation on what had happened.

The Navy was a political animal, the forward projection of the government's power. But it was still a professional fighting force that believed in transparency in after-action reports and keeping all hands informed.

The ship had stayed at Battle Stations Alpha for almost twelve hours before standing down. As soon as the *Bismarck* was hit, Commodore Weinstein, the assistant task force commander, took full command from the new flagship, the *Chakri Naruebet*. He initiated rescue operations, started analyzing what happened, and sent ships, including the *Ark Royal*, after the fleeing French fleet. Other than a few data hits, though, the French slipped away, and the commodore recalled his ships, not willing to disperse his forces.

Marines and sailors were fed and put to the rack, but not many really got much sleep. Hours later, exhausted and still in emotional shock, they gathered to hear the brief.

". . . and remember, these are only initial findings, but we have put engineers on what we thought was the *Jean d'Arc.* As I said, it wasn't even a ship. It was a construct of tubing, propulsion, and launch rails that gave off the same signature as the real ship. We were spoofed into thinking this was the French flagship. I don't need to tell you that this is some pretty sophisticated cyberwarfare, something beyond our present capabilities given the nature of existing sensors.

"The best that we can determine is that the decoy ship was turned off prior to the *Bismarck* opening fire. Only very heavily shielded switches remained, and in the quiet mode. When the meson beams struck the ship, they flowed around the framework, causing no damage as there really wasn't anything to react with.

"When the meson cannon was turned off, the switches remained intact, ready for activation. The *Jean d'Arc*, cloaked but nearby, or possibly another platform, reactivated the switches and powered up their rail guns, which were actually part of the structure of the ship. They waited until the Marines launched, knowing that the AIs would need an override to fire with the Marines between the ship and the target."

There was a rush of murmurs as the Marines took this in.

"At ease, at ease," Gunny Greuber said, holding up his hand. "Let's listen to the senior chief."

"As I was saying they wanted that split-second advantage as they needed the rail guns to power up. Nine inert, non-conductive missiles were launched. We have recovered particles of one from the *Bismarck* and are analyzing it, but it looks to be a dense synthetic. Each one was approximately 40 meters long and massed 350,000 kg. Being non-conductive, the meson beam had no effect on them. They were essentially big rocks being thrown at the ship.

"Travelling at 10,000 kilometers per second, it took five seconds to reach the *Bismarck*. Point defense deflected six off course, but three hit the flagship. Serious damage was done to these three sections," he said as a holo appeared over his head.

Ryck sucked in his breath. This was the first image of the *Bismarck* after the battle that he'd seen, and huge chunks of the ship were simply gone.

"Immediately after impact, the *Jean d'Arc* deliberately uncloaked and fired two BC-8 anti-ship missiles at the *Bismarck*. With her defenses compromised, both missiles struck the ship here," he said as the holo rotated, showing two more chunks taken out of the ship.

Inside the *Bismarck,* all compartments were sealed and fire-fighting measures taken. Within five minutes, the ship was secure, but non-effective. Overall, we lost 9,787 men in the attack. We believe that 6,000 were lost in the initial strike, another 3,000 in the missile attack, and the rest due to exposure to vacuum within moments after the strikes. We should note that most of the remainder could have survived had they been in the correct gear.

"As to the casualties, almost all of the command was taken out in the missile strike, to include Mr. Starling."

"Mr." Starling was telling. The Navy was a fighting force, but it was political, and blame had been laid. "Admiral" had been stripped from him even in death. It was just as well that he had died, though. He would have faced execution had he managed to survive the battle.

"As to Marines," the senior chief continued, and here he stopped to look up and the men facing him. "I, uh, I regret to inform you that only three embarked Marines survived: Sergeant Mark Tillhouse, Lance Corporal Sig Poulson, and Private Spencer Hamilton. These three were bedridden in sickbay on the other side of the ship. Most of the Marines were killed when the *Bismarck* fired on the launch platform. Your Marine command was located with the Navy command when they were hit, and the rest were at the launch hangar when the first strike hit them. I'm sorry to pass that to you."

Some Marines sat in stunned silence, others broke out into exclamations.

Only three survived? Ryck asked himself.

Ryck knew the toll was going to be high. He'd seen the lights turn when the rekis were in the way of the meson cannon. But more than that had to have survived. He knew Mark Tillhouse. They had attended the NCO course together. And he was grateful that he had survived. But that was all? Only three Marines?

They had all been so jealous when they heard 1/9 was going to help salvage a warship. But that mission had been their death sentence.

Ryck was barely aware that the senior chief was continuing, and he had to focus to catch what he was saying.

". . . a lack of leadership, a failure to follow established operational procedures, and most of all, a sense of individual ambition that overcame Navy policy and put his command at risk. Any one of a number of steps would have kept this from happening. The decoy ship was unable to maneuver once it had been set on its final course, so a simple course change would have revealed the plan. One kinetic missile could have destroyed all the launch rails.

Even after the decoy seemed destroyed, sensor readings were off, and a simple recon could have discovered that this was, in fact, a decoy, but arrogant pride wanted there to be a prize to capture, and by wanting it, the command ignored normal warnings.

"This is not the Navy way, and such actions will not be tolerated. Rest assured that procedures will be implemented to ensure this will not be repeated.

"That is all I have for now. I will not be able to take any questions at the moment, but we will issue a more detailed report available for download onto your PAs. The commodore wanted all of you to get an update, though, before we issue our complete findings."

The senior chief and the sergeant major stepped off the platform and walked through the seated Marines. Not taking questions was probably a smart move. He would have been there forever.

Ryck was impressed with the senior chief's candor. There was no question that the blame was on the admiral, but to tell the enlisted so with such candor was rare. Ryck wondered if the officers had gotten the same brief, or if theirs been even more candid.

He stood up, mentally and physically exhausted. Sams was still sitting on the hangar deck, head down. Ryck grabbed him under the armpit and hauled him up.

"Head up, Sams. We've got to get our heads on straight. We're going to get a chance for revenge, mark my words, and we've got to be ready for it when it comes."

FS Intrepid

Chapter 14

Ryck looked across the hold to where Staff Sergeant Hecs was waiting. Their visors were clear, so Ryck could see that the platoon sergeant was in dreamland. Ryck could almost hear the snoring. He nudged Corporal Winsted, more of a bump, given that they were mounted in their PICS, and pointed at their fearless leader.

"How the hell can he do that?" the Third Fire Team leader asked on the P2P.

"Beats the hell out of me," Ryck admitted.

In the midst of a naval battle, where they could be reduced to their component atoms in a second, not many Marines could drift off to sleep. It was an admirable skill, but not one Ryck possessed.

Many things had changed since their last disastrous fight. The battle was broadcast to the populace as a victory, and with three French ships destroyed to one Federation ship, that claim could be made. However, no one in the military thought it was anything other than an ass-whipping. Outnumbered and out-gunned, Admiral DeMornay had managed to take out a Federation battleship. More lives were lost on that one ship than in all three French ships combined. Complacency may have been the order of the day before, but the foe was taken much more seriously now.

Now, the forces were ordered to follow naval doctrine more closely. Of course, the French fleet knew Federation doctrine, but with the Federation's much stronger fleet, there wasn't much the French could do with the knowledge. Only a week prior in the First Quadrant, TF-202 had met and destroyed five French ships without a loss of its own.

One of the changes was that the Marines had been cross-decked to smaller platforms. The loss of an entire battalion, although only a percentage of the total loss of life on the *Bismarck*, had hit the community hard. There were to be no more units that large together on any one ship. Golf Company, along with two Storks, had been embarked aboard the *Intrepid*, an old destroyer.

Another change was that during any action, or possibility of action, all hands were to be in EVA suits, or in the case of Golf Company, two platoons were in PICS. Over two hours ago, the call for Battle Stations Alpha had gone out, and Third Platoon had donned their PICS and entered one of the ship's shuttles. First Platoon was in their PICS hooked up to the two Storks, ready to go if the need arose. Most of Second Platoon were in EVAs, sitting in two 14-man rekis.

In the hangars, the Marines had no idea what was going on. If Ryck stood perfectly still, though, he could feel the subtle "pull" along his body that signified the ship was doing some serious maneuvers. The compensators, arrayed around the ship, kept the men inside the ships alive through the huge G-forces that would crush an unprotected crew. However, G-forces worked along one axis. The compensators reacted in concert, "pulling" to counteract the effect of the G-forces. At any given time, several of them would be working on the body, and that counteraction varied with the distance to the various repeaters. So, the counter-force would be slightly different on one side of the body as the other. Most people said they couldn't feel anything, but Ryck was positive he could. To him, it felt like skin drying with an almost-itch.

About ten minutes earlier, he had noticed a very slight dimming of the ship's lights, something that repeated two more times. Ryck was pretty sure that meant they had fired their plasma guns.

The first time they had gone to Battle Stations Alpha, the Marines had stood in the shuttle for almost seven hours before the all-clear was sounded. It had been a false alarm. Ryck was almost positive that this time, they were all in the middle of another battle.

As if reading his mind, Corporal Winsted said on the P2P, "I think the ship fired her guns a while back. Did you notice it?"

Corporal Winsted was John Beady's replacement, joining the squad when they were cross-decked. He had never seen combat before.

"Yep, sure did. But not everyone noticed it, I'm sure, and as there's nothing we can do about it one way or the other, then no use bringing it up, right? No use getting your team stressed."

"Oh, yeah, right, of course. I didn't mean that. It's just, you know, kinda hard to sit here not knowing what's going on," the Corporal said.

Ryck closed his eyes and said, "Well, I'm going to follow in our leader's footsteps and catch some z's."

There was no way Ryck was going to sleep, but he had to exude a sense of calm. What he had said to Winsted was right, there was no use in stressing out his Marines, and if they knew he was stressed, then they would stress.

Ryck was amazed when, sometime later, he was jolted awake by the skipper's voice. He had no idea how long he'd been out.

"We've got a potential mission. While we've been waiting, there has been an engagement," Captain Davis passed. "A French gunship has been damaged and is trying to escape. The AIs put its probable destination as the planet Weyerhaeuser 23, an uninhabited corporate holding. The *Intrepid* has been ordered to give chase and destroy the ship if possible. If it turns out she is heading to the planet, it will be to offload the crew as the ship itself is too damaged to attempt an atmospheric re-entry. Or entry, I guess, would be more correct. If that happens, First and Third will land and attempt to force a surrender, eliminate them if they don't accept. I will be the operation commander. The XO will be the contingency commander and will be ready with Second Platoon for any possible ship-to-ship boarding. Commander Sukishi has given us a possible launch time of 50 minutes. I know there is not much we can do while we wait, but squad leaders, I want one more check of your Marines' readouts. Gunny Greuber will be downloading the planet specifics, and I want everyone to make themselves familiar with them. Platoon commanders and sergeants and company headquarters, over to the command circuit for your orders. This is Captain Davis, out."

Even with the Marines in their PICS, there was a palpable sense of alertness, if not excitement. Within an hour and a half, maybe two, they could be in action, where they could influence what they did, not just sitting like cargo, wondering if any moment could be their last. Anything was better than not having any control over their destinies. Ryck knew that most of the Marines would be remembering 1/9 and wanting to exact some revenge.

Ryck did a quick check of the squad's readouts. Other than a bump in heart rate and breathing, nothing had changed. They were ready.

The planetary specs came over the link, and Ryck toggled them up. Weyerhaeuser 23 was another corporate holding, this one uninhabited. The huge galaxy-wide conglomerate had seeded vast tracts of the planet with various genmodded tree species some 30 years ago, then left. It wasn't scheduled for a first harvest for another 10 years. Atmosphere was 18% O2, 81% N2, and the remainder trace gasses, and pressure was 95% ES, or "Earth-standard." Gravity was .96 ES. Planetary rotation was 22.4 hours. Temperature ranged from -10 degrees at the poles to 40 at the equator.

These were all very close to ES, and Ryck wondered why the planet was not open to human colonization. He knew that Weyerhaeuser was not in the people business, but comparing this planet to Prophesy, where his family had struggled to scrape crops out of the parched soil, this looked like paradise. It hadn't even needed any terraforming. From what he read, the trees had minor genmods to be able to out-compete the native flora (which had been infected by the company biologists to clear them to help make room for the earth species), the symbiotic-type insect life was released, and that was about it. Seed, then leave until the trees grew into a commercially valuable crop.

There was more to the report, but Ryck had the gist of it. The atmosphere was not going to kill them, they would not burn up nor freeze, and they could move around without issue, even outside of their PICS.

"Everyone ready?" he sent to the squad circuit. "Looks like a nice vacation spot, right?"

"Sure, Sergeant L, I'm ready for some libo[22]," Lips responded.

It really wasn't that funny, Ryck knew, but most of the squad laughed, if somewhat nervously.

Ryck knew the company staff was furiously hammering out a basic plan, adjusting from hip-pocket ops orders that had been developed long before. But for the Marines in the squad, it was sit and wait until the word came down. And that wasn't good. Just being inside their PICS tended to psychologically isolate the men, making them feel alone. Simple chatter helped combat that feeling.

"Uh, Lips, I don't think libo is your strong suit. Why don't you tell the rest of the squad about the Monster Hut?" Ryck told the lance corporal.

There were hoots from some of the other Marines, those who had been in the squad for a while. Lips had been busted for a drunken liberty incident at the bar. Already selected for sergeant, the then-Corporal Holleran was demoted to lance corporal. He was salty enough to understand Ryck's intentions, though, so he launched into a rather exaggerated tale of his demise, bringing in the bar owner, her husband, and two FCDC officers. Even Ryck was laughing, despite knowing that only 20% of the story at best was true.

It was almost disconcerting to be pulled back into reality when the lieutenant came back from the command net to give them their orders, but the tactic had been effective. Almost 20 minutes had passed, 20 minutes when the men were not standing there like statues with only their own thoughts for company.

Their orders were pretty basic, about what Ryck had expected. Until the situation on the ground became clear, it was hard to plan anything concrete or too elaborate. If they launched for the planet, the two Storks with First Platoon would lead the way with Third in the *Intrepid's* shuttle coming in behind. The Storks were transports, but they were armed, and without dedicated Navy air support, they would take the air cover mission. Depending on where anyone might land, the skipper would decide on whether to

[22] Libo: short for liberty, when military personnel are off-duty and off base enjoying free time.

split up or to remain one unit. The opposing forces would be given the opportunity to surrender. If they refused, they would be attacked.

This wasn't really an ops order, Ryck realized as he listened to the lieutenant. At best, it was a vague concept of operations with a list of coordinating measures. But until they knew more, any detailed plan was probably a waste of time.

A few minutes after the lieutenant was done, the skipper came back up on the company circuit.

"All hands, I have an update. We were not able to close with the enemy gunboat in time, and they have reached Weyerhaeuser 23. Two shuttles have been launched and are descending to the planet. Given the class of the gunboat and the listed crew, either each shuttle is only half full or, there was a Legion platoon on board. We are now operating under the assumption that we will be facing the legionnaires. The *Intrepid* could knock the enemy shuttles out of the sky, but we have been ordered to attempt to garner a surrender first, so we will be launching as soon as we get into range, in about six minutes. Second Platoon, you will launch immediately after us and board the gunboat as it orbits. The XO will issue your specific orders in a few moments.

"I charge all of you to be ready, remain flexible, and do your duty. If in fact there are legionnaires among the enemy, they represent a real threat, so it is imperative that we work as a team. We still outnumber them, and we have the *Intrepid* at our backs."

Ryck perked up when Captain Davis mentioned legionnaires. If the legionnaires chose, they could put up a fight. Still, the Marines outnumbered them, and the *Intrepid* was a pretty big stick to wield.

"Platoon commanders, make ready. Let's kick some ass," the skipper said.

Six minutes was a short time in the grand scheme of things, but it stretched out while the Marines waited. Ryck wondered if the French shuttles had landed, and if so, were they preparing to surrender or fight. They would know the *Intrepid* was on their tail, and sitting out the rest of the war sure beat being blasted by a plasma gun. The Legion R-3s might be a great combat suit, but they couldn't stand up to a Federation destroyer.

A Navy sailor in a bright yellow EVA ran up the back hatch of the shuttle, took a reading at a gauge, then scrambled back out as the hatch closed.

"What was that about?" Corporal Winsted asked.

"Just routine. You know the Navy," Ryck responded, even though he was wondering the same thing.

The *Intrepid's* main hangar was a far cry from that of the *Ark Royal's* five hangars. The *Intrepid* was designed to fight, not carry Marines. It barely fit the two Storks along with its two shuttles. In the ancillary hangar, where Second Platoon was loaded on their rekis, the ship's skiff had been pushed to the side just to prep the rekis to launch. With a limited launch crew on the *Intrepid*, launching shuttles, Storks, or rekis wasn't the synchronized ballet that characterized the bigger ship's launch ops.

The Marines were blind in the shuttle's cargo compartment, but a vibration was their hint that they were ready to go. When the artificial gravity disappeared, they knew they were out of the ship and on their way.

After traveling so far in such a short amount of time, it was frustrating for the Marines to know they were so close to the ground, yet they had to wait another 40 minutes until they landed. The physics of atmospheric entry could not be denied. At least the French would face the same timeline.

After ten minutes of uneventful flight, updates began to flash on Ryck's face shield. Both French shuttles had landed close to each other, about 30 km apart. One looked to be in bad shape, making it a miracle that it had even remained in one piece upon landing. The other looked fine. If the French did surrender, only the second shuttle could be used to bring them up to the *Intrepid*. The ship's own two shuttles would be necessary as well.

The glare of atmospheric entry illuminated the hold, coming in from the pilot's station. It was not a steady light, and it made shifting shadows from the Marines across from Ryck. If they were coming through the atmosphere, then they should be landing in less than five minutes.

Their landing points were selected and relayed to each Marine's display. The Storks would land approximately 15 km from the intact shuttle. The *Intrepid's* shuttle would drop Third platoon another 12 kms on the other side of the intact French shuttle.

A message flashed across their displays. The French commander had been contacted by the crew of the *Intrepid*, and the offer for them to surrender had been made. None of the details of the comms was passed, only that the French needed time to consider it. The Marines were ordered to land, but not advance until given the word to do so.

"Looks like there might not be any action," Ryck passed to his three team leaders. "Keep alert, though. Talks could break down."

Despite what he told his team leaders, Ryck throttled back his intensity a bit. It was just as well, really, better, in fact, if the French surrendered. There was no use wasting lives if it wasn't needed—not just French lives, but his Marines' as well. Even a platoon of legionnaires could prove a formidable foe, and if it came to that, not every Marine would be likely to make it home.

They were skimming over the planet still some 200 km from their target. The long route in was actually much quicker and took far less energy than descending straight down from the perpendicular as soldiers and shuttles always did in the flicks.

Ryck pulled up an overlay and placed it over the tactical map. They were coming in over the largest plantation on the planet. If they were going to land, Ryck wouldn't have minded seeing the native plants, but it looked like it was going to be genmodded walnut and teak, two high-value wood species.

The shuttle broke away from the two Storks and started sweeping around to land behind their target shuttle. The back hatch started lowering, flooding the cargo hold with light. Outside, Ryck could see a bright green landscape, undisturbed by any sign of humanity.

"Here we go," Ryck passed to his squad. "We've got the 12 to 4, so move it out and stop. Form on me as to how far to go. Then we just sit and wait while the commands negotiate with each other."

The shuttle was slowing, less than a km out when all hell broke loose on Ryck's face shield display. Four tracks appeared from some three km from the French shuttle, reaching out for the two Storks.

The Stork was a big transport, not a fighting craft. It was armed, and it had defenses, but it was not a fighter. In the second or two it took the hyper-velocity missiles to reach the two aircraft, the lead Stork juked to its right and ejected flares. It wasn't enough. While one missile missed, the other three hit. The lead Stork took one, the trail two. Both icons went immediately grey.

"Get us down!" Lieutenant Nidishchii' screamed over the circuit to the shuttle pilots.

Ryck's adrenaline level surged as he realized what was happening. First Platoon had been knocked from the sky, along with Captain Davis and Gunny Greuber. That would sink in later, if there was a later. Now he had to take care of his men.

"Move to the ramp," he shouted into his mic.

They were about 30 meters above the ground, coming into the LZ. This was probably too high to fall without injury, but it would be better to try that than be inside the shuttle if it got hit. And to protect that shuttle, the Marines had to get out of it immediately.

Ryck saw the plasma signature on his display. The *Intrepid* was answering back.

"All Marines, I want you out in ten seconds so I can fight," the pilot passed on the open circuit. Evidently, he didn't want the weight of a platoon of PICS Marines while he took action. If the Stork was not a fighter, the shuttle was even less of one, but the pilot was going to try.

Ryck led the way, feet at the edge of the ramp, holding on to the hydraulic ramp lift to keep from being pushed out. Someone was on his ass, pushing against him.

The LZ was below them, maybe 15 meters away, when the explosion rocked the shuttle, lifting up her nose, dropping the ass end another five meters. Ryck slid out, falling to the ground with a thud. The shock of the ground was followed by Marines in PICS landing on top of him. There were three or four shocks before Ryck was able to look up. They shuttle was settling, Marines still falling from the ramp. As the shuttle fell, it kept moving forward, so the Marines were not all on top of each other. The bottom of the ramp hit the ground, Marines still jumping out, while the bow was levered into the ground with a vicious slam. The shuttle didn't explode, but the force of the impact collapsed it upon itself.

Ryck tore his gaze away to check his display. An entire platoon was gone. Some of his platoon's icons were light blue, a couple already grey. They were on a planet with an enemy force of an unknown size and strength.

They were in the shit!

Weyerhaeuser 23

Chapter 15

"That's it, then," Lieutenant Nidishchii' said on the command circuit. "The *Intrepid's* down to 70% effective, but it is in pursuit of the French destroyer. We're on our own for now."

"What the fuck?" Sams said. "They're just going to leave us here?"

"They've got over 100 of their own dead, too. The ambush took them by surprise while they were taking out the two shuttles and the first missile launcher. Despite their damage, they've been ordered by the commodore to pursue and finish off the enemy ship. Evidently, it's more damaged than the *Intrepid* and is trying to flee."

"What about Second Platoon?" Ryck asked. "They can't survive for long in EVAs."

"There's been no contact with them for over an hour. Our command is assuming they are lost, too."

"'Assuming? Without proof? Sorry, sir, but that is fucking bullshit," Sams said, his anger evident.

"Yes, it's fucking bullshit, sergeant. So, what do we do about it? Sit here and cry, or get on with our mission? Get a fucking grip on yourself," the platoon commander shouted back.

Ryck had never heard the platoon commander raise his voice, much less use profanity. It took him by surprise.

"Now, I want a complete inventory of what we've got, and I want it in five minutes, no longer. They know where we are, and I don't know what else they've got up their sleeves, but we're getting out of here."

"What about the WIAs, sir?" Doc Grbil asked.

"What's their status?" the platoon commander asked him.

"Roskins, Singh, and Patani are hurt but ambulatory. I've bandaged them up, but they can get back in their PICS and function. Smythe, Tally, Portono, and Justice are pretty bad. Justice isn't going anywhere with that leg, and I've got the other three in ziplocks. Oh yeah, there's the crew chief. He's probably got a concussion, but he's cognizant."

The lieutenant didn't have to ask about the KIAs. Both pilots and five Marines, including Sergeant Paul Pope, Popo, had been killed. Ryck wasn't letting himself think of his friend for now. He would grieve later.

"Staff Sergeant, any way we can get that sailor inside a PICS?" the lieutenant asked.

"We can get him inside one," Staff Sergeant Hecs began.

Each one knew that "one" meant one of the dead Marine's PICS.

". . . but can he operate it? Why don't we leave him here with the KIA and ziplocked WIA? We can move them over there under the trees in case someone lobs something at the shuttle hulk, but I don't think anyone is going to attack one sailor and the wounded. Leave him and Lance Corporal Justice to watch over them."

"OK, do it. You two," he pointed at the two surviving squad leaders, "go get me that report."

As Ryck hurried off, Staff Sergeant Hecs grabbed him and said on the P2P, "Make sure you take the cold packs from the dead."

Ryck momentarily recoiled, but then common sense kicked in. They had no idea on how long they were going to be stuck on the planet. Each Marine had the coldpack in his PICS, then one spare. A coldpack was good for a little more than a day, maybe up to 30 hours. After that, even if the PICS was otherwise battle-worthy, it could not be used. Within 20 or 25 minutes at the most, the Marine inside would go into heat exhaustion. In another five minutes, he would be dead.

"Roger that," he said, calling Rey forward.

He told Rey to collect the packs, both the ones in the PICS and any spares. He then took Third Team and went back into the shuttle to see what could be salvaged.

The door gun on the shuttle was a 300-round-per-minute 25mm KE gun. Without the shuttle's targeting system, it would not be accurate, so Ryck wasn't sure how they could use it, but he told Lance Corporal Martin to take it out of the pintle. It was bulky, and the ammo box added more weight, but it was nothing a PICS could not handle.

Ryck was much happier to see the crate for the M229. This was a small, but compact artillery piece. It could be horsed around by a single Marine, so it was even easier for a Marine in a combat suit. There were only ten rounds for it: five anti-personnel and five anti-armor. Ryck was expecting more rounds, but he couldn't find any.

He was also hoping to find one of the pulse cannons. He knew the company had one, but not where it had been loaded for the operation. The pulse cannon was their only crew-served energy weapon, and if they were going to face legionnaires, and those legionnaires were in R-3s, then they really needed that weapon. He had to get back to the lieutenant, so he gave up the search and moved back out of the wreck.

With comms, a command meeting did not have to take place with each person in a circle facing each other. In fact, that was not tactically sound. Yet that is what usually happened. Ryck, Staff Sergeant Hecs, Sams, and the lieutenant came together and met where they could clear their visors and see each other's faces while they talked.

Staff Sergeant Hecs started it off. "Without counting the four WIA and the Navy crew chief, we've got 26 Marines, 25 from the platoon and Corporal Evans from EOD, and Doc Grbil. All PICS are functioning, but ten are at less than 90%. Lance Corporal Khouri's right arm is inoperable, and his HGL broke right off when he fell out of the shuttle. However, the rest of his PICS functions. Power levels on all suits are still above 95%. All told, I'm amazed the damage to the suits was as light as it turned out to be. We are still combat effective as a platoon."

Sams told the lieutenant that Corporal Evans had only a partial EOD kit, and Ryck reported the status of the M229, which

Jonathan P. Brazee

caught their attention. None of the Marines in the platoon were artillery, but the gun was pretty easy to fire.

"Well, it is what it is," the platoon commander said when Ryck finished. "This is what we have to play with. I want to move over to here," he said, as a spot appeared on their display maps. "I want a good defense put in, then we're going to try and recon what we're facing. After that, we're going to pay them a little social call. We owe them that."

Chapter 16

Ryck lay flat on the ground, his face shield in the dirt. Ahead of him, over a small rise and about 500 meters away, was where they had determined the French were.

PICS were not made for lying down. Once on their bellies, they were not made to rotate the helmet and neck to the right or left. So once down, the Marines inside the PICS were essentially blind.

Ryck would rather have been on his back. At least that way, he could see something. But if they had to move quickly, with their attitude systems turned off, it was quicker and easier to stand up while face down than while face up.

"OK, Ryck, launch it," the lieutenant said beside him.

Ryck, the platoon commander, Corporal Evans, and Corporal Rey's team had left the rest of the platoon some three hours earlier, carefully advancing forward. Judging from where the French shuttles had landed, a few data captures by their sensors, and pure gut instinct, they figured the French had to be close to the position they had identified.

In order to plan an assault, the Marines had to know what they faced—hence, the recon. The lieutenant's AI gave it a 82% probability that there was a Legion platoon there, in combat suits. Staff Sergeant Hec's AI came up with a 77% probability of the same thing.

The other group of French, another 15 kms away, were almost assuredly the Navy crew of the gunship. The Marines were able to capture many more data points, and all pointed to that fact. Of course, Admiral DeMornay had spoofed an entire Federation task force, so spoofing a single Marine platoon was not something too difficult to imagine.

Ryck toggled the dragonfly loose. It rose in the air and then started making its way through the trees. The forest was thick, but somehow sterile. Normal forests had a variety of species, but this one had three plant species: the walnut and teak Ryck had read about online and a hanging moss covered vine that helped regulate water flow to maximize tree growth. The vine-regulated water system must have worked, because the trees were pretty huge for only being 30 years old.

The dragonfly was programmed to flit around like its namesake, but that would only fool a casual observer. It was shielded, so it should escape sensor detection, but anyone seeing it would understand what it was.

The dragonfly could have covered the 500 meters in less than 20 seconds, but that speed would probably give it away to any observers, so it slowly made its way through the forest. It wasn't until it was 30 meters away that it detected movement. Ryck slowed it down and gave it the command to latch itself to one of the trees.

What it captured wasn't good. There was about a platoon of legionnaires there, all in R-3s. They were getting ready for something. That something was most likely an attack on the Marines. The Marines had been using their best shielding technology, but if they picked up slight data points on the Legion, it was likely that the Legion had picked up the same points, if not more, on the Marines.

A platoon of R-3 legionnaires was a very formidable opponent for a platoon of PICS Marines. This was not just in theory. In war games, back when relations were better, the computer referees almost always gave the Legion victories over the Marines when numbers were equal and it was PICS Marines versus R-3 legionnaires. The current PICS was slightly better than those used during the war games, but the R-3s were probably better now as well.

Ryck wanted to be able to assess the full strength of the legionnaires. He counted 12 within view, but he knew there were probably more. He never had the chance for a full count, though, as all the legionnaires in view of the dragonfly suddenly turned to look up at it. One legionnaire pointed up, his arm gunport cover retreating to reveal a snub barrel projector. Then the dragonfly went dead.

"Let's get out of here," the lieutenant said.

All five Marines got up, turned their attitude stabilizers back on, and started to move. They weren't heading directly back to the rest of the Marines, but off at a tangent. Above them, rounds exploded in the canopy. At the second set of explosions, something pinged of Ryck's PICS, but whether that was shrapnel or a piece of shattered wood, Ryck didn't know.

Looking at his display, he could see ghosts appearing behind him. The R-3s were very good and were shielded quite well, but when they were moving, the shielding was less effective. This was opposite from the Marines fractured arrays. They were not as effective when still, but worked better when moving. With the legionnaires in hot pursuit, the Marine AIs could pick up more data points, but as they were still approximations, the icons were not the bright colors of identified objects or people, but wavering off-white circles. Ghosts.

The rounds exploding in the canopy stopped, either because the legionnaires firing them were out of mortar rounds, or they just realized that the rounds were not very effective. A few moments later, though, there was a huge blast behind the Marines, and suddenly, a light red icon appeared on Ryck's display.

A legionnaire was down, his suit's shielding compromised.

"Holy shit, Evans, it worked!" Ryck exclaimed.

They had brought along the EDO Marine because Evans had been sure he could booby-trap their route back for just this situation. Evans had placed five mines, all with passive firing mechanisms. When the Marines ran through the minefield, the mechanisms were bypassed. If anything else lumbered by, the vibrations of the footsteps set off the explosion. The theory was sound, but Ryck had figured that the legionnaires' suits would be able to sense the explosives, if not the mechanism. He was wrong.

"Oohrah!" Evans exclaimed.

The ghosts stopped advancing. The legionnaires had been caught up in the chase, and it had cost them. First blood had gone to the Legion when they shot down the Storks and the shuttle. Second blood went to the Marines, and even if the two were in no way equal, it was a good morale boost for the Marines to strike back at all.

Chapter 17

"OK, Staff Sergeant, you've got them. We'll meet you at the new site in about four hours," Lieutenant Nidishchii' told Staff Sergeant Hecs.

The platoon commander hadn't liked where the platoon had formed up and wanted to move them to something more defensible. There was one piece of high ground that looked promising, but it was too close to where the second group of French was located. Instead, the lieutenant had selected another small rise about 20 km from their present position. It was covered in trees, so it was not much better in terms of visibility, but any advantage had to be taken.

While the platoon was moving, the same group that had reconned the Legion platoon was going to confirm that the second group of French were actually sailors and not combat troops. This was to be a quick recon. The lieutenant didn't want to split his forces, but he had to make sure he understood just what they faced.

Keiji took point. Normally, the HGL gunner would be second in the movement as the HGL itself was not as quick a weapon to deploy as the normal M114, but if they were to face combat-suited legionnaires, then the HGL gave the Marines their best chance to take one of them out.

Reports on the effectiveness of the armor on the Legion R-3s were not conclusive at best, contradictory at worst. The armor was interspaced with circuits that created intense fields whereas the PICS had two field generators that created a sort of bubble around the Marines. The consensus was that the circuit method of generation made for a more effective shielding, particularly against energy weapons.

How effective it was against KE weapons, on the other hand, was not as well known. Some analysts felt that the lighter, more flexible armor of the R-3 was better against physical KE rounds as well. Others felt it gave an advantage in surviving the effects of concussive shock waves. But still others felt the armor was too light and not strong enough to match the older techno PICS in as far as brute ability to withstand KE strikes.

The PICS M114 was a great weapon against softer targets. It fired a stream of 8mm hyper-velocity darts that would pierce ordinary body armor without too much of a problem. However, it would not pierce a PICS. A lucky shot might damage sensors or weapons, but it would not make it through the armor of a PICS to the Marine inside. With that in mind, the Marines could not count on it to be able to take down a legionnaire in an R-3.

When the platoon had been loaded onto the shuttle, they had been given a standard combat load, not one designed to take on other combat-suited soldiers. This had been rather shortsighted given that the Legion possessed combat suits. Since even before the War of the Far Reaches, Marines hadn't faced anyone who had combat suits in their forces, and tactics had evolved without taking the armor into much consideration. Always fighting the last war, however, was a good way to lose the next one.

With their weapons mix, the Marines had a few weapons that could be effective against a legionnaire in an R-3. The HGL might need multiple hits, but it could work. Their shoulder rocket launchers, with the 7.5cm rockets, should be effective. Each Marine, though, had a total of only 12 rockets, six anti-personnel and six anti-armor, and the box could not be reloaded in the field. They had the M229, which would undoubtedly mess up a legionnaire's day, and if they could figure out how to use it, the shuttle's 25mm gun.

Each PICS also had its plasma gun. In an atmosphere, the plasma dispersed quickly, so the distance had to be close, and they took up a huge amount of energy. A fully-charged PICS could maybe fire three times before the suit went dead. With the R-3's effectiveness against energy weapons, and the fact that they had no way to recharge the PICS until back on the ship, those were pretty much a non-starter against the Legion troops.

On the other side of the battlefield, the legionnaires had weapons that could take out a PICS. The weapons of an R-3 remained inside the skin of the suit until fired. This helped with the stealth techno that made the R-3s so hard to acquire with the Marine sensors. Their own version of the hyper-velocity darts wouldn't do much against a PICS, but instead of a plasma gun, they had a hadron gun, miniaturized enough to carry. It was far more efficient than a plasma gun, and it could probably fire for at least a minute, if the Federation math was accurate. It wasn't as powerful as a ship-based hadron cannon, but it didn't have to be. The Marines had been briefed that the R-3's hadron gun would probably take from eight to twelve seconds to "burn" through the PICS' shields.

The legionnaires also had larger KE weapons, and the recording from Ryck's dragonfly revealed what looked to be a portable field gun. Other than that, though, the Marines didn't know with what the Legion platoon was equipped.

Ryck scanned his display as they moved through the trees. He had to watch where he was going, but still focus on his display, looking for the slightest aberration that might indicate a legionnaire was out there. Somewhere in the back of his mind, he marveled at the trees, the spongy surface of the ground. They didn't have forests on Prophesy where he grew up. They didn't have forests like this on Tarawa, either, nor on Alexander, where the division was based.

The lieutenant stopped them several times to stand and scan, but they still made good time to their rally point. All was quiet. Staff Sergeant Hecs reported in from the new position, and Lance Corporal Justice with the WIA and AT3 Fodor, the shuttle crew chief, reported in as well. The legionnaires were nowhere on anyone's scanners.

At least the French crew was showing up on their sensors, about 500 meters ahead of the small recon force. Ryck had taken one of Popo's dragonflies, so he was back up to two. It seemed to synch all right to his PICS, but he decided to launch his remaining original drone.

This far back and in the forest, the lieutenant kept them standing, which was easier. With the others providing security, Ryck was able to concentrate on his dragonfly. He slowed it down as it approached the French, sending it higher into the canopy. This close, it could pick up 15 separate heat signatures. Ryck edged it forward, and the view suddenly opened up to a small clearing. It looked like a tree had fallen, leaving a crease in the otherwise uninterrupted forest.

Fifteen men and women, all sailors were in the clearing, three lying together seemingly injured. Several lean-tos had been built from branches and deadfall, and another few sailors were sitting under them. Ryck counted two sailors, armed with the small French slurp guns, standing guard at either end of the clearing. The rest were engaged in small tasks. There was no sign of heavy weaponry of any kind, either energy or KE.

The little dragonfly had basic sensors, but the PICS, in particular, the lieutenant's PICS-C, had much more sophisticated ones, so after the preliminary scan, the Marines moved forward. They walked their PICS as "stealthily" as they could, which was somewhat of an oxymoron when describing movement in a PICS. Ryck doubted that the sailors had much in the way of sensors, but they had their eyeballs and ears, and they would be able to see and hear a PICS coming through the trees.

At 200 meters out, the lieutenant stopped them. Ryck had the platoon commander's data feed slaved, so he could see the readout. The dragonfly had gotten most of the info already. The French were what they seemed to be: sailors, not legionnaires.

"What do we do?" Ryck asked the lieutenant.

Their mission was still intact. They were to accept a surrender or destroy anyone who refused to give up. There were 15 French combatants up ahead, and with seven PICS Marines, they would stand no chance.

Ryck knew their orders, but he had no stomach to launch an attack. These were shipwreck survivors, in his mind, and the treaties were clear as to how they should be treated. The fact that the two forces were at war, the fact that they were armed, didn't make a difference to him. Ryck didn't know, though, how anal the lieutenant would be with regards to their orders. And if the lieutenant ordered an assault, he would obey.

"They're no threat to us," Lieutenant Nidishchii' said. "Let's leave your dragonfly to watch over them, but let's leave them be. Once we've dealt with the legionnaires, then we can take the crew's surrender."

That was a relief to Ryck. He turned to the lieutenant just as a flicker appeared in the platoon commander's scan feed. An amber warning icon flashed on Ryck's display, indicating an anomaly, but not the red icon of a positive threat identification.

Both Ryck and the lieutenant turned just as a flash illuminated the trees to their right. Their face shields lit up as their PICS identified a Gazelle, the small, man-packed anti-armor missile hurtling at them. From only 100 meters out, barely within arming range, they had no chance. This missile was designed to take out tanks.

Their AIs flashed on each Marine's fractured arrays, but that didn't matter. The missile knew where they were and had locked into their position. Ryck started to lurch to the side, knowing there was not enough time. There was a bigger flash as the missile hit—Prifit.

The missile's exhaust made a cloud from which two legionnaires emerged. The Marines' scans started pulling in data points, but the two were right there in front of them, in plain sight. To Ryck's left, Keiji started pouring his grenades at the legionnaire closest to him. Ryck's first instinct was to open fire with his M114, but he pulled that back and toggled his rocket launcher.

Before he could fire, his alarms screamed as a hadron beam touched him. Immediately his shielding gauge popped up on his display and started to give the numbers as his shield began to disintegrate. Ryck jumped to his right, and his alarms turned off. The legionnaire was targeting the lieutenant, and Ryck had only been caught in a side lobe.

He started to turn back around to take the legionnaire under fire, but to his amazement, Lieutenant Nidishchii' was running, not away, but right at the legionnaire firing at him.

Ryck's display registered an explosion on the arm of the second legionnaire, but he was more focused on the one firing at his platoon commander. He started to fire his rockets, but with the lieutenant between them, he couldn't. He ran to his right further to get a clear line of fire.

At about 50 meters, the lieutenant started firing his rockets, bam, bam, one after the other. The air around him started to glow as his shields approached failure, but he didn't stop.

The anti-armor rockets had limited self-guidance toward metallic objects, but the R-3 wasn't made of metal. The lieutenant was firing his rockets from the hip while running. Each rocket, though, hit the chest of the legionnaire. When the first one hit, Ryck could see the armor actually ripple. When the second one hit an instant later, the rippled became more pronounced.

The lieutenant didn't stop running forward or firing. The third rocket hit in the legionnaire in same spot, but the fourth went over the man's shoulder.

Ryck didn't know how much time had elapsed since the lieutenant had been taken under fire. Seven, eight seconds? His shield was a bright orange, a sure sign of imminent failure.

The lieutenant was only 20 meters from the legionnaire, but he didn't stop. Ryck aimed in on the soldier, who had taken a step back when faced with the charging Marine. Just as Ryck fired, the fifth, or maybe the sixth rocket fired by the lieutenant hit home, this time penetrating the R-3 and blowing a 10-centimeter hole in the R-3's chest. Ryck's rocket skimmed past the lieutenant's head before slamming into the legionnaire's shoulder, but his round was unnecessary. The legionnaire was dead, his R-3 trying to maintain a vertical aspect. Sparks flew out of it, and it slowly collapsed upon itself.

Ryck wheeled to face the other legionnaire, but he was retreating, barely visible through the trees.

"Lieutenant, are you OK?" he shouted into his mic.

There was no response, so Ryck ran forward as the lieutenant turned around.

Ryck shouted out his question again, but the lieutenant pointed at where his ear would be, then shook his head back and forth.

His shield was still glowing, a couple of centimeters worth of cloud around him. It wasn't glowing as brightly as before, but with all that ionized air, it was affecting his comms.

He could see the lieutenant's smile through his face shield, so Ryck knew he was OK. Ryck turned back to check on the others.

Prifit was on his back, and Ryck hoped for the best. Instead, he saw the worst, and that staggered him. The entire carapace section of Prifit's PICS had been blown away. Above the shoulders, the PICS looked normal, as it did below the gut plate. Where Prifit's chest had been though, was a bloody, mangled mess. The anti-armor round, designed to take out tanks, had passed right through his Marine.

Without power, Prifit's face shield was dark, and Ryck was relieved that he couldn't see the lance corporal's face for the moment. He had to prepare himself before he did that.

Ryck turned from Prifit and ordered Keiji to provide security in the direction to which the other legionnaire had fled while he went to check over the dead soldier. The legionnaire was slouched in the dirt in a way a PICS could not. The armor of the R-3, while not pliable, was not as rigid as it was when the man was firing at the lieutenant. From reading published articles in various journals and blogs, Ryck knew the R-3 armor was powered, but it looked like that power gave the suit at least some degree of support as well. Ryck reached out with his foot and gave the legionnaire a shove, knocking him flat to the ground. The feedback sensors let Ryck know the R-3 was still a pretty heavy piece of gear, probably right at the 825 kg reported in the general specs.

The rocket that had blown the hole in the legionnaire's chest did not cause as much damage as the missile that had hit Prifit, but it had done enough. His time as an armorer while still in regen gave him some expertise in combat suits, so he kneeled to examine what the damage revealed. The R-3 armor was thinner than PICS armor, which was to be expected, but Ryck couldn't see any of the circuits that powered it.

"Ryck, are you there?" Staff Sergeant Hecs voice came over the net.

"Yeah, I'm here."

"What the hell's going on? We've got Justice in a panic saying he's heard fighting, and I can't raise the lieutenant. My display's got Lance Corporal Prifit down," the platoon sergeant said.

"We were hit by two legionnaires. Prifit's KIA, but the lieutenant's fine. He friggin' charged one of the legionnaires while taking full fire, but his rockets took the guy out first. His PICS is pretty fried, and I think it's going to need a reset."

There was a moment of silence, then "Prifit's KIA? No chance of bringing him back?"

"Staff Sergeant, no way. His entire chest is gone."

The lieutenant was making a circle in the air with his gauntlet. Back at boot, Ryck had wondered why they spent so much time on hand and arm signals. He never would have thought he would be in the field with a platoon commander who couldn't communicate, though.

"Staff Sergeant, the lieutenant wants me. I'll keep you informed," he told Staff Sergeant Hecs as he went up to his platoon commander.

It wasn't textbook hand and arm signals, but the lieutenant made his intentions clear. He wanted Prifit taken out of his PICS, anything salvaged, then for the Gazelle launcher and the PICS to be destroyed. Ryck grabbed the launcher while Rey and Hartono pulled the pieces of what was left of Tipper Prifit out of his PICS. Ryck tried to avoid looking at what was left inside the PICS, but he managed to take the shoulder launcher and helmet off. He was sure the coldpack was destroyed, and he didn't want to feel around in the bloody mess that was left to confirm that. When he was done, he put the launcher on top of Prifit's destroyed PICS.

Hartono had a buttpack, and what was left of Prifit fit inside of it. Corporal Evans took two of his bullfrogs, the EOD version of the toads[23] each Marine carried, and put one on top of the Gazelle launcher, one on the PICS' codpiece. He lit them off, and the Marines stepped back. All of them stood watching in silence as the bullfrogs ignited and burned their way through the armor. Packing two or three times the punch of a normal toad, it didn't take long.

---

[23] Toad: Slang for the E-559 Self-contained Slow Breaching Device, a high-intensity heat weapon that can be attached to an object and burn through it.

It wasn't until the bullfrogs flickered out, leaving a smoking pile of junk, that they turned and left to rejoin the rest of the platoon.

Chapter 18

Ryck sighed with contentment. He felt naked, his visibility was low in the darkness, and something was digging into his back, but it felt good to be out of his PICS. With power levels down for all the Marines, particularly for the seven who had made the two recons, the lieutenant had ordered a rotating watch, with those off watch out of their PICS.

More vital than the power levels, though, were the coldpacks. With the two per Marine, they had about 50-60 hours of operating time before the PICS became unusable. The lieutenant hoped that the *Intrepid* would be back by then, but it was better to be safe than sorry.

Getting out of the PICS was a calculated risk. If they were hit, it would take up to 30 seconds or possibly longer for the Marines to get back in, sealed, and ready to fight. If the PICS were completely powered down instead of on standby, it would take even longer, but while that would save more power, it increased the risk dramatically.

The lieutenant had sent out three OPs[24], Marines without their PICS and under tarnkappes.[25] Simple vibration sensors were placed to fill in the gaps between the OPs. Even under a full charge by R-3 legionnaires, the platoon should have the time needed to be ready to meet the threat.

Four Marines were in their PICS and on full alert around them—the rest of the empty PICS stood like sentinel statues, ready to come to life.

---

[24] OP: Observation post. One or two Marines sent out in front of the unit's lines to give early warning of approaching enemy.

[25] Tarnkappe: slang, taken from a Grimm's Fairy Tales description of a cloak of concealment, for the S-77 Shielding Blanket. The blanket shields against most sensors as well as from vision.

"Thanks for getting my PICS back up to speed, Ryck," the lieutenant said as he took a seat beside his sergeant.

Ryck? That's twice now, Ryck thought.

With the lieutenant, it was always rank and last name. Ryck wondered if sitting there in the dark in their longjohns affected the degree of formality between the two Marines.

"No problem, sir. It wasn't hard."

Ryck didn't mention that it hadn't been difficult from a technical standpoint, but he had cannibalized the controls from Tipper Prifit's helmet, which had been a bit rough emotionally.

"I guess your time in the armory paid off, huh?" he asked, then continuing before Ryck could respond. "My time as a genhen was in admin, so I can help unscrew a pay problem, but that's about it."

From what he'd heard, the lieutenant had spent almost as much time as Ryck had in regen. He wondered if his platoon commander had hated it as much as he did. Not the discomfort and pain—everyone hated that—but being away from his unit, away from his fellow Marines, and most of all, the feeling of uselessness. At least Ryck had been with weapons while he was a genhen. With all respect and gratitude to the admin types who kept things running smoothly, Ryck thought he would have died had he been locked up in an office somewhere, shuffling papers.

"This might seem odd, given the circumstances, but I've been watching you pretty closely," the lieutenant continued.

What now? Ryck thought.

"What I mean is that you are a good Marine, a good NCO. You think on your feet. That's why I wanted you with me today on the recons. I knew I could count on you."

"Uh, well, thanks, sir," Ryck answered, unsure of where the conversation was going.

"You finished your degree, right?"

"Yes, sir. I received my diploma two months ago."

"Yes, I saw the message. Well, I just wanted to tell you that it's not just me, but Captain Davis had taken note of you, too."

Captain Davis? He's hardly said ten words to me since I've been in the company, and now he's gone.

"My point is, and I just want you to think of it, if you ever want to apply to be an officer, I would endorse you, and Captain Davis told me he would have endorsed you. I can write that endorsement from him as well."

"I . . . I don't know what to say, sir. I mean, it's an honor to hear you tell me that, but I've never even thought of applying for a commission."

That was a lie. He had thought about it, but he kept denying it to the rest of the Marines. For some warped reason that Ryck didn't understand, Marine culture ruled that enlisted Marines who wanted to be officers were suspect, not full members of the "brotherhood."

"Just consider it, OK? The Marines need leaders like you in the officer corps. Anyway, that's all I wanted to say. You make sure to catch some sleep. We don't know what tomorrow will bring, right?"

"Right, sir," Ryck said as the lieutenant stood up and excused himself before walking over to where Staff Sergeant Hecs had bedded down.

"You should be an officer," Sams said quietly beside him, his voice several octaves higher than normal. "Oh really, sir? You mean that? Of course, I want that," he went on, answering himself.

"Fuck you," Ryck said. "I can't help what the lieutenant thinks."

"Sure. You are such a fucking brown-noser, Ryck. I didn't hear you tell him no."

"Eat me," Ryck grumbled.

Despite himself, the lieutenant's words had piqued his interest. In order to become an officer, a Marine had to get recommended by his unit, even if he met all other qualifications. To know he had one, or two, if what the lieutenant had said about Captain Davis was true, opened the door.

He wasn't sure he wanted to become one, though. Sure, it was an advancement in responsibility, not to mention pay, and it would take care of one of Ryck's constant frustrations, that of not knowing what was happening all the time, of being kept in the dark. On the other hand, it would take him farther from his Marines, and there was all the other BS that officers had to deal with that had nothing to do with leading Marines.

Ryck generally liked it as a sergeant, and becoming a platoon sergeant would be pretty awesome. Why take the BS of being an officer when you could get all the good parts as a SNCO?

"Eh, what does Lieutenant Personality know, anyway?"

"You know, Sams, you keep calling him that, but the guy is good. Look at us now. He's put in for every contingency. That's pretty copacetic, if you ask me."

Sams was one of his closest Marines in the platoon, and with Popo dead, there were only two sergeants. Ryck loved Sams like a brother, but his cynical attitude sometimes pissed Ryck off.

"Sure, I'll give you that. But any manual-reading bozo could do that. I don't think he's got the fire that, say, Lieutenant Hargrave's got, or the skipper," he said.

That put an immediate damper on things. Both officers had been killed this morning.

"He had fire today," Ryck muttered.

"What do you mean?" Sams asked.

"You should have seen him. When we both got hit by the legionnaire with his hadron gun, here I am diving to get out of the line of fire. Does the lieutenant do that? Fuck no. He charged the motherfucker. Charges like some knight with a lance. No fucking hesitation."

"He charged *into* the fire? I thought you were supposed to get further away, 'cause the beam dissipates," Sams asked.

"That's for a plasma gun, like ours. But I said hadron gun, which you know the Legion uses. The beam's not going to dissipate for a long, long distance."

"Oh, yeah."

"So I'm getting out of the way, Keiji's shooting like some rabid wolf, and he even hits the other legionnaire's gun port, knocking it out of action— "

"He hits the gun port?"

"Didn't you listen to the debrief? Yeah, one of his grenades hits the gunport that this asshole is using to fire on us, and that knocks his weapon offline. That's why he took off. No weapons."

"Pisspot froggie. Running away," Sams said.

"Yeah, well anyway, I'm trying to get a shot in, and I can see the lieutenant's shield glow, I mean, I can really see it. He's going all orange. But he doesn't stop. Five rockets, no fucking guidance on them. Four hit the legionnaire, and the fourth does it. Bam! He's smoke-checked. And let me tell you, when I worked on his PICS, if that last rocket hadn't hit, the lieutenant would be KIA now. One more second, and his PICS would have been fried. It's because he didn't hesitate, that he went into the attack, that he lived, and maybe the rest of us, too. So, don't tell me he's got no fire, OK?"

"Shit, OK, OK. Back off. I meant, with us, at least, he's like a robot. Never excited. Just does his job."

"He's a good officer. Made his ancestors proud, I bet."

"Something special about his ancestors?" Sams asked.

"Yeah, he's Navaho," Ryck told him, wondering why Sams had to ask.

"And . . . ?"

"Saint Harry on a rope, Sams, don't you keep track of anything? The lieutenant's from Dinétah,"

"Again, and . . . ?"

"You know about Dinétah, right?"

"It's a country on Manitoba. Some of them join the Marines. So? Lots of planets send more than their fair share to the Marines."

"You've never heard of the Code-Talkers?" Ryck asked.

"No, I've never heard of the Code-Talkers," Sams responded, his voice inflected to show his lack of interest.

"You really should. They're part of Marine Corps history. Back in WWII, the Navaho people sent their young men into the U.S. Marines to fight the Japanese, and they were vital in keeping Marine comms secure from being compromised by the Japanese."

"Ancient history, my friend, ancient history. I'm not the one trying to get a history degree."

"It may be old, but it is our history, and when the Navajo relocated to Dinétah, they re-established their warrior culture. So, guess where their best and brightest go? Yep, to the Marines. Like the old-time Gurkhas, only the very top few were able to join the Marines."

"Gurkhas, I know about them. We had a Gurkha gunny before you got here. He had this wicked knife he took everywhere, a cokry or something," Sams said.

"A kukri," Ryck corrected him. "The Gurkhas were big in the old Royal Marines, the Navaho in the U.S. Marines. They both still serve in our Marines. My point is that the lieutenant comes from a long line of warriors, and they only let the best enlist. So, he's made his ancestors proud, today, not just for what he's done when he was an enlisted slob like us."

"Ah, whatever. He may be some kick-butt warrior, but I still think he's got a stick up his ass. He needs to lighten up a schosh. Now, you heard your hero. We've got the get some sleep."

With that, Sams laid back, turning away from Ryck. Within a minute or so, Ryck's friend started snoring.

Chapter 19

The next day, the Marines spent time preparing their position. The hadron comms had been with the skipper, so the platoon had nothing with which to communicate with a ship out of planetary orbit. But the lieutenant assigned Lance Corporal Vargas out of First Squad to monitor all the ground-to-orbit frequencies. When the *Intrepid* returned, the platoon commander wanted to know immediately.

The lieutenant, Staff Sergeant Hecs, Ryck, Sams, and Corporal St. Cyr, the new Second Squad leader, met several times in a mini-war council, going over their options to take the fight to the enemy. It was during one of these that a mass of explosions sounded off to their southwest, possibly 30 km away. The firing kept up for almost two minutes before dying off. Ryck knew there were no Marines there—Justice and the WIA were almost 40 km away to the northeast, and they were the only other Federation forces on the planet. He turned to ask the lieutenant what was going on, but the platoon commander was high-fiving Staff Sergeant Hecs.

"And that, sir, is how it's done," Staff Sergeant Hecs said.

"What was that?" Ryck asked.

"Oh, our good platoon sergeant set up a little decoy last night. It seems like it's not only the French who can spoof."

"And it looks like you owe me 20, sir," Staff Sergeant Hecs said.

"Duly noted, there, Staff Sergeant Phantawisangtong."

The lieutenant got down in the dirt and pushed out a quick 20 pushups.

Ryck hadn't even realized the platoon sergeant had slipped out during the night. If that was 30 km away, then that was 60 km back and forth, quite a trip even in a PICS.

About 30 minutes after the "attack," a voice came over several frequencies at once. The Marines outside of their PICS heard the message over the external speakers of the active PICS.

"Federation Marines, let's avoid any further bloodshed. First Lieutenant Nidishchii'" the voice went on, stumbling a bit over the name, "we are offering you our full guarantee of humane treatment if you surrender your force to us. No one will be hurt, and all needing it will receive medical care. The war is almost over, so let's sit it out. That was a nice feint you pulled, but we have your position locked now. You and your 32 surviving Marines have no air support, no supporting arms, and without those, I am sure you can do the math. You really don't have much chance against a larger Legion force. We outnumber you and outgun you."

There was an explosion of protest from the Marines.

"No need for an immediate reply. No one is doubting your courage. Lieutenant, you have proven your courage time and time again, and several of your men, notably Staff Sergeant Phantawisangtong," the voice said, making even more havoc over the name, "Sergeants Samuelson and Sergeant Lysander, Lance Corporal Westminster, Lance Corporal Laste Holleran, and Private First Class Ling, are well known in the Legion, so this is not a matter of whose balls are the biggest. Most of you have even been of service to the Legion, and you have our gratitude. This is a matter of simply living without needless bloodshed."

While the voice was going on, Staff Sergeant Hecs had wormed into the back of his PICS, and the voice was cut off. He wormed back out and went up to the lieutenant.

Ryck, Sams, and several others came as well.

"How do they know my name?" Ling asked with a worried tone to his voice.

Staff Sergeant Hecs held up his hand, forestalling him, then looking up to the lieutenant.

"Well, that's a nice ni hao," the lieutenant said to them. "Interesting in what they gave away."

"Sir?" Sams asked.

"Well, first, they were specific on us being 32 Marines, and they mentioned every Marine in the platoon who's been awarded a BCS-1 or higher. What does that tell you?" he asked the group.

"Well, Westminster was KIA from the crash," Ryck said.

"Yes, and they have not taken into account that we have seven WIA still alive, and no mention was made of Corporal Evans and HM2 Grbil. Grbil's been decorated, so if they knew about him, they would have mentioned him. What they have is partial intel, and they are guessing the rest. You could have found out most of that from our battalion facebook.[26] By telling us too much, they are revealing their limitations."

"They don't have more men than us, either, right sir?" Staff Sergeant Hecs said.

"I doubt it. We know they lost one and probably two others. If you count the Navy sailors, then yes, they probably have more, but as far as legionnaires, I am guessing we are about even-strengthed."

"But they've got R-3s, and we don't have air now," Vargas said.

"True, but I don't think the R-3 is really that great. I took one out yesterday, and I'm still here, right? And if we make them come to us, maybe we can even out the odds."

"So, do we answer?" asked Staff Sergeant Hecs.

"Can we get a mic out here, out of the helmet?" he asked.

"Sure, no problem," Corporal Evans said.

He took a length of ignition wire, then crawled half-way inside his own PICS. A moment later, he emerged, holding the small chin mic in his hand, the wire trailing from it back to inside the PICS. He handed it to the lieutenant.

"Turn back on the broadcast," he told Staff Sergeant Hecs.

Since Staff Sergeant Hecs had overridden the broadcast from his PICS-C, he had to turn it back on from either his or the lieutenants. He squirmed up inside the back of his, and a few moments, the French voice came back on.

". . . too long before we will be forced to take offensive action."

"Our French friends, if I may interrupt, I do have a response for you. This is First Lieutenant Nidishchii', UFMC."

The voice stopped for a moment, then said, "Uh, yes, Lieutenant. Please go on."

[26] Facebook: a generic reference to any public relations media information for an organization or personal information for an individual.

Every Marine and Doc Grbil had stopped what they were doing and stared at the lieutenant. Slowly, the lieutenant lowered the mic to his ass, and after a moment, let out a tremendous fart, amplified to its max.

There was dead silence before the Marines erupted into howls of laughter, "oohrahs," and "get some, Lieutenant!"

Ryck, trying to control his laughter, looked to Sams and asked, "The lieutenant's got no fire, Sams?"

Chapter 20

"Steve, when we attacked the SOG back on Billiton, they used a mine to take out one of my Marines," Ryck told their EOD Marine.

"Yeah, Yancy Sullivan. I remember," Corporal Evans replied.

"What was the result of the investigation, something about them using wood and an organic explosive?"

"Yeah, the mine body was wood, of all things. For the explosive, they used simple fertilizer. A pressure plate was the trigger. Yancy was pretty unlucky. He stepped right on it."

"Is that something we could do here?" Ryck asked.

"Oh, wow! I don't know. I could if we were back at battalion, no sweat. It wouldn't be as good as one of our issued mines, but it would work. This is real old technology."

"If it was that old, how did it work against us?"

"Because we aren't looking for wood with our PICS. We're looking for all the latest and greatest weapons, not bows and arrows or leather slings," Evans said.

"Do you think it's possible, though?"

"Well, I can take the M887 round casing. They're an organic pulp. Shouldn't be too hard to make a mine casing from them. I can probably come up with something to put inside. All my igniters, though, the legionnaires would be able to pick them up and jam them. I might be able to rig up a pressure plate, but the chances that someone would actually step on it are about nil. The SOG set up over 50, and only one was triggered. So, I'm not sure how we could set them off. A wire is out of the question. I guess we could attach a string or something and try and make it manual, but they could probably see it, and I'm not sure any string would be strong enough to activate any sort of trigger I could come up with. I think we would need a timer of some sort, to activate it. Yeah, that would do it. We could activate a timer with a string, for say, a 20 or 30 or whatever second detonation we want. Yeah, that would work!" he said, his voice getting a little excited as he spoke.

"You mean, like a watch?"

"No, that wouldn't work. Watches are electronic, no moving parts. It would have to be a mechanical timer of some sort, and we don't have any," Evans said, sounding deflated.

Ryck sighed, then took the Rolex off his wrist. This was Joshua's gift to him, intended to be a lifetime treasure. He knew his friend would understand, though.

"Like this?" he asked, holding out the hand-made timepiece.

"Ooh, that's psycho," Corporal Evans said as he reached out to take it. "Yeah, that'll work, but man, that's a shame. This is one beautiful watch."

"Let's do it. As soon as you get the smoke pots up, I want this done. I'll brief the lieutenant, and we'll tell you where we want it."

"No problem, Sergeant L. I'll get on it."

Ryck really, really loved that watch, but not as much as he valued the lives of the Marines around him.

Chapter 21

We've got movement," Lance Corporal Denny sent back on the landline they had rigged from the OP back to the lieutenant's foxhole.

They had set up simple vibration detectors, something very difficult to pick up on a scanner until it was too late and had already been activated, and the landline was pretty much impossible to jam. It could be cut, but that was about it. Between the two sources, the platoon knew the Legion was on the march.

"OK, cover up and wait this out. Do not try to come back," the lieutenant passed.

Ryck sent a quick message out on the squad circuit, "Here they come, from the north."

They had decided if the legionnaires were going to attack, they would come from that direction. It was the most logical avenue of approach, and for that reason alone, Ryck would have picked something different. But the legionnaires evidently had a lot of confidence in their abilities. Ryck hoped that confidence was misplaced.

Unless this was yet another spoof, the Marines were well-arrayed for the incoming assault. They had prepared alternate positions, but the main ones were in a slight horseshoe around the crest of the high ground. If it had been a real hill, that position would not have worked. But by varying the depth of each fighting hole, each Marine had a clear field of fire down below them. Clear except for the trees, that was. They'd knocked down a few, but if too many were down, the legionnaires would simply bypass the area and attack from the flanks where it would be harder to mass fire on them.

The M229 was emplaced toward the right of the line, where a subtle amount of tree removal gave it just a hair more of a field of fire. On the left side of the line, the shuttle's 250mm gun had been lashed onto a tree trunk they had knocked over. Ryck didn't give the gun much credit. There were no working sights, much less a target acquisition control, so it would be blindly firing forward, but at least it was something.

Modern warfare was not supposed to be like this anymore. It was fluid actions across a battlefield with interlocking support and assaults. Marines just didn't go on the defense, either. Sams, for one, had been advocating taking the fight to the legionnaires, not sitting and waiting for the enemy to come to them.

Marines didn't go into the defense, but it had been decades since they had faced a force even equal to them.

The lieutenant merely said, "Whoever is first in the field and awaits the coming of the enemy, will be fresh for the fight; whoever is second in the field and has to hasten to battle will arrive exhausted."

Ryck recognized that from Sun Tzu, and while he didn't think it really fit the situation, it seemed weighty enough to shut up Sams.

"Get the pots going," the lieutenant told Evans.

Evans, in turn, told Private Holderstead, who'd been made his assistant. The private jumped out of his fighting hole and ran forward to the line of makeshift smoke pots Evans had managed to rig up. One smack on the top of each pot and it ignited, sending grey smoke out which rose a meter or so off the ground as it slowly spread. Corporal Evans had tried to explain that it wasn't actually smoke, but it acted like smoke and looked like smoke, so to the rest of the Marines, smoke it was.

It might seem counterintuitive to send out any agent, smoke or not, that blocked visuals when an assault was expected. However, Ryck knew that the legionnaires would not be low-crawling up to their positions, and the lieutenant's reason for the smoke seemed sound. Only time would tell if the lieutenant was right.

The Marines couldn't tell how many legionnaires they faced. Their vibration sensors did not indicate direction, so there was no way for the AIs to triangulate and make an estimate. There had to be over 20, but probably fewer than 40. That was a pretty big range.

When the legionnaires were at 200 meters, Ryck felt his excitement rise. There might have been a touch of fear in there, too, but nothing overriding. He tried to see through the trees, but the legionnaires were still too far away to spot. His sensors were picking up nothing. They probably would continue to pick up nothing until the legionnaires' weapons ports opened, breaking the stealth profile of the R-3's.

Then he saw it, the slightest swirl in the smoke some 120 meters away. The fire team assigned to the M229 saw it as well. In direct fire mode, the gun opened up. A split second later, the anti-armor round impacted, and an R-3 flashed into view as it was blown back.

The battle was on. More swirls in the smoke appeared as unseen legionnaires rushed forward. The M229 fired again, but the round exploded against a tree.

Corporal Evans had laid out ten of his issued mines, but as expected, the legionnaires were able to detect them. They sidestepped them, three coming together and heading right toward Evan's field-expedient mine. Ryck reached down and pulled the string, an unraveled piece of Evan's longjohns. His Rolex started its 10-second count down.

The M229 opened up once more, and it looked like it took another legionnaire out. Then all of the sensors went crazy as the legionnaires opened fire. The first casualty was the M229 team. Something big hit them, and a column of flames lit up the area.

The fractured array shielding should have made the first shots fired at the Marines miss them, but the artillery piece itself didn't have the shielding, and once it fired, it gave up the gun team's position.

With the sensors locking in on the legionnaires, the displays started placing them, and the Marines started to get visuals on them as well. One of the three legionnaires being funneled into the blast area of Evan's field-expedient mine stopped, probably to fire, but the other two kept advancing. The timing couldn't have been better. The mine erupted, a slow, powerful blast that lifted the two legionnaires into the air at least 20 meters before sending them crashing back down.

Another Gazelle fired, but it went over Corporal Rey's head to impact on the trees well behind the Marines. Immediately, at least 20 rockets were fired at the point of launch for the missile.

Ryck couldn't tell if they hit anything, but no more Gazelles were fired.

To his left, the shuttle's 25mm gun opened up. It was not aimed, but it created a stream of fire a meter and a half above the ground. A few trees had been strategically knocked down, so the gun was able to cover the entire platoon front. At least one legionnaire was hit, although Ryck couldn't tell if it was a lethal strike or not. Several hadron beams reached out to it, too many for Ryck's display to number, and ten seconds later, the gun stopped firing.

The legionnaires had something else, something bigger. From way back, there was a blast, followed by an explosion not 10 meters from Ryck. Khouri and Stillwell's icons went grey.

"Khouri, you OK?" he asked, knowing he wouldn't get a response.

The lieutenant was shouting orders over the circuit, trying to get frontage covered as Marines were knocked out. Ryck fired his remaining rockets at the far weapon, whatever it was. The moment it fired, though, it was withdrawn behind a tree, and all of Ryck's rockets impacted on the trees between them. Ryck knew it would take timing and luck to take the weapon out with a rocket. It fired again, but the same trees that protected it gave it a limited field of fire of its own, and it nicked a tree, enough to throw the round off target. It impacted into the dirt in front of one of Second Squad's position, showering the Marines with clods of dirt.

Martin's icon went grey. There hadn't been an explosion, so a hadron beam must have gotten him. Three of Ryck's squad were already gone. Ryck couldn't keep track, of the entire battlefield, but he only knew of three legionnaires down.

The legionnaires' headlong rush had stopped. They had thought to run over the Marines, but the defensive fire was too heavy. However, using the trees as protection, they started a war of attrition. Their big gun, whatever it was, kept pounding away, taking out five Marines from First from the center of the line.

Ryck kept watching the ammo counts of his squad dwindle. Hartono fired his plasma gun, but the distance, coupled with the smoke which lingered, dissipated the beam, and if it hit anyone, the legionnaire's armor was more than able to withstand it. To make matters worse, Hartono's power supply dropped to 38% after firing.

"Hartono, no more P-guns. We're too far. That goes for everyone, only at point-blank range!" he passed.

Ryck leveled his M-77 and chewed up a tree behind which a legionnaire stood. It was only 50 cm across, so it couldn't give the legionnaire complete cover, but it offered a degree of protection. Ryck's 8mm darts quickly chewed through the wood, dropping the tree, and the legionnaire ran to the next one. Ryck knew his darts hit him, but they didn't slow the man down.

Keiji scored another hit on a legionnaire 80 meters away. This was the second hit at the same spot, and it blew off the arm of the R-3.

"The arms are not as strong as the torso," Ryck passed on the platoon circuit. "Try for that!"

"You heard him," the lieutenant followed up. "Aim for the extremities."

With the Marines firing, it was difficult for the legionnaires to hold their hadron guns on target long enough to take out a Marine. The effect was cumulative, though, if they could hit the Marines often enough in a short period of time. Twice now, Ryck had been hit, but each time for only seconds before answering fire made the legionnaire firing at him break off to take cover. His shielding was down to 82%, though.

Their most effective remaining weapon was their HGL. There were only six Marines, though, with functional HGLs, and they were running low on ammo. When those rounds ran out, there wasn't much that would keep the legionnaires from concentrating their hadron guns on them. Ryck didn't know how many charges the hadron guns had, but they could fire much, much longer than the Marines' plasma guns.

"Lieutenant, Keiji and Holleran are down to a 10% load each. Do you think it's time?" Ryck asked?

"They're still too far away," the lieutenant replied. "Too much time exposed."

Another explosion sounded down the line, and two more icons went grey.

"I've got two more down," Corporal St. Cyr passed, his voice fast and excited. "We're getting slammed!"

The lieutenant had put Second Squad in the middle, thinking the two squads with more experienced squad leaders could help support him. Instead, the squad had been taking the brunt of the fire.

"Lieutenant, we didn't figure they'd have some sort of big gun, and it's going to eat us up. Maybe we've just got to go for it?" Staff Sergeant Hecs said.

There was a pause, then the lieutenant answered, "Maybe you're right. OK, Third, tell your two HGL gunners to cease fire. First, tell one of yours. Maybe they'll think they are out of ammo and advance. The rest of you, you know the plan. Get ready. I'll give the command, but it will be soon."

This is crazy, Ryck thought, *but who the hell knows?*

Standing pat was a sure path to defeat, he knew. In previous engagements over the last 50 years, the Marines always had the technological advantage. But this time, the difference in energy weapons was the deciding factor. The R-3 might not be as good as they thought, but the hadron gun was light years ahead of the Marines' P-guns.

Ryck took out his six toads. Ryck was perhaps the only living Marine who had ever taken out an enemy with a toad. They were not designed for fighting but rather burning through things, but watching Evans burn the Gazelle launcher and Prifit's PICS had convinced Ryck that they would burn through the R-3 armor. After getting a close-up look at it, Ryck couldn't believe the R-3 armor itself was stronger than the PICS' LTC[27] armor.

Corporal Evans had given him two of his much more powerful bullfrogs. Now all Ryck had to do was to somehow get them on the legionnaires. Both the toads and bullfrogs were sticky lumps of synthetic pyro, and once put on something, they stuck, so even tossing them at a legionnaire would work. But it was a fair bet that a legionnaire wouldn't just stand there and play catch.

---

[27] LTC: Lutetium Tungsten Carbide

Ryck coated his right gauntlet with the silicon spray that would keep the little hellfires from sticking to his hand. He was ready. Another icon, this one in First Squad, went grey.

"You ready, Ryck?" the lieutenant asked. "I think you'll appreciate this."

Ryck wondered what his platoon commander meant.

"Come on you sons-o'-bitches! Do you want to live forever?" the lieutenant shouted as en masse, the bulk of the platoon got out of their fighting holes and charged forward.

Despite himself, Ryck laughed out loud as he left the slight safety of his hole. They were going "over the top," so what better quote? Dan Daly would be proud. And just as in Belleau Wood so many years ago, the Marines answered the call.

Immediately, hadron beams lanced out at them. If the legionnaires had been surprised at the charge, they certainly recovered quickly. Ryck was aware of the beam, aware of his shields going down, but he pushed forward. He angled to where Evans had set up his own mines, where the legionnaires were avoiding. Then he angled back. He had to get close. It took him only five seconds once under fire to close the distance, and suddenly, there not five meters in front of him, was a legionnaire, stepping backward, gunport open, and covering him with fire.

Ryck leveled one blast of his plasma gun, and the legionnaire collapsed. Ryck felt a thrill run through him. He had been sure the more powerful plasma gun would knock out an R-3 if they could only get close enough.

"P-guns will take them down" he shouted on the circuit as he ran forward.

A shape formed to his left, and as he turned, he saw another legionnaire pouring fire downrange. His plasma gun hadn't recharged, and firing it again might deplete his power, so he tossed the toad in his hand at the unsuspecting legionnaire. The man didn't seem to even know the toad landed on him, but as it sparked and started to burn, he would soon enough. Ryck just hoped that it would be before whichever Marine the legionnaire was firing at went down under the man's beam.

Something hit Ryck in the arm, hard enough to actually jerk it out of position. Ryck was still functioning, so he kept moving.

His display gave the alarm at another touch of a beam, but it stopped as Ryck ran farther, whether from that legionnaire being taken out or because Ryck just ran out of the line of fire, he didn't know. What he did know was that he was down to 28% on his shields.

Then he was past the bulk of the legionnaires, much to his surprise. Of course, that meant that any security forces there would focus on him. Another Marine had broken through, as well. It took a second, but Ryck realized it was the lieutenant. Behind them, more and more Marine icons were going light blue or grey. But in front of them, the only identified red icons were on the gun team that had been wreaking havoc on the platoon.

"Let's get them, Ryck," the lieutenant said as they matched stride in rushing ahead.

Then they got a visual on the gun and two Legionnaires manning it. It looked like a fat mortar, even if it was leveled in direct fire mode. Ryck didn't recognize it, but he didn't have to. All he had to do was destroy it.

With his power down, Ryck didn't know how well his fractured array would be working. He could see that the gun team knew they were coming. They were physically yanking the gun around to face them. Ryck knew they would be able to fire before the lieutenant and he could reach them, and it was still too far away for a P-gun shot.

From beside him, the lieutenant let loose four rockets. He'd rationed his out better than Ryck. Two hit one of the gunners in the chest, the other in the left arm. The legionnaire immediately wheeled around, clutching his arm. He was not out, but down for the moment, at least.

Ryck had nothing, so he continued his charge. He could see the other legionnaire touch something, and Ryck knew this was it. There was a flash, but Ryck kept running. He felt a moment of elation until he realized that the lieutenant was down.

The gunner was furiously trying to reload another electrostatically-jacketed round. If this had been an auto-fire gun,

Ryck would be dead. But this was a single-shot gun, probably to make it more portable. Whatever the reason, Ryck was able to close the distance.

The gun was the first priority, so Ryck slapped one of the bullfrogs on it as he jumped over the gun. He collided with the gunner, who had just started to deploy his personal weapon. Stupid move. If he had done that sooner, depending on what weapon he had, he might have been able to stop Ryck before he reached the man. Instead, the collision with Ryck sent the man flying. Ryck just had to reach over to put a toad on the man's chest. He turned to the one with the damaged arm, who had started to run around his downed buddy. He grabbed another toad just as the screams of the first legionnaire reached him over the man's speakers. The first man heard the screams too, and before Ryck could react, he turned and took off. Ryck threw the toad, but he misjudged the lead, and he missed the man by centimeters. He started to give chase, but it was obvious that among other strengths, the R-3 was also faster. Ryck gave up after fewer than ten seconds.

The circuit was alive with messages. It was only then that Ryck paused to give himself an update. What he saw made his heart fall. He could see that 14 Marines had been greyed out, another eight were light blue. In less than five minutes, 14 Marines had died. He couldn't take time to identify each one.

He ran back to the lieutenant. The platoon commander was down, one leg gone mid-thigh, the other canted at an awkward angle. The bulk of his PICS was intact, and it had started treatment. He was out cold, but alive. Ryck looked back at the now-destroyed gun. Depending on the type of round, the fuze may not have had time to arm, but the sheer velocity of it was enough to cut down the lieutenant.

There was no time to tend him. He had to get back to the fight. He started running forward when he realized that the fighting was slowing down. The legionnaires were pulling back!

There was an explosion as one of them ran too close to one of Evan's mines, but Ryck couldn't tell the amount of damage the mine might have inflicted. Several legionnaires appeared in front of him. Ryck tossed two of his toads. One missed, but the other struck one of the legionnaires on the lower leg. Both fired at Ryck as they passed, and his alarms went off, but they were not going to stop to keep Ryck under fire.

Ryck turned to see the toad ignite, and the legionnaire started kicking out. A chunk of his R-3 went flying, taking the toad with it. The man went to one knee, then got back up and limped off. Ryck watched all of this from less than 40 meters away without interference.

The battle was over, and Ryck went back to survey the carnage. It was more than he expected. Even when faced by a better-armed force, he had expected to come out victorious. And even if the Marines had "won," if they had carried the field, it was a Pyrrhic victory. Fourteen Marines were dead. From his own squad, Corporal Rey and Corporal Mendoza, Hartono and Martin were dead. With Khouri and Stillwell from earlier, Ryck had six KIA just today. Add Prifit, and he'd lost seven Marines, seven friends. Corporal Winsted and Keiji were down, but alive, but Ryck didn't know how bad they were.

Only Ling, Holleran, and Peretti were combat effective. With Ryck, only four men, just a fire team, were left.

Ryck vomited in his PICS. He gut-heaved until there was nothing left.

"Sergeant L, what are your orders?"

Ryck managed to look up, vomit dripping from his chin. Corporal St. Cyr was on a P2P with him.

"What?" he asked stupidly.

"What are your orders? You've got the platoon now."

He'd been so concerned with his squad that he'd barely noticed the rest. Staff Sergeant Hecs and Sams were light blue. HM2 Grbil had the same rank as Ryck, but as a Marine, command fell to him. He was the senior man. He did a quick check. Including the four of them from Third Squad, he had eight Marines and a corpsman. Nine Federation fighting men to hold off a larger Legion force.

He didn't know what to do.

Chapter 22

"So, what do we do about them? Both are probably going to die unless they get into stasis," Doc asked him.

Ryck looked at the two legionnaires. One was missing an arm and was thankfully unconscious. The other was terribly burned, from the shoulder down through his chest and into his gut and hip. Ryck could see organs exposed in amongst the blackened flesh. The smell was overpowering, and it threatened to make Ryck vomit again. The legionnaire was conscious, and he stared blankly up at Ryck.

Using the toads had been Ryck's idea, and it had seemed so logical at the time. Now he was seeing the effects, what it meant on a personal level.

"You can't do anything else for them?" he asked Doc, who was waiting for a decision.

"Not really. I've cleaned around the damage, but they need help, fast. Especially Gary here," he pointed at the burned legionnaire. "Sorry man, but you should know," he said directly to the man.

Shit, Gary? He knows the guy's name? Ryck thought.

"He's got a falling hemoglobin count, renal failure, and is going into dehydration. The pain is manageable because the nerves have been burnt, but I can't keep his fluids going. He needs intensive care and a long bout of regen, and he needs to get in stasis now," Doc went on, addressing Ryck again.

"And we've got only those last two ziplocks?"

"Yeah, that's it. We never, I mean, before . . ." the corpsman started.

"Not your fault. You took your combat issue. If you hadn't split them up and put those in the bottom of your hole, all of them would have been fried," Ryck assured him.

Before the battle, Doc had broken up his kit, putting half in the bottom of a fighting hole—the other half he carried. When he rushed out to pull back Lance Corporal Dodson in the middle of the fight, he'd been taken under fire. He'd been under the hadron beam for about five seconds, enough for his PICS to survive, but it had fried the ziplocks in his pack. Only the ziplocks he'd had in the hole, out of the reach of energy beams, had survived the battle.

Ryck stopped to survey the scene in front of him. Ling and Denny, the Marine who'd been on OP duty and so had missed the fight, were in their PICS and providing security. Corporal St. Cyr was supervising Peretti and PFC Stamos, one of the surviving Second Squad Marines, in the gathering of the dead legionnaires. Despite the low energy levels in everyone's PICS, the lifting required strength, so the two Marines were in their combat suits. Six legionnaires were lined up to the right of the platoon flank. There were five more, including the one Ryck had killed back at their field piece, left to gather.

On their left flank, 14 Marines were laid out. Corporal Rjils, who had survived the fight, had died before he could get into stasis. Ryck knew Doc blamed himself for that, but Lance Corporal Truth in Means had been just as badly off, and Doc picked Truth in Means first.

Behind of the lines, just over the slight crest, eight Marines were in ziplocks, stasis units on. Ryck turned to look at them. Each Marine had his longjohns cut away, and some showed signs of Doc's field treatment. The lieutenant was in the third ziplock, one leg gone, the other in a pressure bandage. He looked small in the bag, not like the warrior he'd proven himself to be. Ryck knew that could have been him in that ziplock just as easily.

Staff Sergeant Hecs had most of his left shoulder gone, as well as the arm. The white bandages stood out in stark contrast to his dark skin. Sams was more of a torso than a human being, the legs and arms of his PICS giving out under a hadron beam. Two of the Marines looked undamaged, but the remaining three showed obvious scars from the fight. They reminded Ryck of photos he'd seen of fetuses in the womb--fetuses who'd been roughed up, that was.

Two Marines were walking wounded, which was somewhat rare. In modern warfare, anything that could take out a PICS usually took out the Marine inside as well. Stefan Wilz' PICS had started to fail, the shielding on the arm giving out just as the hadron beam quit. Stefan's arm had been immediately paralyzed, but the last gasps of the rest of his PICS' shielding had protected his vital organs. His arm was going to have to come off and be regened, but he wasn't in pain and could function for the near term.

Wilz' fellow First Squad Marine, Lance Corporal Cashew, had taken a huge blow to the head that the PICS had withstood, but even with the cradling, his head had bounced back and forth, giving him a concussion. He was groggy and had a headache, but he could manage.

Two legionnaires were also seriously hurt and had been recovered by the Marines, and Doc wanted to know if they should use their last two precious ziplocks to save their lives.

"On the *Marie's Best*, you went into the ziplock with John. Can you do that here?" Ryck asked.

Doc stood back and looked at the two men.

"How much do you weigh, Gary?" he asked the legionnaire.

"Seventy-eight," the man mumbled.

"And let's say another 80 kg for this guy? Yeah, that should be within limits," Doc said.

"OK, we can't let these guys die, so just put them both in one, and that leaves one for us," Ryck said, coming to a decision.

One for 11 men, he reminded himself.

"Roger. I'll get on it," Doc said.

"Thanks, man. I appreciate it," the legionnaire, Gary, said to Ryck, his words slurred, but clear.

Ryck didn't want the guy's thanks. He just hoped that he hadn't put the rest of the Marines in danger.

He went back to where his PICS stood in silence. He'd managed to clean up most of the vomit, but the inside of the suit still smelled. He was down to 22% on his PICS. There wasn't much he could do about that. He could change out his coldpack, though. A suit that overheated was combat ineffective just as much as one that had been fried. This was his last coldpack, but with the casualties, that wasn't something he had to worry about. There were more than enough coldpacks available now for all the surviving Marines. That macabre thought threatened to take over, and Ryck had to force his mind back to the task at hand.

His M77, though, was a total loss. That was what had been hit during the battle, and something had actually broken the barrel, making it hang at an odd angle. Even if he could find a way to reload, that rifle was not going to be firing again.

He could putter around his PICS, but his real task was to decide what to do now. He could strengthen the defenses the best he could. He could move the men to somewhere else and try to keep out of contact. Or he could take the fight to the legionnaires.

He knew what Sams would have done. Sams would have rushed into the attack. He couldn't help but glance to where Sams' barely surviving body was lying on the ground in a ziplock, at death's door, Doc had said. He wanted to go over there to tell him the joke was over, to just get up and get back to business. Irreverent Sams, ladies' man, and one hell of a Marine. More than that, Sams was his friend.

Frankly, Ryck wasn't sure what was the correct action. Honoring Sams' wishes could get them all killed. Maybe attacking was the right course of action, but maybe not. His lack of intel was frustrating. He had to know how many legionnaires were combat effective.

Ryck knew for certain that twelve legionnaires had been killed: 11 here and one back near the French sailors. Two more were ziplocked and out of the fight. At least three more had been hurt, and Ling had reported seeing another three being helped out of the area. So, there were possibly 20 out of the fight, but at a minimum, 14. But how many had they started with? The lieutenant had guessed they'd had close to the Marines' own 32 before the last fight. That meant they could have anywhere from 12 to 18 left. Ryck had nine effectives and two walking wounded left to face them.

"Lieutenant Nidishchii', Capitaine de corvette Benyamina is offering a temporary cease-fire in order to take care of our dead and wounded. If you agree to this, please respond," came over Ryck's PICS' speaker.

Ryck had powered down most of his energy-eating functions, but the comms had been left open.

Capitaine de corvette? That was the Navy equivalent to a Marine major or Federation lieutenant commander. That was probably the correct rank for a gunboat captain, but why was the Navy getting involved? They were out of the fight as far as Ryck knew.

He reached his PICS and toggled the mic. He almost gave his rank and name then thought better of it.

"You've reached the Federation Marines. What are you proposing?" he sent.

"During today's . . ." there was a pause, ". . . *conflict*, 13 legionnaires did not return. We proposed a three-hour truce so we both can recover our fallen. We are open to your terms, of course."

Ryck looked around at their position. Doc caught his eye and began pointing toward their wounded. They had placed the WIA in back of the slight crest of the high ground in an attempt to keep them out of the line of any energy weapons fire. Just one touch, though, and the ziplocks would fail, the stasis fields with them.

"Wait one, Legion," Ryck said.

"What do you think?" he passed on the open circuit to the rest of the Marines.

"If we can get the WIAs out of the line of fire, I'm all for it," Doc responded.

"Vic?" Ryck asked Corporal St. Cyr.

"It's your call, but if they're sincere, we can use the break and take care of our people," the Corporal answered.

Aye, there's the rub, Ryck thought. *Is this a trick?*

In all his dealings with the Legion, they had acted honorably, even if they were at times arrogant. Ryck made his decision quickly. He went back onto the frequency the Legion had used.

"We agree in principle. We have eleven Legion dead here, two severely wounded and in stasis. You are welcome to come get them. We want to move our own WIA to a safe location out of the way of any potential areas of *conflict*," he said, stressing the same word the legionnaire on the other side had used.

"You have two of our wounded? May we know their names and condition?"

Ryck knew he only was required to give the names of enemy prisoners to the Red Cross, but he didn't hesitate.

"One answers to Gary. He was severely burnt. He was conscious before going into stasis, but he's in pretty serious condition. We don't have the name of the second man. He suffered a traumatic amputation of his arm and is in stasis now as well."

There was a pause, then, "We thank you for the care of our wounded. Will you be moving your own wounded to the same location as the rest of your wounded?"

Shit! They knew where the others were.

Ryck would've liked to get all of the WIAs together, but there wasn't any way he could move eight Marines and two legionnaires that distance with the men he had. That didn't even take into account the dead.

"That's a negative. Are you able to take a grid coordinate?" he asked.

Grid coordinates were just arbitrary points, and there was no guarantee that the French used the same ones as the Federation.

"Yes, we can," came the reply.

Ryck picked out a point about 700 meters off the left flank of their position and sent the coordinates. He couldn't transport the wounded far, but he didn't want to give the French any opportunity to view their defenses. And if the French agreed to his next condition, that would close off one potential avenue of approach.

"We will have your wounded and dead at this position in two hours. We require that there is no maneuver on your side until that time. You may approach with whatever size unit you need to retrieve your men, but no shielding will be engaged. The truce will remain for two hours after that. We will be leaving our own casualties at that spot, so after you withdraw, this area, bounded by the coordinates I sent, will remain a no-fire zone. I am sure you can appreciate the effects of energy weapons on our medical stasis units."

Ryck waited until the response came.

"We agree with your terms but wonder on the position. We think it might be close to your present position and possibly within range of collateral fire."

They realized what Ryck intended, he knew.

Tough shit, take it or leave it.

"We have the ability to honor a no-fire zone. I am assuming you have the same ability. This is the area which we have designated," he said.

There was another pause, then the voice came back, "Very well. We agree to your terms. It is now 0245 Paris Time. We will be at your coordinates as 0445. *Merci.*"

Ryck switched to the platoon circuit and passed, "OK, you heard that. We've got a four-hour truce. Everyone, into your PICS. We've got a lot to do and not much time."

He organized the platoon into work details. A PICS had the strength to carry all of their wounded but not the grip. To keep integrity on the ziplocks, to keep the life-saving bags from getting damaged, each Marine could carry only one ziplocked Marine at a time. With Doc trailing like a mother hen, each of the other eight healthy Marines picked up one of the WIAs and followed Ryck, who had the two legionnaires, to the spot he'd picked. It was just a coordinate chosen at random, nothing special from the map, and when they arrived, it looked no different than any other stretch of forest. Once the set down the WIAs, Ryck left Doc and Cashew with the wounded and jogged his Marines back to their position.

He half-expected that the legionnaires would have taken over the position while they were gone, but it was quiet. Each Marine, including Wilz, took the dead man's handle[28] on the back of those PICS that still had them, or if they didn't, on anything they could grab, and lifted their dead comrades to carry them to the no fire zone. They had to help Wilz hoist Corporal Franks to his shoulder, but once up, the one-armed Marine had no problem. It took two trips, but all the Marines had been moved. Ryck looked at the time. They had an hour left.

The legionnaires, with sleeker armor on their R-3s had less to grab onto, and several times, the dead legionnaires were dropped,

---

[28] Dead Man's Handle: the slang term for a handle on the back of each PICS that is used to pick up and carry it should the PICS become immobilized.

but once again with two trips, each legionnaire was carried to the spot.

Ryck took a look at his Marines. They were a grubby lot, the fighting marring their PICS. Ling and Denny looked the best of them, and Denny had the greatest charge on his PICS, so Ryck told both of them, along with Cashew, to stay. He gave Sergeant St. Cyr his orders. He concluded with what St. Cyr should do if this was a Legion trap.

"If that happens, you're in charge. I'm not going to tell you what to do then. You're going to have to make that decision."

The Corporal looked like he was going to say something, but he stopped and followed the rest back to their position.

Ryck looked around him. He had three Marines with him, to face who knew what? He was going to do this in good faith, though. No surprises, no hidden Marines. He checked over the WIAs, then took a position in the center of them. He had the other three Marines stand behind him. Cashew was wobbly and not totally with it, but all he had to do was stand.

At 0425, Ryck's sensors went off, indicating movement in front of him. The contacts slowly made their way forward, slower than expected. He counted three R-3s, then readings for two more people.

At 0446, the group came into view. One legionnaire led the rest. Two sailors, a man and a woman, followed. Behind them were the last two legionnaires.

Ryck stood still as the first legionnaire walked up to within five meters of him. His face shield was clear, as if he had nothing to hide. A ruddy, round face stared at him. Freckles were plastered across his nose and cheeks.

"Lieutenant . . ." he started, then obviously noticed the sergeant's chevrons Ryck had illuminated on his combat suit's shoulders.

"I'm representing the Federation here," Ryck said.

Ryck could almost see the legionnaire's thoughts as the man's eyebrows scrunched together. He would be wondering if the lieutenant was out of action, or if he was back there somewhere, waiting and watching.

"Very well. Capitaine de corvette Benyamina would like to have word with you."

He stepped to the side, making way for Ryck. Ryck walked forward to the older sailor standing there and waited for the man to start.

It was the woman who spoke, and Ryck had to turn and face her. He felt embarrassed. He had often thought that women could serve just as well as men in the Federation military, and here he was, assuming that the gunship's captain had to be a man.

"Do you have a name?" the woman asked.

Ryck hesitated, but as they already knew his name as a member of the platoon, he replied, "Sergeant Ryck Lysander, sir."

Sir? Is it supposed to be ma'am or something like that?

Capitaine de corvette Benyamina didn't seem to notice as she went on, "Sergeant Lysander, thank you for agreeing to this truce. And thank you especially for taking care of our wounded comrades. You and your commander are men of honor.

"With your permission, I would like to check our wounded?"

Ryck gave his consent, and the male sailor, who had on what Ryck only now noticed was the caduceus of the medical service on his collar, walked forward to where the legionnaires, both WIA and KIA, were laid out. If he thought it strange that two legionnaires were in a single ziplock, he said nothing. He peered at them through the clear walls of the bag and checked the stasis readout. He seemed satisfied and said something in French to his commander.

"We will be removing our two wounded men first, then return for our fallen. If time becomes short, may we contact you for an extension?" she asked Ryck.

"Let's see how the time goes. We will be leaving Lance Corporal Cashew here," Ryck said, pointing at the Marine.

That seemed to take her aback, and she said, "This is new to me. I thought this was to be a no-fire area."

"Lance Corporal Cashew has a concussion. He will not be returning with us," Ryck said, keeping his voice steady, and with what he hoped sounded like conviction.

"Yet he is in your combat suit, which you must acknowledge is an offensive weapon," she countered.

Jonathan P. Brazee

"And as I am sure you have been briefed, our PICS have some basic medical capability. Our corpsman has stressed to me that it would be best if Lance Corporal Cashew remain in his PICS."

"If you keep an armed soldier here, I will have to re-evaluate our position for this area at the conclusion of the truce, Sergeant. You may tell your commander that. Our soldiers will not purposely fire on your wounded, but we would have to treat this area as a potential for combat operations. Would you reconsider your position on that? For the good of your wounded?" she asked.

Ryck thought about it. Cashew, although ambulatory, was in no condition to fight. He barely knew where he was. There was a hard and fast rule in the Marines, and that was not to separate a Marine from his weapon. Cashew's rockets were all expended, though, and while he had 52 rounds left for his M77, those had shown to have little to no effect on the Legion's R-3s.

"If I removed his M77, that gun on his arm, would that satisfy you?" he asked.

The Navy officer went silent, most likely listening to what one of the three legionnaires was telling her over their comms. Ryck wondered if one of them would call Ryck on Cashew's P-gun.

He was relieved when she turned toward him and said, "If you can remove it, that will be satisfactory."

Ryck nodded, something that the PICS read and moved the suit up and down in an approximation. He turned and walked up to Cashew.

"Sergeant Lysander, what was that? You're taking my M77?" Cashew asked on the open circuit, his speech still slurred.

Ryck switched both of them to a P2P. "Look, uh, Spence," he said, after checking Cashew's readout to get his first name. Ryck had forgotten that.

"You've got 52 darts left, and they won't do anything against the R-3s. We need to keep our WIAs safe, and that means here out of the line of fire. I want you to guard them, OK?"

"But how, without a weapon?"

"You've got your P-gun, right? They don't realize that," Ryck said.

"Oh, right. But I can go with you and the lieutenant and fight. I'm good to go."

"I know you are, but I need you here, Spence. I need you to watch over everyone. The lieutenant's here, not back there. He needs you here."

Cashew didn't like the idea of not going back, but orders were orders. Ryck went to remove the M77, but realized he hadn't any armorer tools. The Marines didn't know what to do, but finally went with brute force. With Ling and Denny holding Cashew's arm steady, Ryck grabbed the M77, barely getting his gauntlet fingers under it, then gave it six good yanks. On the sixth, the M77 broke free, the barrel breaking off the receiver embedded in the arm of the PICS.

The gunship commander watched closely, and once Ryck held up the barrel of the M77, she nodded. She signaled the two quiet legionnaires, and they moved forward to their KIAs.

"Taking a Marine's weapon, that's a keister kick circus," someone said.

Ryck turned to see that the legionnaire, the first one to speak, had spoken to him through a directional speaker, which from the look of things, could not be overheard by the rest of his team.

"Don't worry, though, I didn't mention his plasma gun. It's a piece of shit, but a man's gotta have something, you know?"

Ryck didn't know how to respond.

"It's not like he's gonna need it. The captain is by-the-fucking-book, but would never go back on her honor, so no matter what happens, we won't be back here. We've left your guys back at your shuttle alone, too. That's some sailor-boy you've got there, though, by the way. The guy was about shitting his pants when we came up, but he stood up to us, telling us we had to go through him to get at your wounded. No weapons, and he's gonna hold off a bunch of us in our Rigs?"

The shuttle crew chief?

Ryck didn't even remember the guy's name, but he'd have to find that out if they ever made it through this. The guy evidently had balls.

Ryck looked at the legionnaire, wondering just what the man's game was. He seemed sincere, though, and that was surprisingly disarming.

"Hey, where you from?" Ryck asked for lack of anything better to say.

The others turned toward him when he said that. Ryck didn't have a direction speaker, and his voice went out in surround sound.

"Why you askin'?" the legionnaire asked, voice suddenly wary.

Ryck did a quick scan of available nets and directed his AI to initiate a P2P with the legionnaire. To his surprise, a direct connection was made.

"You there?" he asked.

"Yeah, so again, why you askin'?"

"It's just, my dad, he always said that, a 'keister kick circus.' He said it was an Ellison thing."

"No farting? You from Ellison?"

"He said that, too, 'no farting,'" Ryck said with a laugh. "No, my parents were from Ellison, but they immigrated to Prophesy before I was born."

"Got out when they could. Smart folks, your parents. Yeah, Ellison born and raised. Took the Legion route out of town, and I've never looked back. Lots of guys do that."

"Not too many Marines from Ellison, though," Ryck said.

"No farting, Castor. We all go Legion. It was the Marines that broke the general strike in '24. Killed lots of folks. So, the Marines are persona non grata."

Ryck vaguely remembered reading about that. Ellison was a true corporate world, and there had been a worker uprising, not a strike, as this guy was saying. Ryck's grandparents on both sides had been alive then, but he'd never heard any family stories of the time from his parents.

"But that's old news. It's a new age. Whoever thought that GF and the Fed would be at war?" the guy said.

Ryck was suddenly struck at how surreal this was. Greater France and the Federation were at war. A few hours ago, Ryck and this legionnaire had been doing their best to kill each other. Now this guy was chatting as if they were long-lost cousins.

He had an urge to ask the legionnaire how he could still be fighting for the Legion. Whatever the Federation did in his grandparents' time, Ellison was still a Federation world.

"Well, the captain is calling. Looks like we're gonna start hauling the cargo. Nice meeting you," the guy said.

"Hey, you know Ezekiel Hope-of-Life?" Ryck asked.

"No, not really. He a friend of yours?"

"My girlfriend's brother. He's Legion."

"No, sorry. But it's a big Legion, as they say. Look, I gotta run. Hope we don't meet again until the politicos get their heads out of their keisters and end this cluster."

"Sure. Uh, good luck," Ryck said to the legionnaire's retreating back.

"Name's Meyers. Coltrain Meyers. Look me up sometime when this is over, and I'll buy you a beer."

Chapter 23

The truce was officially long gone, but through the night and next day, there had been no sign of the legionnaires. Ryck wracked his brain for a way to take the fight to the Legion, but he couldn't think of anything that would give them even a 10% chance at success. He convened a "war council" of the rest of the Marines and Doc, but no one else had any decent ideas, either.

He kept hoping that the Navy would get back, taking the matter out of his hands, but the airwaves remained silent. He had no idea what was happening out there in the space lanes.

Ryck was a Marine, and now in command of a fighting force. He was supposed to be aggressive. Yet, he was secretly wishing that the legionnaires had been hurt badly, too badly to want to tangle again. On one hand, his emotions threatened to take over when he thought about the Marine dead and wounded. He wanted to exact revenge. On the other hand, the rational part of him realized that the legionnaires were just doing their job. Coltrain Meyers was no different than he was, and his comment was telling. The legionnaires and Marines were not fighting each other because of some deep-seated hate. They were fighting because the politicos were playing statesmanship games, maneuvering for a better hand. This was about economics and who was able to pocket the most.

Just because Ryck couldn't come up with a decent plan to attack the Legion, and just because he hoped the two groups would not clash again, did not mean he could just sit there on his butt doing nothing. He had to plan for the worst. And once he decided to stay in their present position, that meant coming up with a better defensive plan. He didn't have much in the way of resources, so he had to out-think any attackers.

They didn't much in the way of intel. They didn't know where the legionnaires were. They didn't know how many there were or what they had left in the way of weapons. But Ryck had formed several opinions that, if correct, might be put to use.

First, the vaunted R-3's, or "rigs" as Meyers had referred to them, were not as invincible as they were made out to be. They had hadron guns, true, and those were as advertised. However, the armor on the R-3 was not as good as that on a PICS. Their stealth capability disappeared when their gun ports opened, and that capability only worked when they were out of visuals, anyway. The fractured array of the PICS seemed to work even when in line-of-sight, leading Ryck to believe the R-3's relied on electronics even when using visuals, unlike the PICS where the eyeball saw what was through the face shield.

Second, the legionnaires seemed pretty confident in themselves. They had hurt the Marines in their attack, but a frontal attack was something you only did when you knew you had overwhelming superiority of numbers or capability. Ryck had been on a number of frontal assaults, but always when they could overwhelm the enemy. He had to think the Legion worked the same way. But the fact that the Marines had taken out so many legionnaires was a good indication that even without air, even without Navy support, man-for-man, the Marines were a match for the legionnaires. His short chat with Meyers wasn't all-revealing, but the man had sounded confident.

How Ryck was going to make use of those guesses and observations, he wasn't sure, but he had to come up with something.

The issued mines were still emplaced surrounding their position. They hadn't worked in the first assault, but they still formed a barrier by their mere presence. Ryck had Evans make two more of his improvised mines, but without a timer, he had to rig up simple pressure plates. That meant a legionnaire would actually have to step on a mine to set it off. There was only a small chance of that, but any chance had to be taken. Ryck had the position of the two mines entered into the PICS of the Marines so that even in the heat of battle, if it got to that, each member of the platoon would know where the mines were. These mines had no way to distinguish between friend or foe.

Ryck had managed to salvage two more dragonflies. He sent these, along with his last one, out to the most probable avenues of approach. The dragonflies had limited power, normally good for about two hours of total flight time, so he landed them on high branches and powered them down, only using enough juice to send back feeds. It wasn't a perfect warning system, but with the vibration sensors still out there, he thought they would get a good warning in case of someone approaching.

The shuttle's 25mm gun was still working. When the legionnaires had fired on it during the fight, they had used their hadron guns. That had killed Corporal Stuyvestent and PFC Bokaw, but the beam had no effect on the gun itself. It would have taken a shipboard hadron gun to put out enough power to slag metal, and as they didn't even have any electronics for the gun, nothing was affected. At the base level, it was just an iron sight weapon, like an old WWI machine gun. Without its advanced targeting system, it was, in a sense, too primitive to be hurt by the most modern weapons technologies. Of course, that old Vickers gun was designed to be fired with the technology of the time, so it would have been more accurate than the 25mm being fired as the modern gun no longer had any targeting capability. Still, the round itself was deadly to anyone in an R-3. If the Marines could hit them, the legionnaires would go down.

The shuttle's gun was still functional. The same could not be said of the M229. Its firing electronics were fused, so even if the barrel and breach were sound, it could not send a round downrange. Ryck had six rounds for it, but no way to use them. With their electrostatic jacketing, Evans couldn't even come up with a way to jury-rig them into something more useful.

Power reserves on each PICS were woefully low. Without the proper tools, Ryck couldn't even switch out powerpacks with those from any of the fallen Marine's PICS that still had some degree of functionality. Technically, there was a way to vampire power from one suit to another, but that required cabling that Ryck didn't have. Ryck kept everyone out of the suits as much as he could, but some of the preparations required the strength of a PICS, and there was no getting around that.

By the middle of the next night, Ryck had a good deal of his preparations completed. He half-expected an attack during the night. With both the Marines and Legion's equipment, night and day made little difference. But his men were dead on their feet, and Ryck needed them combat-effective. He put six men asleep at a time, keeping up a three-man watch. Ryck took the first watch along with Ling and Perreti.

When he awoke the next morning, the sun was already climbing high in the sky. The night had been quiet. Today, he thought, would be an important one.

Ryck had read in the civilian and military journals, which seemed to be enamored with all things Legion, that the R-3's could operate for four days on a single power charge. This was the fourth day. True, the legionnaires could have been getting out of their R-3's and spending time with the suits powered down, but if they were within 60-70 km, the Marine's own sensors should have been able to pick up the cycling of the suits before the shielding was up to power. Ryck was betting that they were closer than that given the speed at which they had met him to retrieve their two WIA's. In addition, they had been in combat, and that would have depleted their power reserves as well. Ryck knew they had field generators, just as the Marines had, but just as the Marine's generator had gone down with the skipper, he thought any generator would have been destroyed when the *Intrepid* took out the French shuttles.

If there was going to be an attack, Ryck was sure it would happen today. Anything after that would be Marines in longjohns attacking legionnaires in their version of combat suit underwear with pointy sticks.

Ryck looked at their position. It was good, he thought. Possibly enough. But he had to do more. He just couldn't think of what.

"Evans, come here a sec," he called out.

The EOD Corporal walked over and asked, "What's up?"

"I was just thinking, could we take those arty rounds and hoist them up in the trees over there? Then if they come, drop them on top of their heads?"

"Sure, I could rig something up. But we could do that with rocks, too. All it will do is piss them off."

"But the 889 can take out an R-3. We saw that two days ago," Ryck protested.

"Yes, an armed M889 round will destroy an R-3. An 887 would probably, too. But it takes 10 g's of pressure after the breach initiates the sequence to arm one of them, and dropping one from five meters high just won't do it. Sorry, Sergeant L, it just won't work," Evans told him.

"Oh, OK. I'm just trying to think out loud here."

"Look, Sergeant L, me and Nance, we were talking this morning. You've done a great job here, and we think we've actually got a chance if it comes to that. None of us two would've come up with half of this. So, no matter what happens, even if the worst, well, we, I would say all of us, we're proud to be here with you."

Ryck was floored. He'd been feeling like a failure for not coming up with anything better. If the others were counting on him, well God help them with that, but it made Ryck feel honored. If this was going to be his last day, at least he was with men he respected, men about whom he felt proud.

"I . . . it's me who is proud. All of you," he said, speaking louder and addressing the rest of them. "All of you, I couldn't wish for a better group of Marines, of brothers. I am proud to be here with you."

There was a chorus of oohrahs from the Marines, from *his* Marines.

As if on cue, the alarm sounded from his PICS. Ryck ran over to it and clamored inside. The feed from one of the dragonflies was dead. Ryck ran back the recording, and just a few moments ago, it picked up the slightest movement in the trees before going dead. Ryck went back and froze it at the last second it was live, then had his AI enhance it. He couldn't see anything concrete, but he didn't have to. They were on their way.

"OK, Marines, enough of this mutual love fest. They're on their way. Everyone into your positions, now!"

There was the slight, almost inaudible hum as his PICS powered up. Ryck checked his power level first: 14%. This was going to be it, whatever *it* turned out to be, with this particular PICS. He checked the other suits as they powered up. None were over 22%.

PFC Ling and Private Peretti stopped in front of him and saluted. Ryck brought his PICS to attention and returned the salute to the two Marines standing in front of him in their longjohns. They were not going to be in their PICS. They had volunteered to man the 25 mm. Each had a tarnkappe. A dead PICS had been dragged over in front of the gun, hopefully providing cover from any Legion sensors. Behind the gun, the two Marines were to hide under their tarnkappes, and when they had targets, they were to fire. Without their face shield displays, though, their AI's could not get enough data points to form an image of the legionnaires, so they would have to wait until the legionnaire's gun ports opened, spoiling their stealth profile. With the naked eye, though, even when under full stealth, the R-3s gave enough hints so the two Marines should be able to pick up something.

If they made it out of the fight, Ryck would make sure Peretti regained some of his lost rank and Ling got a meritorious promotion as well. If *anyone* made it out of this, Ryck would fight for meritorious promotions.

The Marines had no surprises downrange, unless someone stepped on one of the mines. They just had to sit and wait. A surprisingly small number of vibration sensors sounded—Ryck hoped that meant that the legionnaire numbers were few.

From over 500 meters out, Ryck's display started picking up readings. The AI's quickly identified them as two R-3s. There was no way they should be able to pick them up. That meant that either this was part of their cyberwarfare games, or more hopefully, that those two R-3s were damaged. Even if that were the case, Ryck still didn't know how many undamaged R-3s were out there.

They were not coming in from the same direction, into the teeth, such as they were, of the defense. They were working from the flank, evidently trying to roll up the Marines. Ryck had guessed correctly, but that still didn't ensure anything. He'd had two other contingencies depending on the legionnaire's approach, but this way, none of the Marines had to move to alternate positions.

Keep it steady, he silently thought to his men.

The legionnaires didn't stop their advance. Previously, their field piece had taken a deadly toll on the Marines, and if they had another, Ryck's plan would be stillborn. However, nothing was fired, and as the legionnaires closed to within 300 meters, Ryck let out a breath he hadn't realized he was holding. He now doubted they had another field piece.

Ryck's AI picked up another R-3. Its shielding was obviously in better condition, but not good enough. That was at least three legionnaires, by his count, all with some degree of damage, or at least degradation, to their suits.

Ryck watched his display closely, looking for any surprises. If the three in front were a feint, a force attacking from either side of them could be disastrous. With the legionnaire's this close, the Marines could not move to their alternate positions without giving themselves away.

A few moments later, the first legionnaire opened fire, suddenly appearing on Ryck's display. That was the fourth legionnaire identified. One of the previously noted legionnaires opened fire, too.

Steady! Ryck willed to the rest.

Nine seconds later, the PICS 20 meters to Ryck's right front started to send up sparks before dying.

"Hell yeah!" he whispered excitedly to himself as the two more legionnaire's opened fire, one, someone brand new.

Five legionnaires were in the attack, firing at Marine PICS unheeded. The current target lasted only five seconds before going up. That was longer than Ryck had hoped. That had been Staff Sergeant Hecs' PICS, and it had been a miracle that they'd even been able to get the thing powered up. It had to have been leaking like a sieve, so the legionnaires couldn't have missed it.

Within moments, seven legionnaires were advancing, firing their hadron guns. In quick succession, four empty PICS were fried. The Marines only had three more that they'd managed to power up, or at least make them seem to be powered up, and then the seven of them that had the Marines and Doc inside, so Ryck was relieved when the legionnaires quit firing. They'd finally noticed that no one was firing back.

Come on, baby, come one, he thought. *Just a little closer.*

Ryck watched them on his display. They had stopped about 50 meters out. He wished he could listen in, but he imagined them trying to figure out what was up, what trick the Marines had planned.

After a few moments, two of the legionnaires retreated, as if to provide security.

Grubbing shit! thought Ryck.

He wanted them together, checking out the apparently abandoned position.

Five of them did come forward. Ryck crouched in his fighting hole, waiting. They were on complete passive sensing. They couldn't talk. Ryck knew there was no way the legionnaires could listen in to one of their circuits, but the mere fact that there was a transmission would be enough to alert the legionnaires that not all of the PICS power emissions were from empty combat suits.

Come on guys, it's up to you, he pleaded with Peretti and Ling.

He was tempted to open up a comms link. They were the ones to initiate the attack.

When the 25 mm gun opened up, despite expecting it, Ryck about jumped out of his skin. With more of a scramble than a leap, he was out of the extra deep fighting hole he had dug.

In an instant, he saw that two of the legionnaires were down, the rest darting out of the way. Ryck threw the toad he had ready at the legionnaire nearest him, not even 15 meters away. The toad struck the legionnaire on the shoulder before bouncing off.

What the . . . ?

They'd adapted. They knew what a toad was, and had applied some sort of lubrication, like what the Marines used on their gauntlets to handle the toads, to their R-3's.

Their adjustment wasn't perfect, however. To his left, a toad was burning a hole in the hip of another legionnaire. The R-3 started to split open as the legionnaire inside initiated an emergency molt.

Ryck's alarms went off as a hadron beam touched him, but then the beam was gone.

The 25 mm continued its chatter, but unless the targets were already in the line of fire, it was hard to horse the thing around and aim it. One of the legionnaires leveled his arm at it, but instead of a beam, the muzzle of a KE gun appeared. It looked too big for the Legion version of the M77, so it was probably their 10 mm gun. The legionnaire fired a burst at Peretti and Ling, but then the guy took a direct hit from Cowboy, Lance Corporal Manteo Silver, their last HGL gunner.

The legionnaire spun around, quicker than Ryck thought possible in a combat suit, and returned fire. Ryck started sprinting forward, but another hadron beam touched him, and he had to stop to throw his last toad. He missed the 20-meter throw, but the legionnaire saw the toad coming and stopped firing to get out of the way.

Meanwhile, Cowboy and the legionnaire traded shots like old-time duelists until one of Cowboy's grenades broke through, and the legionnaire fell back, smoke pouring from what used to be his belly.

Things were happening quickly, and it was hard to keep track of events. Ryck saw Ling jumping over the PICS that had been used to mask the 25 mm, his gloved hand holding one of Evan's bullfrogs. In his longjohns, even the slightest touch of a hadron beam would kill him. Ryck wanted to tell him to get back, but Ling had taken matters into his own hand and had launched the bullfrog. Ryck couldn't see where it landed or even who was the target.

Ryck tried to find another target when beside him, Lance Corporal Denny exploded, blood and PICS parts pelting Ryck. Ryck stared for a moment in shock. One moment, Denny was there, the next, he was in pieces. One of the legionnaires, one of the two who had retreated to provide security, had charged back into the fray. He had another KE gun deployed, but what did they Legion have on its R-3's bigger than their 10 mm?

Anger flowed through Ryck. Denny was gone, just like that, and this mother grubbing fucker was to blame. The legionnaire had swung about to take another Marine under fire, and Ryck charged.

He had one weapon left, his plasma gun. His energy charge was at 9%. That had to be enough, he hoped with all his might. But he had to close the gap. He was too far away. He flipped off his attitude stabilizers to be able to coax the last bit of speed out of his tired PICS.

It took only seconds, but time slowed down. Twenty meters, fifteen. At 10, the legionnaire realized what was happening. He started to swing his gun around.

Too late mother fucker! Ryck thought with glee as he triggered his plasma gun.

And nothing happened.

Ryck's PICS simply didn't have enough power, which meant that without a weapon, Ryck was charging a fully armed legionnaire in an R-3.

By instinct, Ryck's training kicked in. MacPruitt's MCMA class flashed through his brain. He dropped down, almost to the ground as the legionnaire fired, the round going off over his head. From that position, he lunged forward as hard as he could as the legionnaire took a step back, another round going high.

Ryck hit the legionnaire in the chest with the force of a small tank. The R-3 had pretty powerful stabilizers of its own, and they increased power to keep the legionnaire upright, but they were not designed with a charging PICS in mind. Ryck and the legionnaire crashed to the ground, Ryck on top of his enemy.

"You mother fucker!" he screamed in almost inarticulate rage as he pulled back his gauntleted fist and smashed it into the legionnaire's face shield.

The legionnaire tried to struggle, to throw Ryck off of him, but his own R-3's attempts to right him back to his feet interfered with his efforts.

Ryck reared back and hit again, his mind losing itself in animalistic, single-minded violence.

"This is for Denny!" he screamed, hitting again.

"This is for Rey!" he shouted as he struck.

"This is for Hartono, for Priffit, for Khouri!"

Bam, bam bam. The face shield began to crack.

"Mendoza, Martin!"

The face shield shattered. As Ryck pulled his gauntleted hand back again, a ruddy, freckled face looked up at him, bloody and in sheer terror, mouth open to plead for his life. Ryck didn't hesitate.

"And this is for my friend Sams!" he shouted, driving his fist through the face shield mount and through the head of Coltrain Meyers, pulverizing it. Hunks of brain matter, bone splinters, and blood spattered over him, covering his own face shield and blocking most of his view.

Ryck didn't stop, again and again he struck, each time, going through the list of men, of brothers, who had fallen, not just here on this godforsaken planet, but since he'd been in the Corps.

Davis, Wan, Nbele, Smith, Peale, Popo--damn it all—Coudry, Rjils, Greuber, Dodson, even going back to recruit training with Yount and Hyunh. Stuyvestent, Bokaw. With each name, he pounded the legionnaire's corpse.

"Sergeant L, Sergeant L, it's over. You can stop," a voice finally registered.

The voice had been yammering on for a while, an incessant whine, but it only then started to coalesce into something he recognized as human speech. Ryck finally paused in his assault and looked up. He tried to wipe some of the mess off his face shield, but mostly just pushed it around. He could see Ling standing there though, in his longjohns. Two Marines in PICS stood beside him, but Ryck's face shield was too smeared to make out who they were.

"Huh?" he said in a daze.

"It's over Sergeant L," Ling told him, speaking slowly and clearly as if to a child. "It's over, and we won."

Ryck rolled off the dead legionnaire and slowly got to his feet. Tears and snot were flowing down his face.

It's over?

Ling said they'd won, but it sure the hell didn't feel that way, that anyone had won.

Chapter 24

Ryck stared at Doc Grbil. The corpsman's face had finally relaxed. It had been a rough hour, and watching Doc pass had been painful, but Ryck was numb. He had no more tears to shed.

The son-of-a-bitch didn't need to have died. Three Marines had been killed in the final battle: Denny, Stamos, and Yuan. Peretti had been hit by shrapnel and suffered a serious head wound, and he needed stasis. One of the two surviving legionnaires, the one who had molted from his burning R-3, had also been seriously hurt with third-degree burns over a good portion of his body, and much of his flesh had been burnt away. Doc and the other legionnaire had also been wounded, but Doc assured Ryck that they would make it, and he needed to double up Peretti and the burned legionnaire in the last remaining ziplock. Despite his misgivings, Ryck gave the OK, not that Doc needed it on medical matters, where he could overrule Ryck if he so chose.

Several hours after the two were put into stasis, Doc had collapsed. He had hidden the extent of his wounds. His gut had been torn apart. He had to have known how serious his wounds were, that he had to get into stasis if he was going to have a chance to survive, but he hid that, giving up his own life to save a grubbing legionnaire. That was not a fair trade by any stretch of the imagination. The four Marines stood by helplessly as Doc suffered until he couldn't take it anymore and agreed to a pain block. Doc's last hour was better, if only in a relative sense. He took one final breath, then no more.

Ryck had boarded the *Intrepid* as part of a Marine company. Of that company, over the last few days, Second Platoon probably died abandoned in space. Third, First, part of Weapons platoon, along with company HQ, had launched for the planet's surface. Only Third actually landed with the rest blown out of the sky. Of those who made it down, Ryck had managed to keep only three other Marines alive and unhurt. Four, if he was counted. Four Marines out of an entire company.

A Marine company was nothing in the grand scheme of things. When entire ships the size of the *Bismarck* were lost, with thousands of sailors and Marines onboard, what was one company? Third Platoon had been trapped on Weyerhaeuser in their tiny slice of the war while hundreds of Navy ships slugged it out. He looked over at the legionnaire, Legionnaire de 1ere classe Khalid Ramzy. One of the 25 mm rounds had pierced his R-3, creasing his chest and cutting his pecs open. Doc had sprayed the gouge shut and told Ryck the wounded man would survive. The legionnaire had seen what Ryck had done to Coltrain, though, and now refused to look him in the eye. His fear was almost palpable.

The legionnaire's fear was misplaced. Ryck's anger was spent. He knew Khalid was just someone trying to get by, just as Coltrain had been. He'd used the Legion to escape the corporate madhouse of Ellison, never imaging that someone with Ellison roots was going to smash his brains out on yet another corporate fiefdom.

Ryck regretted it now. If he could take it back, he would. But there were no mulligans in war.

Of the four Marines, only one PICS had any power left. They had only their small 2 mm Rugers. If the French sailors mounted an attack, Ryck wasn't sure they could fend them off.

Ryck was tired. He gave Ling, who seemed to be a fountain of energy, the first watch. He lay down on the dirt and had drifted off to a dreamless sleep when Ling shook his arm, waking him.

"Sergeant L, we've got company," Ling told him.

The other two Marines were groggily waking up when a huge shape passed over them, instantly wiping away any dregs of fatigue.

At first, Ryck thought the *Intrepid* had made finally returned and had sent down a shuttle to pick them up. That momentary flash of joy was dashed, though, when the make of the shuttle became clear. It was French.

"Shit," Corporal St. Cyr simply said, succinctly reflecting all their feelings.

They looked to Ryck. If he told them to fight, he knew they would fight. But to what end? He'd probably get court-martialed when all this was over, but he wasn't going to waste the three Marine's life on a futile gesture.

"Hey Khalid, it looks like your buddies are here," he started, before a voice poured down from the above.

"Federation Marines, we are from the Greater French ship *Forbin*. Please do not fire upon us. The war is over. We repeat, the war is over. We are here to retrieve all French personnel. We already have retrieved your wounded and dead from the other site, and we've been informed that you have more in this area. We offer you the same courtesy. If you have any French personnel with you, please make them available. Please acknowledge this on Universal."

Ryck stared in shock as the shuttle kept circling, moving in and out of his line of sight because of the trees. The voice started repeating the same message.

"Well, what do you think?" he asked the other three. "Is this a trick?"

"If it is, I'm not sure we can do anything about it," St. Cyr said. "I think a squad of girl scouts could probably handle us about now. We're out of any real weapons, and almost out of supplements. Besides, I've heard the French Navy chow is pretty good," he said bitterly.

The three waited for his decision. There really wasn't any decision to make, though. Circumstances had made it for him.

"Khalid," he said again, "if this is another French trick, I hope you remember that we gave you medical treatment, you and your buddy there."

He walked over to St. Cyr's PICS, the only one with any power left, reached in, and toggled the Universal.

"French shuttle, this is Sergeant Ryck Lysander, United Federation Marine Corps. We have two legionnaires here, both wounded, one in stasis. You are welcome to land and pick them up. As for us, if we can hitch a ride back to a Federation ship, we would sure appreciate it."

Alexander
February 27, 311 (Standard Reckoning)

Chapter 25

Ryck stared at the Navy Cross, hanging crookedly on the chest of his dress blues blouse. He was torn about it. As he'd said during the ceremony after the commandant had pinned it on him only an hour ago, this was for those who hadn't made it. In that manner it was a fitting tribute. However, Ryck knew the award had also been a political statement.

At the conclusion of hostilities, the Federation had rushed to declare victory. Buckets of medals had been awarded, and all in record time. No less than 18 Federation Novas had been awarded, mostly to Naval commanders, but Doc Grbil received one posthumously, and a living Marine captain in 2/3 had been awarded one. Normally, the Nova took up to two years to be vetted and awarded, but those 18 had flown through the process in less than five months.

Lieutenant Nidishchii' had been awarded the Navy Cross, too, presented to him earlier in the morning at his bedside in regen. Every other Marine in the platoon had been awarded a Silver Star. Ryck had done a quick search, and never in the history of the Corps had an entire unit been awarded Silver Stars. Now, his platoon and the entire company from 2/3 had received them. The whole thing reeked of politics.

That was not to say that Ryck didn't think his Marines deserved to be commended. They had kicked ass in a very trying situation. They deserved whatever they got. It was just the political grandstanding tainted the awards, Ryck thought.

The Federation declared victory, and merely going by numbers of men and ships lost, there was a basis for that claim. The

Federation had lost 12 capital ships, the largest being the *Bismarck*. Over 20,000 sailors had died, as had 1,914 Marines. The Greater French alliance had lost 38 ships, 25,000 sailors, 2,400 legionnaires, and a handful of allied soldiers and Marines. The numbers were heavily skewed to the Federation, which wasn't surprising given their overwhelming superiority in naval forces. Actually, it was surprising to Ryck that the numbers weren't even more lopsided.

But what had been gained? Greater France was still not a full member of the Federation. They still had their government in Paris. Not only that, but they had also managed to extract a concession on tariffs. Only they could place import or export tariffs on goods going into or out of their territory. This had been one of their key complaints that had led to the conflict.

The French had remained mostly quiet about the terms of the peace agreement, just issuing the obligatory comments about regretting any misunderstandings and hoping for a prosperous and cooperative future. The blogosphere was live with accusations of the Federation "capitulating," but from Greater France itself, the media was mostly quiet.

Ryck knew the real reason that the war had ended so abruptly, though. When the Legion suicide team had taken the Siren Corporation's mine on New Lancashire, the Federations largest source of erbium, the vital rare earth needed for the manufacture of ship hulls, fighter craft, and even parts of Marine PICS, they threatened to set off a dirty bomb, which would somehow chain react, contaminating the resource. Without a source of erbium, commerce would dry up as shipbuilding would cease, and those already in service would eventually lose their ability to use bubble space.

Of course, it didn't help that Siren Corp was owned by retired and current admirals and a few other high-ranking government officials. The Council was willing to spend Navy and Marine lives to "bring Greater France to the negotiating table," but threaten their individual financial bottom lines, and the war was over, just like that.

There had never been a way for the French to win a conventional war with the Federation. But they had figured out how to hurt the men in charge, and that was enough to get their basic demands met.

The legionnaire who had led the assault on the mine, breaking through the FCDC officers protecting it, was none other than Commandant Nicholas Gruenstein, the ex-liaison to Third Marine Division. Ryck guessed that the major had pretty much erased any black mark the Legion had given him for the failed negotiations on Soreau.

Ryck removed his medal bar and the free-hanging Navy Cross medal that had just been pinned on his chest. He needed to switch to a medal bar which held each award in place. He'd already had two of them made, with all his previous awards as well as the new Navy Cross, both different in only the last medal on the bar. He considered both for the hundredth time, then chose the second one, pinning it to his blouse. The bar was getting a little crowded. Any more medals and he'd have to go to two rows.

He checked the time. He was tempted to try a quick cam with Hannah. Things had been a little strained after they found out that Ezekiel had been killed on some unnamed moon in the Second Quadrant, but things between them were getting back to normal. He wanted to make a stop before the ceremony, though, so he figured he didn't have enough time.

He took the blouse off the hanger and put it back on, checking himself in the mirror. The rocker under his chevrons looked good, he had to admit to himself. Staff Sergeant Ryck Lysander, meritoriously promoted, turned and left his quarters.

He had to stop as other SNCO's offered their congratulations as he walked, or tried to walk, down the passage. The SNCO barracks, the "Holiday Inn," was packed as Marines were getting into their own blues, and it seemed as if each SNCO had something to say to him. It felt weird to have gunnies, even the master and first sergeants, treating him like that. He made it through their gauntlet and out into the quad. Passing between C and D barracks, it was only 50 meters to Franz Hall, the home of the gen hens.

It felt like he'd never left as he entered the front hatch. He'd spent over a year as a guest there, and it held mixed memories—mostly bad though. The corpsman on duty looked up, then when he saw who it was, went back to his PA. Ryck had a routine that he tried to follow each day. He checked on each of the Marines from the platoon. Peretti was still in an induced coma and back at the hospital, and Justice and Tally had finished regen and had been released back to their units. Sams wasn't even on Alexander—he'd been casevac'd all the way to Earth, something of a miracle that he was still breathing. The rest, though, except for the lieutenant who was at the officers' quarters, were there.

Ryck started his rounds. Most of them had already left for the ceremony. Keiji was going to be standing in formation, by his special request, but the rest were going to be in the bleachers with the rest of the gen hens. Corporal Winsted and Lance Corporal Cashew were there, though, and Ryck chatted with them for a few minutes. Both had their Silver Stars mounted, and both commented on Ryck's Navy Cross.

Checking the time, Ryck made his excuses and took the elevator to the fifth deck. This was the SNCO's deck, and seven of the twelve quarters were occupied. Two men, a gunny and another staff sergeant, had been discharged only this morning to get them back with their units for the ceremony.

He knocked on one of the hatches.

"Come in!" a voice shouted.

He opened the hatch and walked in. Staff Sergeant Hecs was getting ready to put on his blouse. The left sleeve of his blues had been removed due to the heavy regen cage that surrounded his growing arm, but still, getting the arm and cage through the sleeve opening could be difficult.

"Hey, good timing. Can you help me with this thing?" he asked Ryck.

"Sure, Staff Sergeant," Ryck answered, stepping up to help.

"What the hell, Ryck, what have I told you? Two weeks already with your rocker, and it's still staff sergeant to me?"

Ryck hadn't too much trouble with the other SNCOs, but even after fighting side-by-side with the man, Ryck still tended to see Staff Sergeant Hecs as his hard-ass heavy hat DI.

"It's Hecs, Hector, Asshole. Even 'King Tong.' Just not 'Staff Sergeant.'"

Ryck grimaced. No matter what, "Hecs" was still, in many ways. "King Tong" to him.

"Of course, I knew what you called me. You think you were the first to come up with that oh-so-clever name? You've got to remember, you were my fifth platoon, and each one thought they had come up with it."

"Well, uh, it kinda fit. You were rather, uh, animal on us," Ryck said sheepishly.

"Sure was. You negats needed it. You seemed to have come out OK," Hecs said, before continuing. "You know what, though? None of you little wannabes knew something. You called me King Tong, but you know I am Thai, right?"

Ryck didn't know, but he nodded.

"In Thai, 'ting tong' means crazy. So Ting Tong King Tong. I just thought that was pretty freaking funny. Hell, I called myself that. I had to keep from laughing anytime I overheard you guys. Did you ever see my I Love Me Wall?"

Ryck had seen it, of course. He'd never really looked at it in any great detail when he was a sergeant. NCO's didn't pry into SNCOs' lives.

"Go take a look at my drill field plaque."

Ryck walked up to it, saw the drill field emblem, then below it was his name:

Sergeant "Ting Tong King Kong" Hector Phantawisangtong
Feb 22, 306 to July 3, 309

"See, we even had it put on the plaque. We all put our nicknames on them. If you make it there, and I am recommending that you do, you'll get your own, I'm sure."

"Really? You think I should go to Camp Charles?"

"Damn right, I do. You would do great there, and frankly, it's a stepping stone you need if you ever want to make sergeant major."

"I don't know. I've got my best buddy there, and he hates it. He keeps wanting to get into combat."

Hecs eyeballed Ryck's chest and said, "I think you've got enough combat for now, Ryck."

Hecs looked closer at Ryck's ribbon, then said, "I see you went with your *Croix de guerre.*"

"Yeah, I had two bars made up, one with and one without. I was torn. We just fought them, for God's sake. We lost good men. But I don't know. It wasn't like the legionnaires chose to fight us, just like we didn't choose to fight them. We all were just following orders. Orders that were there for grubbing bank accounts, not for freedom or defense."

"Oh, sounding cynical there, Ryck. I think Sams would approve. He always thought you accepted too much, you know?"

"Yeah, fucking Sams. He's a cynic, that's for sure. I miss that bastard," Ryck said quietly before asking Hecs, "You think I shouldn't wear it?"

"Look at mine."

Ryck only then really looked at Hecs' blues. There, the last medal in his row, was his *Croix de guerre.*

"Fuck them if they don't like it," Hecs said. "So, you here to gab, or are you going to help me get this thing on?"

Ryck held the blouse, maneuvering it around so Hecs could slide his arm through. They checked each other's uniforms, making sure each was squared way, then left to attend the ceremony.

The Birthday Remembrance was held on February 27 each year, the anniversary of the forming of the *Infantería de Marina* back in 1537, Old Reckoning. While the November 10 Birthday Celebration was just that, a celebration, the February 27 ceremonies were more somber occasions. While a toast might be lifted to fallen comrades, drunkenness was frowned upon. The most important activity during the day was the reading of the fallen. Each and every Marine who had died during the year had his name read aloud in front of those still left behind.

This year's reading was going to take a long time. Ninth Marines had lost 1,214 Marines and sailors, most in 1/9 and the regimental headquarters. That would take about an hour and a half to read the names.

As they arrived in back of the parade deck, Ryck said goodbye to Hecs and started walking to where 2/9 was forming. A face in the regimental headquarters caught his eye, a Marine who had not deployed but who had stayed back with the rear party to assist in sending forward replacements.

Ryck walked up to the sergeant and stood there until the sergeant noticed him.

"Staff Sergeant," he said to Ryck, looking stiff and uncomfortable.

"Sergeant MacPruit. You can be a royal asshole. You know that, right?" Ryck asked.

MacPruit locked his eyes over Ryck's shoulder, focusing on nothing.

"But, and I say this with all sincerity, you saved my life on Weyerhaeuser. "

MacPruit broke his escape gaze to stare at Ryck in confusion.

"I know you were getting back at me back in your class when you broke my arm. But the class was effective. I don't know how much you were told about what happened, but when I was weaponless and faced with an armed legionnaire, of all people, it was you who came to me, telling me what to do. I reacted, just as you had taught. And because of that, I'm here today. I just want to thank you."

Ryck held out his hand, and MacPruit hesitantly took it.

"You're still a grubbing asshole, but I would be proud to serve with you anytime," Ryck said, and he meant it.

MacPruit colored, his face turning red, and he said, "You made us all proud. The whole Marine Corps knows you. And if you say I helped at all, well, thank you. I am humbled. I may be an asshole, like you say, I know. But I do respect you, and thank you for your words."

He seemed to want to say something else, but then let it go. He could imagine MacPruit's guilt, alive only because he had been left in the rear with the gear. Ryck hoped MacPruit would realize that he had contributed after all.

"Well, we're forming up. I've got to go," Ryck said, then hurried back to Golf Company.

Captain Quartermain was the new company commander, but commander of a gutted company. Second Platoon was at full strength. Not one of them had died. They had boarded the abandoned French ship, then basically sat out the war after managing to return life support to the aft crew spaces and holing up there until rescued. Ryck had thought they were all dead, and to find out that each Marine had survived had been a welcome piece of news.

With five new Marines, Third Platoon's formation was up to nine with Keiji joining them again for the ceremony. Ryck was the acting platoon commander. There had been talk about disbanding the platoon, even temporarily, but Ryck had fought that, saying both the platoon commander and platoon sergeant were still alive, as were a number of the rest. As a "war hero," his opinion had actually carried some weight.

First Platoon, though, had been disbanded. It would be reinstated later, once the personnel situation had stabilized.

The regiment formed up, and led by a single drummer, his leopard skin draped in black, marched onto the parade deck.

The regimental headquarters led the way. Following them was 1/9. Sergeant Mark Tillhouse carried the battalion colors, a black streamer joining the other battle streamers, signifying their unit awards over the battalion's years of service. Behind him, the other two surviving Marines marched. They were in turn followed by the new cadre staff of about 30 Marines.

Slowly, the rest of the regiment marched in. No music was played. Only the steady beat of the drummer kept a lonely cadence. When the regiment was formed, the Commandant of the Marines marched forward, taking the new regimental commander's salute. With the *Bismarck* Marines constituting the single largest loss of life, the commandant had travelled to Alexander for this year's ceremony. He was accompanied by a large news contingent that was anxious to film the reading of names. Rumor had it that the commandant had wanted to make this a closed ceremony but had been overruled. It took someone very high on the pecking order to overrule the Marine commandant on something like that.

Without an order being spoken, the regimental sergeant major's voice rang out with "Ninth Regimental Headquarters: Jerome William Able."

For a last call, ranks were never given. A Marine was a Marine.

Master Gunnery Sergeant Teleste was next with "John King Accord."

Then it was back to the sergeant major with "Antonio Salcedo Pious Accounte."

Back and forth, one after the other, they took turns, solemnly reading out each name. Ryck recognized a few. The colonel, of course. The sergeant major. Several of the NCO's. When they got to 1/9, Ryck could feel the tension increase. He knew the news hounds would be salivating, the reading of the Marines of the "Lost Battalion."

Ryck's back started to bother him, but he stood stock-still. He hoped Keiji was doing OK. Regen took a lot out of a person.

The list of names went on: Kellen Lin Huang . . . Francis Kipriyanov . . . George Victor Lodgepole.

Finally, the sergeant major intoned "Second Battalion, Ninth Marines."

Ryck and the rest tightened up their position of attention.

All the Marines in the headquarters and 1/9 had their names read out in alphabetical order as they had died at the same instant, more or less. With 2/9, things were different. It started the same, with the company headquarters and First Platoon Marines' names being read in alphabetical order, then those killed when the shuttle went down.

Ryck had to swallow when he heard the master guns call out "Paul Pope."

Rest in peace, brother, Ryck thought, the tears that had been welling in his eyes beginning to stream down his cheeks.

After "Francis Sylian Westminster," the last of those who had died on the shuttle, though, each name was read in the order in which he had fallen.

"Tipper Prifit," the sergeant major said, the first of Ryck's squad.

Ryck felt dizzy as he heard the name. He wanted to take a knee. It took an extreme amount of willpower to remain at attention.

"Botros Khouri."

"Jeb A. Stillwell."

"Uriah Sampson Martin."

Those were the first three to fall in the first battle.

"Priest Randall Hennesy . . . Giant Luck . . . Griffin L. Holderstead . . . Lin Chan Ho. . . Rosario Gambino" from First and Second Squads.

"Tizzard Fu Rey."

Ryck could see his corporal, sitting in ships berthing laughing uproariously at one of his own stupid jokes.

"Hartono."

Hartono was always a boot to Ryck. The guy only had one name, for goodness sake, and fervently avoided any nickname. It was against his religion, he maintained.

"Albert Gomez Smith," from First Squad.

"Jorge Jesus Jacamba Mendoza."

The last of his squad to fall. But all the Marines were his, not just those in his squad. He was in command when the next five fell.

"Jan Rjils."

"Pacscal Stamos."

"Evan John Denny."

"Lawrence Peter Yuang."

And finally, "Harris Theodore Grbil."

These were men that Ryck had led, led them to their deaths. Ryck swore to himself that he would etch their names in his memory. As long as he remembered them, they were not gone.

Ryck felt a surge of guilt, guilt that had been building up since he had been taken aboard the French shuttle and flown off the planet. Why had he survived, without really a scratch, when so many had died? Was he really meant to be a leader? Everyone was telling him he was some sort of hero, but he'd just been lucky. Only he wasn't so sure that was a good thing.

He'd killed human beings. Not crazed terrorists like the SOG. Just normal guys. If Ezekiel Hope-of-Life had been facing him, Ryck would have cut him down in a heartbeat. The brother of Joshua, the brother of Hannah. He'd have killed the man, simply because Ezekiel had turned right instead of left into the Legion office back when he'd enlisted.

He'd killed men, beating one to death with his fists. Civilized people just didn't do that.

More damning, he'd gotten his own men killed.

Lost in his thoughts, Ryck hadn't noticed that the long list had finally reached the end. The sergeant major and master guns, their voices hoarse, stood back. A lone Marine marched onto the parade deck.

The classic Amazing Grace reached out as the Marine bagpiper poured his soul into his music. The mournful sounds reverberated among the Marines, and somehow, they cleansed Ryck's thoughts. When the last notes faded away, Ryck stood up straighter. He would miss his men, his friends. But the best way to honor them would be to become a better Marine, a better leader.

Could he have done a better job? Could he have brought home more of his Marines? He was sure of it. And if it ever came to that again, he was going to be better prepared, he would make better decisions.

There was no march in review. The regimental commander saluted the commandant, then turned to dismiss the regiment. There would be six services at the two chapels, a service for each recorded faith of the fallen Marines and sailors, and Ryck decided he was going to attend each one.

Prophesy

Epilogue

"You don't want to see your sister first?" Joshua asked.

"No, I cammed her before we landed. She understands." Ryck said.

"OK. I just thought you'd want to get cleaned up first."

"I'm grubbing nervous enough as it is. Waiting any longer will just make it worse," Ryck told his friend. "Do you really think this is the right thing to do?"

"You kidding me? Of course, it is."

"Yeah, but now? With, you know?"

"Look, Ryck. Shit happens, and this has been a horrible year. Not your fault, not my fault. The guys on top, they play their games, and it's the troops in the trenches who pay the price. It's always been that way, from the Greeks to us here now."

"Yeah, but . . ."

"But nothing. Life goes on. If things are meant to be, they are meant to be," Joshua went on.

They sat in silence as the cab brought them closer. The taxi driver was studiously ignoring them, but Ryck could catch him glimpse at them in the mirror every so often.

Both men were in civvies. Ryck hadn't even brought a uniform with him. But they had the air of soldiers about them. Prophesy was behind the Federation, and most people had bought the Federation's grand claim of victory. The driver had to be wondering if the two were Marines, Navy, or Legion. If he said the wrong thing, he could be jeopardizing his potential tip.

"So, what do you think?" Ryck asked, pulling his thoughts away from the driver.

"Don't rightly know," Joshua said matter-of-factly.

"But she's your sister. Hasn't she said anything to you?"

"Hey, she likes you. But after that, who knows? She's pretty strong-willed, and she doesn't come running to her big brother with every little thing."

"Big brother" sobered them up. With Ezekiel gone, Joshua was in fact the big brother of the family, something pretty important in Tortie culture.

"What about you, you ready?" Ryck asked.

"Born ready. No matter what happens, don't come knocking on my door for at least a day. I'm taking Hope, and we're locking out the rest of the world."

Joshua had spent the war at Camp Charles, but all dependents had been required to leave Tarawa and go back home for the duration. The recruit training surge had continued after the war as the new recruits cycled through training, and this was his first opportunity to see his wife. The fact that it coincided with I-Day was a happy coincidence as it meant he could travel with Ryck back home, but Ryck knew Joshua's only goal was to spend time with Hope, not attend I-Day celebrations.

"You guys in the war?" the taxi driver asked, his curiosity overcoming his common sense.

"Yep," Ryck said, offering nothing else. For once he wanted to leave the Corps behind him for a few days.

The taxi driver was waiting for more details, but Ryck turned back to Joshua and asked, "So are you happy being a married man? Last time we were here, you were a little nervous."

"Yeah, I am. I think of her all the time. I think of little Ester, too. She's growing by leaps and bounds, and I can't wait to see how big she's grown."

"I'm married. Me and the wife's got three," the driver said.

Joshua keyed up the privacy screen.

"It was the best move I've made. If I make staff sergeant, I can get married quarters, so Hope doesn't have to sit in some apartment out in the ville. Maybe we can start on number two, a little guy?"

"Holy shit! If you do, you better hope he takes after Hope and not you!" Ryck told him.

That started a smack-talk session that hadn't ended by the time they reached the Hope-of-Life compound. Ryck only had his backpack, so he took the driver's meter and swiped it while Joshua grabbed his suitcase, full of presents for his family.

The driver's surly attitude at having been cut off changed when he saw the tip Ryck keyed in.

"When you want to leave, you call me, OK?" he said, slipping Ryck his card.

Ryck absentmindedly pocketed it as he followed Joshua to the main house. A rocket streaked out, slamming into his friend, knocking him back a step. Hope clung to his neck, her face buried into his shoulder. They both were crying.

Joshua's mother followed at a more leisurely pace, a small girl on her hip. When Joshua opened his eyes, he saw her, then reached out for the little one, who recoiled slightly at the strange man hugging her mother.

"It's OK baby, that be your papa," Mrs. Hope-of-Life said.

"Papa?" the little girl asked, clearly getting excited.

She squirmed down from her grandmother and rushed to hug Joshua's leg.

Ryck felt out of place, like an intruder.

"Why don't you come on inside," Mrs. Hope-of-Life suggested. "Leave these three for a piece. I imagine you be thirsty. I also imagine you be wanting to see Hannah?" she asked, a twinkle in her eyes.

"Uh, yes ma'am," Ryck said.

"Yes to what?"

"Uh, both?"

She laughed, a deep throaty laugh.

"Of course, I just be teasing. Come on in. I'll fetch Hannah."

Ryck left the small family in front of the house and followed Mrs. Hope-of-Life inside. She got him a home-made lemon squash, telling him how much better it was for him than what he could get at the stores. She left him there nursing it.

This really is pretty good, he thought as he sipped the drink before a slender form moved in front of him.

"Ryck, Joshua didn't tell me you be coming. I . . . where be your sister? I think Joshua will be a mite busy to be socializing with you. Maybe you should be with Lysa?"

"I didn't come to be with Joshua, and Lysa knows where I am," he said.

Her eyes narrowed.

"And why be you here?"

"It's I-Day in two days. I promised you I would be back to see you this I-Day."

"That you did, Ryck."

"Did you forget that?" Ryck asked, suddenly less sure of himself.

"No, of course, I didn't. But soldier boys make many promises to girls. Most promises are not kept."

Her face clouded over while she said that. Ryck wondered if Ezekiel had made a promise to come back.

"Well, I'm here," he said.

"So you are."

She didn't seem talkative. Ryck wondered if things had changed between them. Her brother had been killed by Marines, after all. Did she blame him for that?

"Well, so what will you do now that you be here?" she asked.

"I wanted . . . I wanted to talk to you. I wanted to ask you something."

"OK, then ask," she prompted.

"Uh, not here in the kitchen," he said, pointing out her sister who had just come in and opened the fridge.

"How about the library?" she asked.

He followed her to the library, where she sat down, pointing to a plush chair for him to sit. He sat, but it was very deep, pulling him away from her. He scootched forward and sat on the edge of the chair.

"I'm . . . I mean, I, well, this has been a very rough year, for both of us. I'm sorry I couldn't get here for Ezekiel's funeral, and all."

Shit, this is hard!

She sat silently, waiting.

"Anyway, I've been thinking of you. Of us. I really like when we're together. I feel comfortable with you."

"Comfortable?" she asked, arching her eyebrow.

"No, not like that. I mean, I care for you. I mean, I love you, and I want to marry you."

That's not how I wanted it to go!

She sat there, not saying a word.

He started to panic. She wasn't jumping up to agree, like the women did in the flicks.

"Ryck," she began. "I care for you, too. Maybe I love you. I never meant to. I was just going out for fun. You be Joshua's friend, and I wanted to see the kind of man he would love. Somewhere in there, I think I fell a little in love with you myself. You are strong, yet kind. You have a gentle heart. I've watched you with your nieces, and I know you would be a good father."

His heart gave a little jump of hope.

"But I told you long ago that I am not a soldier's girl. I am not like Hope, bless her heart, ready to follow her man from base to base, sitting in apartments, waiting for him to show up."

"But I'm a staff sergeant now. I can get base housing."

She held up her hand to stop him.

"I be a little more than a year away from my Ph.D. This has been my goal since I was a little girl. I am going to make something of myself. I love and respect my mother dearly, but I am not going to be the matriarch of some household. I have my dreams. And I will not marry someone and have them taken away from me."

"Why would they get taken from you?" Ryck asked, heartbroken in the direction this was taking.

"You be not a Torritite. That be OK, and I respect your beliefs, but your kind do not suffer women to make their own way in life."

"Why do you think that?" Ryck asked, confused.

"Because of the laws. Making women little more than chattel. You don't have women in your precious Marines, right?"

"Hannah, I think you are mistaking things here. Sure, the Federation is behind the times on things, to include women in the service. But that's not what all people think. Of course, you should finish your degree. And whatever you wanted to do in your life, I would support you. I can't promise that I will be home every night. I can't promise that I wouldn't be gone for long periods of time. But if I am going to be gone, do you think I would be attracted to a woman who needed me every minute of the day to make every single decision? Part of the reason I love you is that you are so capable. You are strong."

Hannah looked at him in shock, surprised by his outburst.

"I . . . I'm sorry I threw this at you, especially now. Maybe I should have waited. Or maybe it was never going to be. Just don't say no just yet. Think about it. If you do love me, like you said, we can work out anything. If not, then I will always wish you well. And if you change your mind, if you want to marry me, then I will be waiting for your yes."

He stood up then, looking at her for a moment before bending over and kissing her forehead. He left her there, sitting in the library. Mrs. Hope-of-Life was waiting in the kitchen. Her eyes lit up when Ryck appeared, but that faded when she saw his expression. She didn't say a word as Ryck opened the door and walked outside.

Joshua was just coming in, one arm around Hope, the other hand holding Ester's little hand. He looked at Ryck, eyes questioning.

Ryck shook his head and gave a thumbs down. He didn't bother to say anything.

He felt the taxi driver's card in his pocket. He hadn't expected to need it so soon. He pulled it out and called the man who happily said he'd be right back.

This had been one shitty year. He'd lost friends, close friends. He'd fought against men with whom he had no beef, and in doing so, had revealed a savage side to him that he hadn't known he'd had. A side of him that shamed him. And now, just when he'd hoped for an anchor for all his troubles, he'd been cast adrift.

Maybe that was the problem. A marriage should be because of love. A marriage shouldn't be because a man, or woman, needed something, be that financial support or emotional support. That was a contract, not a marriage.

The taxi driver appeared down the road, his fans kicking up dust as he turned and made his way down the drive. Ryck would call Lysa as soon as he got in to tell her the news. She'd be disappointed, of course, but she'd hide it and try to make him feel better. Lysa might not have a degree, might not ever set the world on fire, but she was strong in her own way, too.

The taxi pulled to a stop and sank down. Just as Ryck was opening the door, he heard his name called in back of him. Turning he saw Hannah, hair streaming in back of her while running pell-mell after him. She was shouting one word.

"Yes!"

Thank you for reading *Sergeant*. If you liked it, please feel free to leave a review of the book from wherever you bought it.

Please continue with Ryck's story in the next books of the series, *Lieutenant*.

If you would like updates on new books releases, news, or special offers, please consider signing up for my mailing list. Your email will not be sold, rented, or in any other way disseminated. If you are interested, please sign up at the link below:

http://eepurl.com/bnFSHH

Other Books by Jonathan Brazee

The United Federation Marine Corps
Recruit
Sergeant
Lieutenant
Captain
Major
Lieutenant Colonel
Colonel
Commandant

Rebel
(Set in the UFMC universe.)
Behind Enemy Lines (A UFMC Prequel)
The Accidental War (A Ryck Lysander Short Story Published in
BOB's Bar: Tales from the Multiverse)

The United Federation Marine Corps' Lysander Twins
Legacy Marines
Esther's Story: Recon Marine
Noah's Story: Marine Tanker

Esther's Story: Special Duty
Blood United

Coda

Women of the United Federation Marines
Gladiator
Sniper
Corpsman

High Value Target (A Gracie Medicine Crow Short Story)
BOLO Mission (A Gracie Medicine Crow Short Story)
Weaponized Math (A Gracie Medicine Crow Novelette, Published in
The Expanding Universe 3, a 2017 Nebula Award Finalist)

The Navy of Humankind: Wasp Squadron
Fire Ant (2018 Nebula Award Finalist)
Crystals
Ace
Fortitude

Ghost Marines
Integration (2018 Dragon Award Finalist)
Unification
Fusion

The Return of the Marines Trilogy
The Few
The Proud
The Marines

The Al Anbar Chronicles: First Marine Expeditionary Force--Iraq
Prisoner of Fallujah
Combat Corpsman
Sniper

Werewolf of Marines
Werewolf of Marines: Semper Lycanus
Werewolf of Marines: Patria Lycanus
Werewolf of Marines: Pax Lycanus

To the Shores of Tripoli

Wererat

Darwin's Quest: The Search for the Ultimate Survivor

Venus: A Paleolithic Short Story

Duty

Semper Fidelis

Checkmate (Originally Published in The Expanding Universe 4)

THE BOHICA WARRIORS
(with Michael Anderle and C. J. Fawcett)
Reprobates
Degenerates

SEEDS OF WAR
(With Lawrence Schoen)
Invasion
Scorched Earth
Bitter Harvest

Non-Fiction

Exercise for a Longer Life

The Effects of Environmental Activism on the Yellowfin Tuna
Industry

Author Website
http://www.jonathanbrazee.com

Made in the USA
Middletown, DE
02 March 2020